WHEN THE BEAT DROPS

WHEN THE BEAT DROPS

ANNA HECKER

Sky Pony Press
New York

First Edition

This is a work of fiction. Names, characters, places, and incidents are from the author's imagination and used fictitiously.

Sky Pony Press books may be purchased in bulk at special discounts for sales promotion, corporate gifts, fund-raising, or educational purposes. Special editions can also be created to specifications. For details, contact the Special Sales Department, Sky Pony Press, 307 West 36th Street, 11th Floor, New York, NY 10018 or info@skyhorsepublishing.com.

Sky Pony˚ is a registered trademark of Skyhorse Publishing, Inc.˚, a Delaware corporation.

www.skyponypress.com

10 9 8 7 6 5 4 3 2 1

Library of Congress Cataloging-in-Publication Data is available on file.

Cover design by Kate Gartner
Cover photograph: iStockphoto

Print ISBN: 978-1-5107-3333-6
Ebook ISBN: 978-1-5107-3334-3

Printed in the United States of America

*For anyone who's lost their mind and
found their tribe on the dance floor*

CHAPTER 1

The clock ticks in 4/4 time. It cuts through the scrape and shuffle of students putting away their instruments, dragging us six minutes closer to the end of the school year and one minute closer to the moment I've been waiting for.

"Class, we have a very special end-of-the-year treat for you." Mr. Gillis, the band teacher, pushes his wire-framed glasses up his nose. The shuffle suspends.

"You're letting us out early?" Jamal Robeson asks from behind his bass drum. Next to him, the percussionists titter.

"Even better." Mr. Gillis beams at me. "You're about to witness the world premiere of an original jazz trio written and performed by our very own Mira Alden, with Nicky Soriano on piano and Crow Cutler on drums. Put your hands together for 'Lou's New York!'"

All around me, people deflate.

"*Loser's* New York?" Gabriella Lawson jokes, tossing her stick-straight, shiny auburn hair over one shoulder and sending a gale of laughter through the flutes and clarinets.

"By Sad Trombone?" Jamal adds, and the laughter ripples through the rest of the band.

A memory whirls back to me: grass and dirt in my mouth, my eyes red and hot. *Stay cool,* I remind myself as I pick my way to the front of the room. It's what Miles Davis, my personal hero and the best trumpet player who ever lived, would have done. He never let critics get to him. He always played it cool.

On the other side of the room Crow adjusts her fedora and wheels her upright bass around the splayed-out feet of people who refuse to let her by. Her pale skin looks almost translucent under the band-room lights, and a man's herringbone blazer flaps around her shoulders. Nicky sets his sax on his chair and heads for the drums, his head held as high as it will go on his 5'3" frame. His pristine, preppy outfit is a stark contrast to Crow's thrift-store duds. His chinos actually swish as he walks.

"Mira, do you have any words to share about your piece?" Mr. Gillis prompts.

Miles Davis never talked on stage. He believed the music should speak for itself. So I don't tell the class that Lou was my grandfather, who turned me onto jazz when I was just a little girl. That this piece is a tribute to the hours he used to spend on Metro-North going into the city to hear his favorite jazz combos, often staying so late he missed the last train home and had to wander Grand Central Station until dawn. That it's a thank-you for believing me when I said I wanted to play like Miles Davis, for buying me my first trumpet and coming to all my recitals even when his emphysema was so bad he could barely applaud.

That it's a memorial, because as of September Grandpa Lou isn't with us anymore. That the man Gabriella Lawson just called a "loser" was my favorite person who ever lived.

I don't say any of that. I nod at Crow and Nicky, sweat gathering on my palms.

"A-one, a-two, a-one-two-three-*four*!" Crow counts, slapping her bass.

I raise my trumpet to my lips and feel forty pairs of eyes on me, just waiting for me to give them new material. *Please don't let me fall on my face*, I pray. *Not again.*

Somehow, I find my breath. My fingers seek the valves and as the opening phrase echoes through the bell of my trumpet the band room fades away and we're in Grandpa Lou's living room in New Haven, the carpet scratchy against my bare knees as I lean up against his speakers, soaking in the horn. Nicky starts in with the snare, gaining speed like the train chugging into Manhattan. As the sound builds the three of us break into a fast, wild bebop riff and we're in Harlem in 1944, when Miles Davis first came to New York and spent his days studying at Juilliard and his nights jamming uptown at Minton's with Dizzy Gillespie and Charlie "Bird" Parker.

My notes intertwine with Nicky's riffs and dart around the reverb from Crow's bass. We're weaving with Miles in and out of the clubs on 52nd Street, setting the soundtrack to Greenwich Village as beat poets snap their approval over black coffee and rotgut wine.

Nicky drops out for a moment and I launch into a solo that has the beatniks leaping to their feet and shedding their cool.

"Get it!" Crow hollers, spinning her bass in a full 360 just as I ease back into the refrain. Nicky's snare slows until we're sitting with Grandpa Lou in the front row of a tiny jazz club in Harlem, a cigarette in his hand and his smile like a halo, lighting up his whole face. My lungs feel like they're about to burst by the time I hit the final high note, and I slowly lower my trumpet from my lips as the song's last vibrations float through the air.

I can practically smell Grandpa Lou's aftershave. My lips un-pucker into a smile and Nicky gives me a mock salute from the drums. Crow tips her fedora. I wait for applause to crash over me like a wave.

All I get is another tick of the clock. I tumble back to reality and find half the students zoning out, staring into space or checking their phones. Others just look confused—or, worse, unimpressed.

"What even *was* that?" Gabriella asks in a loud, fake *sotto voce*.

"Weirdness from a weirdo?" Jamal ventures.

Mr. Gillis brings his hands together in pointed, enthusiastic applause. Some of the students join him half-heartedly, but then the bell clangs and everyone is out of their seat at once, stampeding for the door.

"Don't forget to practice over the summer!" Mr. Gillis calls to a nearly empty room. As the last student thuds away, he turns to me with a sigh.

"Sorry about that, Mira. I guess your material was a little . . . advanced for them."

Nicky stands, shaking his head in disgust. "Can those cretins appreciate *anything* that's not an arrangement of some crappy pop song?"

I watch Mr. Gillis try and fail to hide a smile. "They might not get it now," he says diplomatically. "Maybe someday they will."

"They would have gotten it at Windham." The words slip from my mouth before I can stop them. So much for keeping my cool.

Mr. Gillis's smile disappears. "I'm sorry about that, Mira," he says. "I tried to pull strings for you. I really did."

"I know," I say. "Thanks anyway."

I turn away from him and clean my trumpet's spit valve so he can't read the bitterness in my eyes. I'm more than *sorry* about missing all eight weeks of Windham Music Camp this summer; I'm furious. Furious that my parents didn't realize we couldn't afford it before the scholarship application deadline passed. Furious that I emptied my savings account and spent the last two months hosting bake sales only to come up short. Even a tiny bit furious at Crow and Nicky because they still get to go, even though they helped with the bake sales and none of this is their fault.

"It's such crap." Nicky follows Mr. Gillis around the room, breaking down music stands with small, precise movements. "All those summers gushing about your talent, and they can't even scrounge up a little extra scholarship money? Go romance a rich donor or something?"

"Especially *this* summer," Crow half wails, stuffing her bass into its giant case. "With our audition coming up. When you need to practice the *most*."

Even though Crow's just repeating everything I've said for months, her words tie my stomach in a knot. The three of us are applying early admission to the world-renowned Fulton Jazz Conservatory in Harlem: the only college I have any interest in attending. There's a two-part audition process, and our first is in mid-August, so people can fly in without having to miss school. Even with the summer yawning in front of me like a stale, empty trap, it doesn't feel like enough time.

"Oh, I'll still practice." My voice sounds scorched. "Probably even more than you guys. It's not like I have anything else to do this summer."

"You three will nail it." Mr. Gillis assures us. "By the time I see you in September, Fulton will be begging you to go there."

I snap my trumpet case shut. "I hope you're right," I say quietly. I wait for Crow and Nicky to finish packing up their instruments, already bracing myself for the onslaught of stupidity beyond the band room doors.

"Have a good summer!" Mr. Gillis calls after us.

"I'll try," I say, even though I'm pretty convinced that no summer spent folding towels at my parents' moldy, failing gym could possibly be *good*. "You too."

Out in the hallway the cacophony swallows us, a thousand students cleaning out their lockers. A cluster of guys from the JV basketball team uses one of the trash bins as target practice; a brown-skinned banana flies by, missing my ear by millimeters.

"Watch it!" I call, ducking.

Brian D'Angelo, second-string forward, tuts his tongue. "Close call there, Sad Trombone. Hate to see you faceplant on *that*."

A bitter bubble of shame bursts in my stomach as the memory floods back, stronger this time. *Crisp fall air biting at my nose as I take my first-ever marching band solo at the homecoming game. My toe hitting a divot in the football field and notes skidding sideways from my trumpet, crowds of blurred halftime faces jeering as I fly face-forward into dirt and grass. The taste of tears as Nicky helps me to my feet, the red eyes and heaving shoulders and mess of snot as I begin ugly-crying in front of a thousand jeering spectators. The nickname that's followed me ever since.*

Next to Brian D'Angelo, Brad Eaton raises a pretend trombone to his lips. "*Whomp-whomp-whaaaaaa.*"

I stare straight ahead and keep walking, reminding myself to play it cool. The Monday after the Halftime Incident I began channeling Miles Davis, keeping my head high and my face blank as cries of "Sad Trombone!" dogged me through the halls. It still hurts, even after three years. But I'll be damned if I ever burst into tears in front of a crowd again.

Behind me, I feel Nicky stop. "For the millionth time, you cretins, she plays the *trumpet,*" he says in his withering, nasal drawl.

Brad pretends to look shocked. "Oh, what're you gonna do about it? Beat me up with your tiny little gay hands?" The whole hallway bursts out laughing.

Nicky rolls his eyes. "You *wish* I'd touch you with my tiny little gay hands," he shoots back. "Call me when you come out of the closet, 'kay, sweet pea?" He holds an imaginary phone to his ear and blows Brad a kiss.

"Ew." Brad cowers back, the smile wiped from his lips. "Gross."

Now it's our turn to laugh as we link arms and continue down the hall.

"Jesus." Nicky shakes his head. "I can't wait to never have to come back here again."

"Just one more year, kiddos." Crow's voice is pure steel. "And then we'll be in Manhattan, jamming with the *real* cool cats, and we won't even remember these losers existed."

"If we get in," I remind them.

"Of *course* we'll get in." Nicky lays a comforting hand on my arm.

"How can they resist us?" Crow adds, and I force a smile. Our collective plan for the future has always been so clear, hatched after the Halftime Incident and polished until it was as smooth and solid as a marble statue. The three of us together at Fulton, studying jazz with the greats. The off-campus loft we'll share; all-night jam sessions fueled by black coffee and Chinese takeout. All we have to do is get through the next year of high school . . . and get in.

We pause at a junction in the hall. Crow and Nicky's lockers are to the left, mine to the right.

"So I'll see you guys tomorrow?" I ask. "Windham road trip?"

"You're sure you want to drive us?" Nicky's voice is gentle.

"My mom said she'd do it if you change your mind," Crow pipes in.

"I'll do it," I say, even though the words feel like swallowing acid. "I want to see everyone."

"You mean you want to see *Peter*," Crow taunts.

"Naked," Nicky agrees.

"That is classified information," I inform them. Even though it's true, I *do* kind of want to see Peter Singh naked. We almost got that far last summer, but we both chickened out at the last minute.

This summer was going to be different. *Was.*

"Anyway," I say, too briskly. "I have to get to work. See you guys tomorrow."

Crow gives me a quick hug while Nicky stands on tiptoe to air-kiss my cheek. Then they turn and walk away, Crow loping behind her bass and Nicky hustling to keep up, his saxophone case swinging from his hand. I turn and head to Locker 1279, which is easy to spot because someone scratched

"Sad Trombone" into the orange paint job. For a while I tried to cover it up with a picture of Miles Davis—playing the *trumpet*, to make a point—but it kept getting torn down and finally I gave up. Nobody's going to call me Sad Trombone in Manhattan. People there have better things to do.

I spin my combination and start sorting through ripped-out notebook pages, old tests, and sheet music. Only the music is worth keeping. I shove everything else in the nearest trash, and I'm almost out the door when a familiar face stops me. She's grinning from a newspaper photo inside one of the trophy cases, one arm around her co-captain and the other raising a massive trophy. The trophy itself stands next to the photo, gleaming dull gold. *Connecticut State Soccer Champions*, it reads. *All-State MVP, Brittany Alden.*

Even though the display has been up since last spring, I slow down and watch my reflection float over Britt's photo. Despite the fact that we have the same light-brown skin, springy chestnut-colored curls, and dark eyes flecked with gold, people have trouble believing we're sisters. Britt has an easy smile, a million friends, and a soccer scholarship. I have giant feet and a trumpet.

I haven't seen her since she left for college in September: plane tickets from LA to Connecticut were too expensive for Christmas, and lately she's been so busy with finals she hasn't even been texting. But she's coming home tonight, and knowing she'll be here makes missing camp just a little easier to bear. I can't help thinking that maybe this will be the summer we stop being Britt the Soccer Star and Mira the Weird Jazz Nerd and can just be us again, like we were before high school.

I may not be going to camp, but maybe this will be the summer I finally get my sister back.

CHAPTER 2

I inherited Grandpa Lou's car when he died. It's a 1990 Buick LeSabre in a two-tone brown that Nicky refers to as "fecal chic," its exhaust smells like toxic death and the seats give you automatic swamp-ass. But if I inhale deep enough I can still smell Grandpa's cigarettes and aftershave, and his collection of scratchy jazz cassettes still litters the seats and floor.

As I slide into the driver's seat after my front-desk shift at our family-owned gym, The Gym Rat, Mom comes running across the parking lot.

"I'm coming with!" she calls, stashing a rolled-up piece of poster board in the back seat. "My class was canceled so—girls' trip!"

"Oh?" I ask as the car gurgles to life.

"Yeah. No one showed up." She pulls a cosmetic bag out of her purse and adjusts the side mirror, using it to brush shimmery shadow over her hazel eyes.

"Uh-oh," I say. The six o'clock Cardio Jam class used to popular with commuters on their way home from Manhattan, but attendance has been down ever since a brand-new Crunch opened next to the train station.

"Oh, well." She rims her eyes in brown pencil. "I'd rather see Britt, anyway!"

I nod and push an Ornette Coleman cassette into the finicky tape deck. We're only two exits down the highway when Mom leans over and turns it off.

"Sorry, hon," she says, flicking mascara onto her lashes. "This stuff sets my teeth on edge."

I bite my lip and spend the rest of the trip listening to her rant about how she wishes we could afford mini trampolines for the gym. As soon as I park she leaps out of the car and grabs the poster board, hurrying to the terminal. My beat-up Adidas slap a dopey counterpoint to the squeak of her sneakers and I try to ignore the heads turning to look at us, peoples' eyebrows scrunching as they try to figure us out. There's Mom in her gym clothes and full face of makeup, with her pale, toned arms and fine, strawberry-blond hair. Then there's me, bare-faced and natural-haired, curls bouncing in every direction as I walk. Even though Britt and I inherited Mom's lanky build and freckles, nobody ever believes we're her daughters.

"Give me a hand, Mir-Bear?" Mom unrolls the poster board as we join a crowd waiting for Arrivals at the base of an escalator. I take one end, sending a waterfall of gold glitter fluttering to the floor.

Welcome home Brittany! the sign reads in the cheery bubble letters Mom uses for the DIY motivational posters she's always posting around the gym. *Alden Family MVP!*

The words claw at my neck.

"What's wrong?" she asks.

I can't believe she doesn't know. "Alden Family MVP?" I ask.

Mom looks from me to the sign, and her eyes go wide. "Oh, I didn't mean it like that!" She shakes her head. "Oh my god, you don't really think that, do you? It's just because of the championships. . . . You know, how she was state soccer MVP last year?"

"It's fine," I shrug it off, playing it cool. "It's a cute sign. She'll love it."

Mom reaches over to pat my shoulder. "You know you two are *both* my best girls, right, Mir-Bear?" she asks.

"I know," I repeat. Although I don't, necessarily. Not always.

But Mom's already craning her neck at the escalators, looking for Britt. "There she *is*!" she cries, her voice rising up the scale. I catch a glimpse of my sister in a navy blue Pepperdine T-shirt and cutoffs, half-hidden behind a couple with a wailing baby.

"Britt! Britt, honey! Right here!" Mom waves her hand and I feel people turning to stare. But then her arm drops, and the smile falls from her face.

"Oh my god," she whispers. "What did she do to her hair?"

As the couple and baby step off the escalator, I get a better look. Half of Britt's long, tight, always-perfectly-moisturized curls are gone, the entire left side cut close to her skull with spiral designs shaved into the soft black fuzz. From the expression on Mom's face, you'd think Britt had tattooed *QUEEN BITCH* across her forehead.

"Wow, you guys made me a sign!" Britt's smile is a flute refrain, clear and playful and sweet. She spreads her arms for a hug, but Mom stops her.

"What happened to your hair?" she demands.

Britt's smile flickers. "I cut it?" she says, like it's a question. "Am I seriously getting the third degree before I even get a hug?"

Mom clenches the sign at her side. "It's a bit of a shock. I thought you loved your hair."

Britt rolls her eyes, embracing Mom's stiff shoulders. "The girls in my dorm think it's cool."

"*I* think it's cool," I add.

"Well *thank* you." Britt disengages from Mom and pulls me in. She smells like airplane peanuts and vanilla body spray. "See?" she says to Mom. "Other people like it."

I link my arm through hers and she chats about finals on the way to the car, then calls shotgun while Mom's still loading her bags into the trunk.

"You're making your own mother ride in the back?" Mom asks, pretending to be annoyed. But I can tell, now that the shock of Britt's hair has worn off, she's happy to have her older, favorite daughter home again. She's already leaning forward as I pull out of short-term parking.

"I hope you're ready to teach your old cardio classes," she says, patting Britt's shoulder. "That stupid Crunch may have all sorts of shiny machines, but they don't have *you*."

"Mmm," Britt says, poking at the stereo. She finds a pop station that fills the car with wailing auto-tune, and even though this is *my* car and I normally hate cheesy pop, I put up with it now because it's Britt and I haven't seen her since September. Mom, in the meantime, launches into a story about how she ran into Britt's old soccer coach and he offered to work with her over the summer.

"For *free*!" Mom sounds triumphant. "Isn't that great?"

"You talked to Coach?" Britt's head whips around.

Mom nods, pursing her lips. "He wants you to have a good season. We all do."

Britt shifts in her seat, the vinyl sucking against her thigh. "I just wish you'd talked to me first."

I watch in the rearview mirror as Mom's eyes cut to Britt. "I'm talking to you now."

"Right. Sure." Britt turns up the radio and chats off-handedly about finals and her flight until our wheels sigh into the driveway and Dad runs out to greet us, still in his athletic shorts and purple Gym Rat T-shirt. Late-afternoon sun glints off his shaved head, bringing out the coppery undertones in his deep-brown skin.

"Dad!" Britt leaps out of the car and rushes at his open arms.

"Baby!" He picks her up easily, swinging her around until her legs fly out behind her and she squeals to be set down. "Missed you."

"Missed you too."

He holds her at arm's length, evaluating. His smile falters when he gets to her hair. "That's a new look."

She shrugs. "Mom hates it. Right, Mom?"

"It's not my favorite." Mom brushes past us, one of Britt's bags tucked under her arm. "Lee, did you start dinner? I need protein, stat."

He grabs her and plants a kiss on her cheek. "It's almost ready. Let's get these inside."

Britt and Dad each take a suitcase before I can offer to help. I follow them into the house, closing the screen door behind us with a piercing squeal. Our house is small and painted a dingy yellow, chosen mostly for its bargain-basement price and proximity to The Gym Rat. The stairs whine under our feet and the door to Britt's room opens with a musty pop.

"Aw, it's exactly the same!" Britt looks around at the smiley-face comforter on her neatly made bed and the row of soccer trophies on her dresser. Her room is tiny (we used to share, but Dad put up a wall when Britt started high school so we could have our own space), but it's impeccably organized. Unlike mine, where every surface is cluttered with books and sheet music and the walls are covered in gray egg-crate foam that I stapled up so I wouldn't drive the rest of the family nuts practicing the trumpet.

Dad frowns. "You thought we'd redecorate?"

Britt laughs and unzips her suitcase. I linger in the doorway as Dad leaves, watching her remove armloads of wrinkled clothes and dump them into her hamper: a jumble of Pepperdine and Coletown tees, limp jeans and tangled socks and underwear. But there's other stuff mixed in there, too, stuff that seems very un-Britt: a pair of rainbow knee socks covered in unicorns, some neon green booty shorts, a black top that's sheer except for a pair of *X*s over the nipples.

"What's this?" I ask, intercepting something blue and slinky.

Britt turns, and her lips twitch into a smile. "Just a dress. It's fun, right?"

I hold it up. The dress is smaller than my T-shirt, and covered with cats shooting lasers from their eyes.

"Since when do you wear stuff like this?"

"Since college." Her smile widens. "Try it on. It'd look cute on you."

"Absolutely not." I lob it at the hamper, missing by a good two feet. Britt laughs, retrieves it, and lands it in a single, graceful arc.

"Can I borrow your car tonight?" she asks, tossing balled-up athletic socks into a drawer.

"Where're you going?"

"Just out. Meeting up with a friend from college."

"Can I come?" I ask, falling into our old rhythm as if she hadn't just been gone for almost a year. In a minute she'll look up at me, smile, and tell me "next time." Except there won't be a next time—there never was. Britt and I may be sisters at home, but once I got to high school we were practically strangers in public. She hung out with the jocks, I had Crow and Nicky, and our orbits rarely crossed beyond a secret smile when we passed in the halls.

She says something, and I nod automatically. "Sure, next time," I say, still lost in the past.

"Um, Mira. Hello?" Britt laughs, a tinkling laugh that always goes one note up before falling down a chromatic scale: a-*ha*-ha-ha-ha-ha. "I said yes."

"Wait, what?" I return to the present. "Really?"

"Sure." She's grinning, smoothing wrinkles from a purple mini tutu that just emerged from her luggage.

"Since when do you invite me to things?"

"Since college." She tosses the tutu into her closet as I try to process this new side of Britt, a side that wears purple tutus and is willing to tolerate her dorky little sister tagging along when she goes out. "Seriously, you should come. It'll be fun."

"I guess I can clear my schedule," I say, trying to play it cool even as my heart begins pounding.

She throws a pillow at me. "Thanks for penciling me in, dork."

"Anytime," I shoot back. Then I change the subject quickly . . . before she can change her mind.

CHAPTER 3

"I'm driving," Britt announces as we leave the house.

"But it's my car!" I protest.

"But I know where we're going," Britt counters, reaching for the keys.

I hold them above her head. "I know how to use Google Maps."

"But . . ." Britt stands in front of the driver's side, blocking the door. "But I'm your big sister who you love and haven't seen in nine months and who really, really wants to drive your car right now!"

I can't help it. I crack up.

"Fine," I say, handing her the keys. "But stay under the limit and no checking your phone."

She nods, already sliding into the driver's seat.

"You're sure you want me to come?" I ask for the thousandth time as she pulls out of the driveway. I spent all of dinner boiling over with excitement, but now doubt is beginning to creep in. If Britt's college friend is anything like her buddies from high school, she'll be some gorgeous, polished jock who spends the whole night pretending I don't exist.

"Would you be here if I didn't?" Britt rests her elbow on the open window, looking as effortlessly cool with her new hair as if she were in a music video. Still, my palms start to sweat as shopping plazas, car dealerships, and fast-food restaurants whip past. A couple of towns over, in a leafy neighborhood full of big, old houses, Britt pulls up to a sprawling Victorian and honks the horn. A second later the door bursts open and someone comes swooping down the front walk like a giant bat, a nest of dark, tangled hair trailing behind her. She opens the passenger's side door, sees me sitting there, and shrieks—a perfect A-sharp.

"Oh, look at *you!*" she cries. "You could be Britt's *twin*, she didn't tell me she had a sister who could positively be a *twin*. You two are so goddamn beautiful it's unfair! And can I have shotgun? I hate riding in the back seat. I say it's because I get carsick but actually I just like being up front. Do you mind?"

I turn to Britt, my jaw falling open. This girl is so different from Britt's high school friends, it's hard to believe they're the same species.

Britt tries to suppress a laugh. "Mira," she says, "this is Yelena. My friend from college."

Yelena is skinny and skittery as a daddy longlegs, with porcelain skin and huge amber eyes. She's wearing a black bandeau top, a vinyl miniskirt, and giant patent leather boots that come up to her knees. A thin silver belly chain shivers as she talks.

"It's *my* car," I mutter. But still, I unbuckle my seat belt. When I step outside I notice Yelena's wearing a backpack made out of an old baby doll. A zipper bisects the body; there are straps sewn crookedly to the shoulders and its round blue eyes stare blankly into the distance. If this were a horror film, it would definitely come to life and terrorize a group of coeds.

"This is Emma." Yelena catches me looking. "I made her myself. Isn't she freaky? Say hello, Emma!" She moves Emma's arm in a jerky wave and then folds herself into the passenger's seat, rummaging in the doll's belly and pulling out a phone. A moment later a blast of drum machines tears through the car, racing at nearly two hundred beats per minute. It makes my entire body go rigid but it also suits Yelena somehow; she seems like the kind of person whose life should have a soundtrack.

"So where're we going, anyway?" I ask for the zillionth time as Britt puts the car in drive. But the music drowns me out and Britt turns to Yelena, chattering at a mile a minute about her plane ride home and a bunch of people I don't know as we pull onto the highway. We pass one exit, then four, and by the time we cross the border from Connecticut into New York I can't keep my questions to myself anymore.

"Where are we going?" I yell over the music.

Yelena pokes Britt. "You told her, right?"

"Umm." Britt bites her lip. "Maybe not exactly."

"Oh, please tell me she's a virgin!" Yelena bounces up and down in her seat. "I love breaking in virgins. They usually freak the fuck out!"

A million alarm bells ring in my head. "*Excuse me*?!" I shout.

"Not that kind of virgin," Britt says quickly.

"A warehouse party virgin!" Yelena screams, flinging her arms in the air and laughing.

"A *what*-house what-what?" It sounds like Yelena said "ware-house party," but that can't be right. Maybe she meant a house party, like the kind Britt was always going to in high school.

"Oh, she's a virgin!" There's a manic sparkle in Yelena's eyes as she turns to me. "You're going to *love* this. Everybody loves their first warehouse party. It will absolutely change your world."

"What if I don't want my world changed?" I mutter as Britt slows at a tollbooth. I realize we're almost to the city, and little pinpricks of dread start to puncture my excitement. When Britt invited me out I pictured the kind of party she was always telling me about in high school: finished basements, rum and Cokes, sloppy make-out sessions, and tearful confessions in the bathroom line. A warehouse party sounds way out of character for Britt.

Then again, so are purple tutus and a half-shaved head.

"Oh, you definitely want your world changed," Yelena assures me. "Even if you don't know it yet."

Britt flicks her turn signal and we peel onto an exit, snaking through a labyrinth of industrial streets. Everything around us is gray: the cracked sidewalk, the pockmarked pavement, and the endless low buildings that, at this time of night, sit silent as dozing bears. Only sickly yellow streetlamps punctuate the gloom, puddling light on the concrete.

The dread that began back at the tollbooth blossoms into full-on, chest-pressing panic. I'm far from home, in an unfamiliar neighborhood, with no way to escape. Coming out was a bad idea. Not only should *I* not be here but I don't think Britt should, either.

"We're clearly in the wrong place," I announce. "We should go. Like, home."

"Don't be ridiculous," Yelena chirps. "It's right around the corner."

Britt turns onto a street that looks like it hasn't been touched since 1920. Trolley tracks run down its center, and the LeSabre's wheels patter a drumroll over cobblestones. Old brick warehouses with broken windows and peaked glass roofs rise up on one side of us; on the other, the East River flows silently behind a concrete divide, Manhattan's lights rippling softly on its surface.

"Grab this spot." Yelena points to a gap between a rusty Honda Civic and a VW Bug painted in psychedelic swirls. Britt crookedly parallel parks. The engine sputters to a halt as she grabs the backpack she brought with her: the one I'd assumed, based on Britt's going-out habits of the past, was full of rum and fruity mixers.

"Here." She tosses me a ball of slithery blue fabric. "Put this on."

The fabric pools on my knees, and I see that it's the dress from earlier: the one with the cats shooting lasers. "No way!" I tell her. "This thing is tiny."

"Come on. It'll look cute!" Britt pulls her Pepperdine T-shirt over her head, revealing a bright red tube top.

"You're wearing *that*?" I choke.

"Hell *yeah* she is!" Yelena lines her lips in heavy black pencil. "That thing is the shit, Britt. Whoa, I just made a rhyme!"

Britt rests her foot on the dashboard and adjusts a striped sock around her knee. "C'mon, Mir-Bear, put it on already. You'll thank me later."

I know that voice. That's the let's-draw-on-the-wall-with-crayons voice, the swap-Mom's-almond-milk-with-heavy-cream voice. But I'm not falling for it this time.

"Nope." I set the dress on the seat next to me. "Absolutely not."

"Fine." Britt uses the rearview mirror to apply a thick coat of glitter to her eyelids. "God, I forgot how stubborn you are."

"Are you ready?" Yelena is practically jumping up and down in her seat. "I can hear the party from here—I totally have so much FOMO right now."

"Fear of Missing Out," Britt explains. "It's Yelena's greatest affliction."

I turn the phrase over in my mind, conjuring images of Windham Music Camp's vaulted concert hall and spacious, sunny practice rooms. Fear of Missing Out could basically describe my whole summer.

Britt snaps a gold fanny pack around her waist and opens the car door. Yelena slings the baby doll backpack over her shoulders and gives me a what-are-you-waiting-for look.

My legs feel like cement as I step outside. I can hear the party somewhere ahead of us, bass chattering the cobblestones.

"C'mon!" Britt takes my hand and pulls me down the street, the bass growing louder with every step. I look up and see one of the warehouses is lit from within; green and purple lasers leak through its grimy windows, chasing each other across the sky.

When we reach it, Yelena yanks open a heavy black door and we duck inside. We're at the end of a long, dark corridor that smells like damp concrete and old cigarettes. A graffiti arrow directs us around the corner, and suddenly we're at a folding table littered with paper printouts, strips of wristbands, markers, and a cashbox. A girl with a constellation of piercings in her left cheek smiles at us through orange lipstick while Yelena hands her a fistful of bills.

"Welcome to Electric Wonderland." She stamps our hands. "Have a great night!"

"Electric Wonderland?" I repeat as we push through the doors. I don't like electric *anything*. I'd still be composing to gaslight if I could.

Britt opens her mouth to respond, but the party swallows her words. The party swallows *everything*.

The bass, which was loud outside, is now a full-body experience. It stops me in my tracks, vibrating into my feet and radiating up my legs, pumping my heart and pulsing blood through my veins. The beat feels ancient and futuristic at the same time, and as my eyes adjust to the thick smoke-machine fog I can see the way the dancing crowd flings itself toward the music as if the beat is the moon and they're the tides, pushed and pulled by its rhythm until their bodies are no longer their own.

I've heard electronic music before, on TV and through tinny car speakers in the high school parking lot, and it never made any sense. I never understood why people would want to listen to music made by a computer when the sound from real instruments is so much richer and more complex . . . so much *better*.

But this music isn't the same as the major-key, 4/4, utterly predictable drum-machine songs that underscore every car commercial on TV and Dance Blast class at the gym. This beat is everywhere, percussion lines woven together in colorful tonal textile before unraveling just enough to keep the crowd on their toes, hints of distorted cello and bright, pure vibraphone darting in and out of the beats like playful fireflies.

Britt takes my hand and I stumble forward, the bass thrumming in my veins as we make our way through the crowd. This is how this music is meant to be played, I realize: not over car radios but from speaker towers that are taller than our house. It's so loud I don't just hear the music; I can actually feel it inside of me, vibrating my bones.

Yelena's hair bobs ahead of us, weaving past a row of vendors selling T-shirts and glowsticks and water, dodging luminous dancing bodies. Video projections swirl across a far wall, a mash-up of Disney's *Alice in Wonderland* and girls Hula-Hooping in the desert, and there's a geodesic dome covered in color-changing LED lights.

On the other end of the room, in a raised booth flanked by massive speaker towers, a DJ with waist-length hair hollers into a microphone.

"I'm DJ Headspin," he screams, "and I'm here to make your head spin!" The crowd goes nuts. It looks like he's conducting a psychedelic symphony and everyone on the dance floor is an instrument, and I wonder what it must feel like to hold that kind of power, to be able to make so many people move.

"Come on!" Yelena shouts through the wall of music. She takes Britt's hand and Britt grabs mine and we snake through clots of people dancing around backpacks piled on the floor, their movements creating rhythms on top of rhythms, adding layers to the music that have never been there before and will never be there again. I brush past limbs glistening with sweat and mumble apologies nobody can hear. A girl in a furry hat with teddy-bear ears backs into me, stepping on my foot. She turns and places a damp hand on my arm.

"Are you okay?" she screams, inches from my face.

I nod. Her pupils are huge, with only a thin rim of green peeking out. Her jaw works frantically over a wad of gum.

"I'm glad you're all right!" she calls after me as Britt tugs my arm, dragging me forward. "I love you!"

My eyes dart back to the girl, who is already dancing again, bouncing up and down like she's on a pogo stick. I must have misheard her. Why would a stranger say *I love you*?

I'm still mulling it over when a tidal wave of sound crashes down on us and I realize we've made it to the front of the room. I crane my neck, following the speaker towers to a bridge where DJ Headspin flips switches on what looks like the flashing motherboard of a spaceship, one giant headphone pressed to his ear. The song he's playing sounds like robots dancing and soda fizzing, like a storm of metallic rain.

Directly in front of us, heavy curtains block the area next to the stage. Yelena says something to a bouncer the size of a house, and he shakes his head. Anger flashes across her face and she releases a torrent of words; I can't hear anything, but I can tell by the way her arms are flailing that she isn't pleased.

The bouncer shakes his head again, and she blows out a frustrated stream of air and steps aside, fishing out her phone and typing furiously.

"Can we go?" I whisper to Britt. "That bouncer looks like he wants to eat us for breakfast."

Britt shakes her head. "When Yelena wants something . . ." she begins.

But I don't catch the rest because at that moment an arm slithers out from a break in the curtain and taps the bouncer's shoulder.

There's an entire world tattooed on that arm: stylized animals and climbing vines, craggy mountains and crashing waves, all of it woven into a tapestry that glides smoothly over taut, tan muscles.

The bouncer leans toward it, listening. He glances at the three of us, nods once, and opens the barrier just wide enough for us to slip through.

Britt's fingers close around my arm. I feel the bouncer's meaty glare on my back as Britt pulls me forward, through the break in the curtain, to the unknown world backstage.

CHAPTER 4

It's quieter back here, with the speakers facing away from us and the *thump-thump-thump* of the party muffled by the heavy velvet curtain.

"Hey, you finally made it." I turn toward the voice, blinking in the sudden glare of work lights. It's the owner of the arm, a college-aged white guy with full-color tattoo sleeves under a black T-shirt. There's a walkie-talkie clipped to his jeans.

My gaze makes its way from his wrists to his neck to a face like a Miles Davis song: calm and chaotic and sharp and sweet and sad all at once. I instantly want to listen to him on repeat, to run my hands through his messy dark hair and trace the indentation below his cheekbone. I want to touch every picture on his arm as he explains them to me one by one, and then I want to go back and start again. This feels less like my tingly little crush on Peter Singh at camp and more like the first time I listened to *Kind of Blue* all the way through, like the music was slicing me open and turning me inside out.

"Derek Ryan!" Yelena flutters her fingers. "Aren't you happy to see us?"

"Yelena Andreyev. Of course." He gives her a hug and his eyes find mine over her shoulder. Even in the darkness, they're a shocking blue.

My knees turn to soup. I grip a nearby pole for support.

"Who're your friends?" Derek asks, releasing Yelena without releasing my eyes. His voice is warm and grainy, like sun-baked sand.

"Duh, of course! This is Britt—we go to school together—and that's her little sister, Mira. It's her first party, can you believe it?"

Derek extends his hand. His touch turns my skin to hot lava, makes me want to melt into the floor. Maybe I'm remembering it wrong, but I don't recall touching Peter Singh *ever* feeling like this.

"You like it?" he asks. "Your first party can be a little overwhelming."

Overwhelming is an understatement. "It's . . . loud," I say idiotically.

"Mira!" Britt throws her hands in the air, but Derek laughs, a big, boisterous laugh that fills every corner of the room.

"I hear you," he says. "We love our subwoofers, not gonna lie. But here." He fishes something out of the pocket of his slim, dark jeans. "Catch."

"Don't—" I start to say as he tosses me a tiny cellophane package. I reach for it, thinking maybe this one time my hand-eye coordination will do its job. The package glances off my fingertips and skitters to the floor.

My cheeks burn, but I force myself to stay cool as I crouch to retrieve it. "Must have left my reflexes at home," I joke.

"Earplugs," Derek explains as I stand. "Don't want you going deaf at your very first party."

"Thanks." I turn them over. "You just carry these around?"

He starts to reply but a voice erupts from his walkie-talkie, something about a security situation at the door.

"Be right there." Derek turns to us. "Sorry, duty calls. Catch you ladies later."

"Wait!" Yelena's hands flutter by her face. "I'll walk with you, okay?"

Derek nods, and she adjusts her backpack and shoots Britt a look I can't quite interpret. "Be right back."

Before he leaves, Derek's pale blue eyes find mine and hold them for a long beat. "Hey, remember," he says, backing away slowly. "You only get one first party, so make it count."

Then he's gone, Yelena bopping along next to him. Britt leans against a wall and I follow her lead, trying to look like I hang out backstage at giant warehouse parties every night of the week. I pull out my phone to check the time, which seems like a cool, casual thing to do—until it actually registers and I do a double take.

"Crap, Britt." I show her my phone. "We have to get home. We're going to miss curfew."

"Like they'll notice?" Britt raises an eyebrow. Even though we technically have an eleven o'clock curfew, our parents are always asleep by then—they get up at five a.m. to open the gym, so they go to bed early and sleep hard. In high school, Britt went out every weekend; some nights I'd hear her come home and follow her into the bathroom to hold her hair while she puked. It was enough to turn me off heavy drinking for good, but if our parents noticed, they never let on. Sometimes I wondered if they were ignoring it on purpose, hoping Britt would just slow down on her own. Or maybe they really didn't care, as long as she kept her grades up and kept winning soccer trophies.

"Yeah, but still . . ." I begin. I have to get up at seven tomorrow to drive Crow and Nicky to camp. If I don't get to bed soon, I'll have giant bags under my eyes when I finally see Peter again.

Just then Yelena bursts through the curtain, her cheeks flushed.

"I'm back, bitches!" she calls. "Let's go dance."

My stomach clenches. I've tried to avoid dancing in public ever since the eighth grade, when my aunt Shonda joked that I clearly got my dancing skills from my mom's side of the family.

"Hold out your hands," Yelena commands.

I stick my arm out, hand down. Maybe Yelena wants to do some kind of team-building cheer, like Britt always does before soccer games.

"Um, Yelena?" Britt looks suddenly nervous. "I don't think you should. . . ."

"Here you go, darling." Yelena grasps my arm, turns it over, and sticks a pill in my palm. It's a clear gelcap, about three-quarters full of brownish-white powder.

"What is this?" I ask.

Yelena does a theatrical double take. "Seriously? You don't know?" She turns to Britt. "Did she think we were all coming here to play Parcheesi or something?"

"Not exactly." Britt bites her lip. "I was going to tell her. Just . . . not like this."

"Then how, exactly?" Yelena perches a hand on her hip. "Engraved invitation? Singing telegram?"

Britt's eyes dart back to me.

"Tell me *what*?" I look from the pill to Yelena to Britt, who's twisting one of her remaining curls way too tight.

"Mira, honey." Yelena closes my fingers around the pill. "This is molly. It makes you want to dance."

"Molly?" I still don't get it.

And then I do.

The dancers with saucer-sized pupils. The psychedelic visuals projected on the walls. It all makes sense now. I feel like an idiot.

I flash back to a PSA I saw on TV: a guy at a concert taking a pill, then sweating through his clothes and saying all of these crazy, paranoid things. A diagram showed the pill dissolving in his bloodstream and eating holes in his brain, and it ended with minor-key organ music and a somber voice-over intoning: "Say no to drugs. Or else."

"You mean drugs." I scowl at Yelena. "You want me to take drugs?"

Yelena dissolves into laughter. "Oh my god, you sound so straight-edge, it's adorable. I *love* your sister!" she says to Britt.

Britt isn't laughing. She looks mortified.

"*You* do this stuff?" I whirl to face her. I can't believe it. My golden girl sister—beautiful, popular, gliding through life as easily as she cuts through opponents trying to block her on the soccer field—takes drugs?

Britt looks down at her feet, kicking at the floor. "Sometimes," she says. The music drops into a breakdown, a low bass rumble that sounds like a groan.

"Why?" I ask finally.

"Um, because they're *awesome?*" Yelena cuts in. "It's not like she murders puppies or anything. It's just fun."

Britt looks up, and her gaze shushes Yelena fast. Her eyes meet mine, round and almost pleading. "It *is* fun," she says. "But: it's more than that. It kind of makes everything come together in this really beautiful way."

"Aw." Yelena throws her arms around my sister and gives her a peck on the cheek. "You're so poetic, Britt. You know what that makes me want to do?"

"Molly," Britt and I sigh at the same time.

"Bingo." Yelena sticks out her tongue, a pill cradled neatly in its crease. She closes her mouth, swallows hard, and gives us a cat-that-ate-the-canary smile. "Britt?" she arches an eyebrow. "You want in or not? And, Mira, don't tell me you're not just a *little* curious?"

"Nope." I shove the pill into Yelena's hand. My heart is racing. This is a side of Britt I've never seen before, a side I didn't even know existed. "No way. N-to-the-O. That stuff eats holes in your brain."

Yelena lets out a howl of laughter, and even Britt cracks a grin. "That is such bullshit!" Yelena cries. "Where'd you hear that, a PSA?"

Heat snakes up my neck. "What?" I ask. "You only have one brain."

Britt shrugs, finally looking me in the eye. "You only have one life," she says.

CHAPTER 5

Back out in the party, surrounded by jumbles of gyrating bodies, I try not to stare at my sister. It's been about twenty minutes since Britt took the pill, and I keep checking to see if her pupils are growing, and wondering if she'll start sweating buckets like the guy in the PSA, or telling strangers she loves them.

Instead she's just dancing the way she always does: like the music's coming from inside of her, and her hips have a mind of their own. Aunt Shonda never had anything bad to say about *Britt's* dancing skills.

"C'mon!" She catches me looking. "We're supposed to be having fun!"

"I *am* having fun," I mutter. But the truth is, I can't focus on the music when I'm also worried about Britt. Drugs took down too many of my jazz idols. What if they ruin my sister's life, too?

"Liar." Britt grabs my hands and spins me in a circle. She throws her head back, teeth sparkling white in the lights, and even though I can't hear it over the music I can see the shape of her laugh. There's a thin sheen of sweat on her face and she looks happy in an open, childlike way, like when we were little kids catching fireflies on warm summer nights. That was before my parents bought the gym, when we still lived in New Haven on the same block as Grandpa Lou, in an apartment building with a big backyard where all the kids would play together and trap lightning bugs in glass mason jars.

We moved out of that apartment and bought the gym ten years ago. Was that the last time I saw Britt like this, so open and happy and free?

"Oooh!" Britt drops my hands. "Something's happening!"

I lean in to get a better look at her pupils, but just then a spotlight flicks on, illuminating a woman in a spangled leotard balancing on a trapeze suspended from the ceiling.

"Cool!" Britt breathes. The pounding bass stops and a tinkly piano piece comes on as the trapeze artist pitches forward into a swan dive, falling face-first toward the floor.

I gasp along with the crowd. But the dancer catches herself, swinging over the sea of faces. I crane my neck and watch her flip above our heads, always coming a hair's breadth away from plummeting into our arms. Each time she dives we suck in our breath; each time she catches herself, we let it out again, our breathing as synced as the senior jazz ensemble at music camp.

The silvery piano music spikes into a crescendo and the trapeze artist whips her body in circles until she explodes into a triple somersault, light bursting around her as she lands with graceful bow by the DJ booth.

I clap hard as the plodding bass kicks back in. "That was amazing!" I turn to gush to Britt.

But my sister is gone.

"Britt?" I spin in a circle, looking for her half-shaved head or Yelena's creepy backpack. Nothing.

Irritation zips through me. Britt promised we'd stick together. How am I ever going to find her in this crowd?

Snaking around hordes of sweaty dancers seemed easier with Yelena leading the way. On my own the dance floor is all sharp fingernails and jabbing elbows; clusters of people dance hip to hip, too close to let me through. Saying, "excuse me" doesn't work. Nobody can hear me over the beat.

I make it to a wall and sink against it, fishing out my phone. A *No Service* message laughs back at me, and my irritation boils into anger. Is Britt ditching me again, pretending I don't exist just like she always did in high school? The bass grows more insistent, a jackhammer pounding between my eyes. I have to get out of here.

I push back into the crowd. My toe hits something soft, throwing me off balance. I windmill my arms, trying to catch myself, but the floor comes screaming up at me, hard and concrete and moving way too fast.

Not again, I think as my body hits cement.

Pain surges through my knee and my tongue throbs, my mouth pooling with blood. It takes a moment to gather myself: a moment I spend facedown on the floor, a pile of backpacks under my ankles.

Someone taps my shoulder and I look up to find a circle of faces peering down at me. A guy wearing dozens of plastic beaded bracelets grasps me under the arms and helps me to my feet. A girl in an Alice in Wonderland costume offers a hand so I can steady myself. I wince as I grasp it.

Something wet and sticky trickles down my shin. I'm bleeding through my jeans. A girl with a white bandana around her neck follows my eyes. Without a word, she unties it and hands it to me.

I can't just bleed all over a stranger's scarf. I try to give it back.

"Keep it!" she insists, her mouth close to my ear. "I have more."

Her friends press in close. They make shapes with their mouths that I guess are supposed to be comforting words as I dab at my knee, tie-dyeing the bandana in blood. My throat feels thick, my eyes itchy and full; not from the pain, but from falling on my face in front of a bunch of strangers. Again.

Somehow, the fact that they're being so nice only makes it worse.

"I'm all right, thanks," I say, glad they can't hear my voice crack over the music. I even manage a wobbly smile.

"You want a hug?" the guy with the bracelets asks.

I shake my head. I just need to get away from this party and these way-too-kind people. I need to get outside.

"Feel better!" he calls after me as I put my head down and tunnel through the throngs, limping toward the exit. It seems like a century before I'm back in the long, dark hallway, pushing past the line of people waiting to get in. Finally I'm outside.

I take a few deep breaths. The fresh air dissipates the lump in my throat and whisks the moisture from the corners of my eyes. My sneakers slap cobblestone, the receding bass matching the throbbing in my knee. I turn right, then left, finding the LeSabre and sagging against its hood.

A gust of wind rips off the river and ruffles my hair as I settle into the unfamiliar soundscape: the distant whoosh of traffic on the freeway, a truck engine idling with a gravelly *chukka-chukka-chuk* a couple of blocks away, an empty Doritos bag rattling down the sidewalk. I text Britt that I'm out here, but my message doesn't go through.

"Dammit!" I say out loud, slamming my hands against the hood of the car and wincing as the sound rings through the deserted neighborhood.

"Damn what?" a voice responds, high-pitched and out of breath.

My head shoots up. I guess I'm not alone out here after all.

CHAPTER 6

A girl around my age hurries toward me, lugging a pair of large, black flight cases that bang against her ankles with every step. They're covered with stickers: unicorns, record labels, a Puerto Rican flag.

"I thought I was alone out here," I say.

"Yeah, you and me both. I've been lugging these around for, like, hours." She sets the cases on the ground and shakes the cramps out of her hands, jingling the gold chains around her neck. She's short and plump and, I'm guessing, Puerto Rican, with a bow-shaped mouth and heavy cat's-eye makeup surrounding velvety brown eyes. "Do you know where the party's at? I'm running mad late. My mom was working late and I couldn't leave my sisters alone and my ride left without me and I had to take the subway and . . . anyway, sorry." She stops and wipes a trickle of sweat from her forehead. "I'm lost, is what I'm saying."

"It's back that way." I gesture behind me. "Go to the end of this block and then take a right, then a left, then a right . . ."

Her brow wrinkles. "Left, then right, then . . . ?"

"No, the other way around." I turn and point.

"Sorry. I'm all mixed up." She removes a shiny gold ball cap and rakes her hand through candy-pink hair. Her expression reminds me of how I felt inside the warehouse: lost and stressed and all alone.

"I can walk you back there, if you want," I offer.

Her face relaxes into a smile. "Really? Sweet!"

"No problem." I reach for one of her flight cases.

"Oh, girl, no!" She tries to swat my hand away. "They're heavy as fuck."

I lift the case and grunt. "What's in here, rocks?"

"Equipment." She makes a grab for the handle but I shoo her hand away and start walking. I've spent enough time as a musician to know the code: if you have an extra hand, you carry someone's case. "The gear at these things sucks, so I bring my own," she continues. "I'm Shay, by the way. *DJ* Shay. And you are?"

"Mira."

"Mira, Mira, on the wall, who's the dopest of them all?" she singsongs. "Sweet name. Musical."

"Thanks." I slow my pace so Shay can keep up. Her legs, like the rest of her, are short, her feet kid-sized in zebra-print high-tops with bright pink laces. "So you're a DJ?"

She grins. "Yep. I'm on next, actually. Which is why I'm freaking the fuck out about being late."

We turn a corner and the warehouse looms into view. Shay eyes the cluster of people outside the door and shakes her head.

"That looks like a nightmare," she says, disappearing around the side of the building. "There's gotta be a side entrance somewhere." She tries another door and it swings open, releasing a blast of drums and synthesizers. I follow her down a dusty passage and suddenly we're backstage, approaching the DJ booth from the back. As Shay climbs a set of rickety stairs I look around for Derek, thinking maybe he's hanging out back here again, but all I see are piles of cables and bolts of cloth.

Shay disappears through a curtain at the top of the stairs.

"I still have your gear!" I call.

Nothing. I start up the stairs, the flight case banging against my leg, and peek through the curtain. Light pours into my eyes, temporarily blinding me. Music surrounds me like a flock of bats released from a cave.

"There you are!" Shay grabs me and pulls me through, and suddenly I'm standing in the center of the world and everything is hot and bright and alive. The music vibrates my bones and I can feel the crowd below me dancing in the dim lights, their energy pulsing up to the stage. In the center of the booth DJ Headspin whips his waist-length hair to the beat.

"Good crowd!" Shay sets her flight case down and rubs her hands briskly, her eyes shining. I can see the dance floor now: the clouds of dust and thick pockets of fog, glow sticks and LED toys like bioluminescent butterflies.

She sees me looking. "Ever been in the DJ booth before?"

I shake my head. I've been onstage dozens of times, for recitals and music competitions, but the rows of parents sitting quietly in folding chairs were nothing like this.

"Oh, well, shit! You should hang here. You'll have the best view."

"Really?" I ask. The DJ booth isn't quite as appealing as my bed right now, but it's a safe distance away from that cruel concrete floor full of flailing arms and deceptive backpack piles.

"Sure!" She grins, revealing a gap between her front teeth. "It's not like I have backup dancers."

"Thanks." I back into a corner and try to make myself unobtrusive, keeping an eye on the dance floor for Britt or Yelena . . . or Derek.

Shay snaps open one of her flight cases to reveal the fanciest-looking CD player I've ever seen: a giant slab of black plastic covered in screens, knobs, and buttons. *CDJ*, it says in big silver letters on the side. Her face softens as she sets it on the table next to DJ Headspin's laptop, giving it a friendly little pat. The way she touches her equipment reminds me of how I handle my trumpet.

DJ Headspin lifts his laptop and Shay slides the CDJ under it, then flips open her second flight case and scuttles around under the table with a handful of audio cables. A moment later she pops up and grabs a pair of pink, rhinestone-studded headphones.

"This is the cool part," she tells me, dropping back. "Ten bucks says you can't tell when I transition in." She slips on the headphones and turns a couple of knobs, her hand poised over one of the CDJs.

If she hadn't told me it was coming, I wouldn't have noticed. But as soon as Shay's hand touches down I hear a new beat layering in, running parallel to the song that's playing. She touches a slider and the beat grows louder. Soon a funky bass line joins in, meandering up and down a five-note phrase like a happy bullfrog.

DJ Headspin slams his headphones on the table and raises his hands in the air. Half of the crowd cheers, but the other half, the half that's too busy dancing, doesn't even notice.

Shay gives the slider a triumphant push all the way to the right and a rich, flirtatious vocal fills the room.

"Just a little lovin', early in the mornin'," the disembodied voice sings over the beat.

I spring forward. I can't help it. Shay has one side of her headphones off as she squints at her equipment.

"That's Carmen McRae!" I exclaim. "From the *Just a Little Lovin'* album in 1970. It's a classic!"

She turns to me. "You know this sample?"

"I'm kind of a jazz nerd," I admit.

"Cool! I *wish* I knew more about jazz." Shay fiddles with a few nobs. "But hey, check *this* out."

She bobs her head, counting until the sample comes up again, and then presses a button that says *LOOP*.

"Now gimme a few . . ."

She spins a wheel, flipping through a long list of song titles. Finally, her face lights up and she selects one. She shrugs the headphones back on and I watch her react to the music in her ears.

This time I'm listening for it. I hear the new track come in, a soulful, sweet instrumental with trembling electric strings. It seems to throw the dance floor into a trance, bodies moving dreamily as seaweed. Then the beat picks up, and Shay gives me a big grin.

"Now, check it," she says. She hits the LOOP button and Carmen McRae's voice soars through the speakers. The crowd goes insane, leaping in the air, and I feel a smile spread across my face.

"You want to try?" Shay asks.

My mouth falls open. "Really?"

"I mean, just the loop part. It doesn't really matter where you put it, but it would sound better at the beginning of an eight-count. You know what that is?"

"A measure?"

She raises an eyebrow. "You know your shit."

"You'll really let me try it?"

"Go to town. I gotta find my next track."

Shay returns her attention to the digital readout and my heartbeat expands until it's as loud and full as the bass shaking the speakers. I count four measures, and then another two, and then I go for it.

I hit the button.

"Just a little lovin', early in the mornin'," Carmen croons.

The dancers catapult to life. Their shouts echo through the warehouse, tangling in the rafters.

A jolt of pure pleasure sings through me.

I just made people jump.

I just made people scream.

I just made people *dance.*

CHAPTER 7

"So you saw your sister on drugs?"

Crow leans forward, craning her head around the curve of her bass. It fills every spare inch of the LeSabre, and the three of us are folded around it like tissue paper tucked into a package. I've spent the better part of the trip to Windham telling Crow and Nicky about my night. It probably wouldn't have taken so long, but they kept interrupting me with questions.

"Was she super high?" Nicky crosses his legs in the passenger seat, dangling a loafer from his toes. "Did she act crazy? Did she even recognize you?"

"Of course she recognized me." I reach for my extra-large iced coffee and take a long swig. I ended up only getting three hours of sleep, and my head feels like it's full of mosquitoes. "And she wasn't acting that crazy. She was actually being really sweet."

I managed to find Britt and Yelena once Shay's DJ set was over, after Shay texted me her number and said we should hang sometime before disappearing into a knot of well-wishers. When I finally ran into Britt again she gave me a huge hug and said she'd been looking for me for hours, which was a very

Britt-type thing to say even if it probably wasn't one-hundred-percent true. Then she fell asleep while I was driving us home and drooled on the window.

Crow's brow furrows. "You don't sound that upset. Are *you* going to start taking drugs?"

"Crow!" I slam my cup back into its holder. "Of course not."

"I don't know," Nicky says dreamily. "It sounds kind of magical . . . everyone acting all lovey and all those lights and a lady on a trapeze. I might try it."

Crow leans forward and smacks him on the arm. "No you would not. And it's not like anyone's asking *you* anyway."

"Touché." Nicky says as I slow at a sign announcing the turnoff for Windham Music Camp. A low, mournful ache starts in my stomach, growing as I follow the winding gravel road into a parking lot jammed with cars and parents, campers and suitcases and instruments.

"We're here!" Crow opens the door and leaps out. "Oh hallelujah, this blessed day has . . . oh." She stops mid-jump and looks at me. "Crap, I'm sorry, Mira. I forgot. . . ."

"It's fine." I chug the rest of my coffee, even though it's definitely not helping the ache in my stomach. Crow's still staring at me, her face creased with pity, when a blur of tangerine hair sideswipes her into a hug.

"Regina!" Crow wraps her arms around her, smiling ear to ear. "Oh my god, your hair got so long! Are you in the same cabin again this year?"

"Yes! You?" The sour note in my stomach becomes a deafening blast as they hug. I stand and stretch, trying to play it cool, but Regina sees me and barrels over.

"Miraaaaaa!" she hollers. "You're in our cabin too, right?"

"Um, actually, I'm just dropping them off." I examine my fingernails like they're the most interesting things in the world. There's a heavy layer of dirt beneath them even though I showered this morning, and I wonder if it's from the warehouse. I also came home with rings of soot around my nostrils.

"*What?!*" Regina bleats.

"I have to work this summer." My voice comes out froggy. "So. No camp for me."

"That stinks," Regina clucks. "We'll totally miss you. . . . Oh my god, Brian!"

Her gaze shoots past my shoulder, and a moment later she's bounding across the parking lot and launching herself into the arms of a surprised-looking cellist.

"Come on." Nicky appears at my elbow with a sympathetic grimace. "Let's get our crap out of your car."

I try for a smile, glad to have something to do with my hands as we wrestle Crow's double bass from the LeSabre. It takes several tries and sweat pools in my armpits, making dark crescents on my T-shirt.

"One, two, three, *heave!*" Nicky cries, and I stagger back, the instrument nearly falling on top of me. I let out a dyspeptic *oomph* as I bang my hip against the side mirror, still struggling to keep the bass (and myself) upright.

"Hey, you."

The voice stops me cold. It's the voice that grew hoarse with desire in my ear last summer, the voice I spoke to on the phone every night for the first month after camp. After the first month every night turned into every few days, then every few weeks, and eventually just the occasional text message.

It wasn't that anything happened. It just turned out that a long-distance relationship required more maintenance than either of us had time for.

"Peter." I peek around the bass, my hands flying to my head in a useless attempt to tame the frizz. He's thinner than I remembered, with pointy elbows and big, bony knees, dusky skin and thick black hair. His Adam's apple is almost the size of a real apple in his skinny throat.

"Uh, how's it going?" He crosses his arms awkwardly over his red Forensics Society T-shirt.

"Good?" It comes out like a question. I shift Crow's bass so it leans on my shoulder.

"*Crow!*" Nicky hisses, dragging her by the elbow. "Why don't *you* take *your* instrument and we can, um . . . go bring it somewhere. . . ."

"What a swell plan!" Crow says with all the subtlety of a bulldozer, giving me a giant wink. I glare at her as I hand it off, then turn back to Peter. I'm waiting for my heart to start beating out of control, for my knees to jellify and my palms to pour sweat, but instead I just feel hot and tired.

"So, uh, how's it going?" Peter says again, clasping his hands behind his back.

"Okay. You?"

"Pretty all right."

I nod. I don't know what else to say. I've been fantasizing about this moment for almost a year, but now that it's here it doesn't feel the way I thought it would. I don't want to throw my arms around him and kiss him, or take his hand and drag him into an abandoned practice room and take his shirt off. And no matter how hard I try, I can't help comparing him to Derek.

"So, uh, I heard you're not here this summer." Peter leans awkwardly against my car.

"Word travels fast."

His laugh is a nasal toot. "So I guess we won't get to . . . you know. Hang out."

He actually looks disappointed. From the way he says, "hang out," I know he really means, "hook up."

Do it now! part of my brain screams. *It's going to be a long, dry summer. Fool around while you still can!*

But something's changed since last summer—or maybe just since last night—and suddenly Peter Singh doesn't look as appetizing as I remembered.

"Yeah." I shrug. "Too bad."

He leans closer, a spidery hand on my arm. His breath smells like Funyuns. "I missed you," he says.

"Umyeahmetoo." I take a step back, leaving his hand dangling. "Listen, I have to help my friends unload this stuff, so . . ."

"Yeah." Hurt and confusion crease his face, and I instantly feel bad. It's not Peter's fault he's gangly and awkward. Last year I loved the fact that we were gangly and awkward together. Maybe if I weren't so tired and out of sorts, I still would.

Britt would know exactly how to handle this situation; she was always politely fending off advances from guys. But I'm coming up blank. Finally I just shrug and turn away, grabbing Crow's tweed suitcase from the trunk.

"See you around," I say, giving him a lame half wave as I practically run toward the cabins. I can feel his disappointment like a sunburn on my back as the camp spreads out below me, a deep green hill dotted with rustic cabins and a covered amphitheater that reminds me of all the recitals I won't be playing over the next eight weeks. Seeing them only adds to the ache in my stomach, the feeling that I only have a few hours to soak up everything I love about being here and I am definitely blowing it.

I catch up to Crow hauling her bass into the cabin.

"That was quick!" she says brightly. "Are you still a virgin or what?"

"I don't want to talk about it." The coffee isn't working. I'm grumpy, and exhausted, and everything about being here seems wrong.

"That bad?" She jabs me in the ribs. "I bet he'll last longer next time."

"Jesus, Crow!" I explode. "We didn't bone. We didn't even kiss!"

She steps back, looking hurt. "Okay, jeez. Sorry I asked."

"No, I'm sorry. I'm just tired." I push open the door to the cabin and its familiar smell rushes in, wood and violin-bow rosin and the peppermint-scented cleaner they use in the bathrooms. It brings back every memory of giggling with my friends here past lights-out, our impromptu jam sessions and good-natured feuds over the shower. It seems impossible that I'm not staying for another eight weeks of this. Impossible, and hugely unfair.

Crow follows me and makes a beeline for the corner, flinging her laundry bag onto the top bunk. "My bed is still free! Claimed for the Crow dynasty! Victory at last!"

I follow more slowly, her suitcase growing heavier with each step. As Crow scrambles up the ladder I'm drawn to the bunk below, the one that used to be mine. But instead of my old green blanket, there's a bright pink bedspread splashed with yellow daisies. A pink plastic alarm clock sits on the shelf where my headphones should be, and a pair of yellow Tweety Bird slippers peeks out from under the bed.

"Ugh, I forgot how hard it is to make a top bunk," Crow complains.

"Yeah." I try to shush the cellos playing a self-pitying dirge in my stomach, but the more I look around the louder they get. If I stay here one more minute, I'm going to completely lose my cool. "Hey, Crow, I gotta go."

She peeks over the edge of the bunk, blinking behind her thick glasses. "You're not staying for lunch?"

"I'm not hungry."

"So just have ice cream."

The memory of the soft-serve machine in the cafeteria only makes the cellos play louder. I loved that ice cream, and the fact that I could eat it anytime I wanted after a lifetime of my health-nut parents forbidding processed sugar from ever entering our home. A ball of helpless rage rises in my throat. I'm about to lose it.

"I actually—don't feel good," I say, my voice thick. "I better go. I'll see you at Visitors' Weekend, okay?"

I turn and find the doorknob, tears clouding my eyes.

"You don't even want a hug?" Crow is saying, but I can't stay here, not even long enough for that. I shake my hair into my face and half walk, half run back to the car, praying nobody will recognize me and see me losing my cool. I don't want their comfort or their pity. I just want to be alone.

Finally I'm at the parking lot, the LeSabre's sticky vinyl seat burning my thighs. I back out fast, gravel spraying metal with tiny pings, and draw a long, shaky breath as I put the car in drive, leaving Windham's frigid lake and throngs of excited music nerds in my rearview mirror.

The summer yawns in front of me, empty and lonely and stale. There'll be no soft serve, no jam sessions, no making out with Peter Singh, no music theory grad students offering insightful comments on my compositions. All I have is the gym and Britt and an audition to prepare for, and the memory of a tattooed, blue-eyed party promoter who may or may not have held my gaze for a beat too long.

Halfway down the road I slam my foot on the brake and pull onto a shoulder. I yank out my phone and find Shay's number, staring at the way it shimmers on my screen.

Hey, it's Mira from last night, I type. I hit Send and then I'm back on the road again, driving forward into the loneliest summer of my life.

CHAPTER 8

Shay wants to learn about jazz. She tells me this in a series of text messages peppered with unicorn GIFs and blinking emojis, offering to give me DJ lessons in exchange. So after work that Tuesday I drive down to her place in the Bronx, parking in front of a big brick building that looks just like all the others on her block. The old men sitting outside eye me curiously as I trudge by with my trumpet case and laptop, their voices a rough melody over the smack of their dominoes.

I find the buzzer marked *Perez*, and as I make my way up to her apartment in a rickety old elevator I worry for the thousandth time that things will be different with Shay in broad daylight. Will she realize what a dork I am compared to all the glittery people on her Instagram feed? Will she take one look at me, make some excuse about how she's too busy to hang out, and never text me again?

"Mira Mira!" She opens her door wearing a loose white tank top that says *diva* across the front in rhinestones, her hair in a messy pink topknot. The warm singsong of her voice immediately eases my fears, and I smile at her two younger sisters as they glance up at me from the TV in the living room.

"DJ Shay." I smile back.

"Man, that never gets old." She hands me a glass of sweet, bright-yellow lemonade. "Want to see my glamorous home studio? It's in the basement, where all the really rich and famous DJs keep their equipment."

I laugh. "Do I need a VIP wristband?"

"No, girl. You're rolling with me." She shouts at her sisters that she'll be right downstairs and to stay out of trouble as I follow her back to the elevator, which spits us out in an underground room filled with rusty metal dividers.

"Storage units," she explains as we weave through a maze of little metal rooms filled with moldy cardboard boxes and couches spilling stuffing. Some are packed to the ceiling, but Shay's is impeccably clean. She's organized it like a tiny studio, with her flight cases and speakers resting on a table made from plywood laid across two sawhorses. She's even added a pair of beat-up bar stools and a fluffy pink rug. "Baller, right?"

"The very lap of luxury." I perch on one of the stools. "So you want to learn about jazz?"

She nods, twisting a pink strand of hair around her finger. "It's so dope you knew who that sample was. I want to know shit like that."

"Well." I power up my laptop. "You've come to the right place."

"Get out." She leans in closer. "You made a PowerPoint?"

My cheeks go hot. In addition to working at the gym, practicing trumpet, and working on compositions for my audition, I've spent the past four days creating a beginner's history of jazz for Shay, complete with photos and audio clips and even a few historically accurate trumpet solos. Looking at it now, I realize how insanely, obsessively nerdy it must seem. I wait for her to start laughing, or tell me to get out again but mean it literally this time. Instead her eyes soften, and she holds a hand to her heart.

"You didn't have to do all this." She looks delighted. "I was just thinking you'd play me some tracks or something."

"Yeah, well . . ." I turn back to my laptop, hiding my smile. "Let's just start."

With that I dive into the roots of jazz, starting in New Orleans with the blues and ragtime and Dixieland, then heading north for swing and big band and detouring into Harlem for bebop. Each song fills me with aching familiarity; these are the tunes Grandpa Lou played for me when I was just a little girl, too young to know what the music was but old enough to know I loved it.

Grandpa Lou never played an instrument—when he was a kid there was never money, and when he grew up there was never time. Instead he listened, and when I came along he made sure I had the opportunities he never got. I've always loved jazz thanks to him, but now it's more than just a sound or a set of skills. It's how I keep his memory alive.

Shay taps her feet to Scott Joplin's ragtime and closes her eyes at Billie Holiday's smoky, sorrowful vocals. Sometimes she asks questions but mostly she just listens, taking it all in. When I pick up my trumpet for a Miles Davis riff she shakes her head, her eyes sparkling.

"Damn, you're *talented*!" she says, and the compliment warms me down to my toes. "Play more!"

"Really?" I ask, picking up my trumpet again. I play a few more songs, including my part from *Lou's New York,* and her eyes go wider with each note.

"You *wrote* that?" she asks.

I nod, pride swelling inside me. It feels good to share music with someone again; Crow and Nicky have been so busy settling into life at camp that we've barely had time to text, let alone talk about jazz.

"Shit." She shakes her head. "I don't know about teaching you to spin now. What if you show me up?"

"You don't have to," I say. Honestly, it's more than I was expecting this summer to be able to share jazz with someone who really listens and actually cares. But Shay is already flipping open flight cases and pressing buttons. She turns on the speakers with a pop and sizzle and the room seems to come alive; I can almost feel the electricity pulsing around us.

"I totally do," she says. "I offered, right?"

The turntables stare up at me and I remember the zing of excitement when I pressed the LOOP button at the warehouse, the way DJ Headspin commanded the crowd like the moon guides the tides. I think of Crow and Nicky at camp without me, and my empty room at home; the itch in my fingers to jam with people who aren't here and the long, boring hours minding the front desk at The Gym Rat.

I shrug. "May as well."

Shay presses a button and her equipment lights up, a rainbow of colored buttons and blinking LED screens. A beat like popcorn bursts through the speakers, kick drum and snare echoing off the concrete walls. "So the whole point of DJing is to keep people dancing," she says over the music. "And the only two things people won't dance to is silence, and music that sucks."

She plugs in her headphones. "Your job is to choose good music and keep it playing. Basically, you never want to give your dance floor an excuse to take a break."

She points to the CDJ on our right. "This is Channel One. The mixer—this box in the middle here—has two channels, and you can toggle between them using this slider—it's called the crossfader. Right now it's all the way to the right, so there's only music coming through Channel One. Got it?"

I nod. So far, it's not exactly rocket science. Sibelius, my music composition software, is way more complicated.

"This track is 128 beats per minute," Shay continues, "but I can use the pitch slider to speed it up or slow it down. Try it."

I pinch the cool metal between my fingers and push it all the way up. The beat goes into hyperdrive, the melody distorting into rapid Minnie Mouse squeaks.

"Yikes." I yank my hand away.

"Crazy, right? Now try pitching it down."

This time I'm slower. The track goes sluggish, until it sounds like it's struggling through tar.

Shay grins. "That's the basics. I'm gonna queue up a track on Channel Two, but you'll only be able to hear it through the headphones. It won't come through the speakers. Got it?"

She slips her pink rhinestone headphones over my ears. Suddenly my head is a mess of beats, drums smacking against each other like waves hitting rock. I grimace.

She reaches over and stops the turntable to my left. My ears clear.

"So your job is to match the beat from Channel One with the beat from Channel Two," Shay tells me. "You can use the pitch sliders or the jog wheel—that's this part here that looks like a record spinning. If you do it right, nobody will even hear the transition. And if you do it wrong . . ." She releases the turntable, sending the beats into chaos again.

I nod, stepping up to the rig and settling the headphones over my ears. This ought to be easy with my musical background. I hit START on the CDJ to my right and the now-familiar beat fills the room. I let it go for a few bars before bracing myself for the new beat to come through my headphones. Then I press START on Channel Two.

A gust of noise sweeps through the basement like a five-car pileup, rattling the metal storage cages.

"Aaaagh!" I leap back, throwing the headphones onto the table. "What the . . . ?"

I can tell Shay is trying not to laugh.

"Oh." I deflate. I forgot to move the crossfader, so now I'm playing both channels at once.

"Try again," Shay says encouragingly. "Nobody gets it the first time."

I turn away from her, my face burning, and settle the headphones over my ears. At first it's just a jumble of sound: rhythms circling and raising fists and wrestling each other to the ground. I have no idea which beat goes with which song.

Sweat starts to tickle my forehead. This is not as easy as I thought.

Shay places a tentative hand on my arm. "I'll give you a hint," she starts.

I shake my head. I don't want any hints. I should be getting this. I'm a musician, dammit.

My hand feels like a spider creeping toward the pitch slider. I ease it down to zero, then nudge it just a little more. My pulse slows with the beat and soon I'm able to pick out the new track in the thicket of noise, like finding and following a ribbon in a braid.

"Oh!" I turn to Shay.

"See?" she mouths.

The beats are almost the same speed now, only off by a fraction of a bar. Shay mimes touching the jog wheel, and I rest my fingertips on it. The beat pauses. I pick it up and it starts again. From the corner of my eye I see Shay nodding, tapping her foot in time to the song.

I release my fingers and let the track spin through to the end of a phrase. I can feel the purr of the machine under my fingertips, trembling like a greyhound at the gate. I check the crossfader, making sure it's still all the way to the right. And then, with the first track almost over, I release the jog wheel and begin edging the crossfader to the left, bringing the second track in nice and slow.

Shay's mouth goes slack. She raises her eyebrows, and when I take off the headphones I can hear my mix in the speakers, the beats perfectly synced. I let them stay there for a few measures before sliding the crossfader all the way to the left.

"Daaaamn," Shay says slowly. "You're picking this up really fast."

My face flushes. This feels like the first time I composed a full jazz piece on Sibelius, in my Intro to Composition class at Windham. The teacher, who was notoriously stingy with compliments, played it for the class and called it "remarkably good."

"Let's try another," I suggest.

Shay cues up a song, moving aside so I can mix it in.

"Am I getting it?" I ask as the songs blend together, mellowing into a single groove.

She nods, her lip between her teeth. "Damn. It took me, like, a week to learn this."

"Beginner's luck?" I joke, even though I'm not sure it is. I've always picked up music quickly—it's the only thing I'm really good at.

"Yeah, maybe." There's a shade of dusk in Shay's voice but she keeps going with the lesson, teaching me how to play with levels and when to bring in the highs and lows and mids. A couple of times I almost trainwreck, which is what Shay calls it when the beats stop running parallel, crashing off the tracks like a train derailing. But mostly I manage to keep the tunes going, and as song blends into song I feel my body ease into the music like it's a warm bubble bath. I stop stressing about my Fulton audition, stop missing Crow and Nicky and all my friends at camp, and let the music engulf me and my mind telescope inward until there's nothing in the world but these songs and knobs and sliders and buttons. It's like learning to play the trumpet all over again, and as I master each new skill I shed a piece of the pain and anger of my Windham-free summer. It feels good to be learning something new—even if it's not the type of education I was expecting.

"Alright, that's enough." Shay finally snaps off her system with a loud pop. "It's getting hot down here, right?"

"Sure," I say, gathering my laptop as she slides her equipment back into its cases. "I'm starting to see what you like about this."

"No shit. Cause you're good." The door to her storage cage rattles as she bangs it shut behind us. "Just don't go stealing my gigs, 'kay?"

"Never," I assure her. "I don't even want to be a DJ." But even as I say it I'm remembering the way it felt to make an entire warehouse full of people jump in the air at once.

"Sure you don't." Her sneakers squeak against the cement floor. "Everyone wants to be a DJ."

"*Everyone*?" I raise an eyebrow. "Like, your mom and stuff?"

"Okay, *almost* everyone." She gives me a playful shove. "Cause it's dope as shit, right? And if you do it right, you can make serious money."

"Really?" My ears perk up. Money is one thing I can always use more of. My parents can only afford to pay us minimum wage at the gym, and every penny of that goes into my car or my college fund. "Are you making money now?"

"Not yet." Shay presses the button for the elevator and taps her foot to some beat only she can hear. "Warehouse gigs pay, like, fifty bucks. I made way more selling molly, but who wants to do *that* all night?"

Molly. My shoulders tense at the word. A few days ago it was innocuous, melodious even: a girl's name with a sweet little trill. Now it's eating holes in my sister's brain.

"You sold molly?" I ask. Shay seems like the opposite of a drug dealer, small and sweet and open instead of big and shady and mean.

She stares down at her toes, scuffing them against the floor. "Not a lot. Just until I bought my CDJs. My ex had a hookup, so it was easy. Besides, it's not one of those nasty drugs like crack. It doesn't kill people."

I still can't get over the fact that the bubbly girl in front of me used to be a drug dealer. "Weren't you worried about getting caught?" I ask.

"Hell yeah. That's why I stopped." The elevator arrives with a sigh and Shay sends us groaning upward. "He said cops would never arrest me 'cause I'm a girl, but I was still scared as hell."

The elevator doors wheeze open and I realized we're not on Shay's floor. Instead we're at the base of a dark stairwell with a metal door at the top. *Fire Exit Only*, a big sign on it warns. *Alarm Will Sound.*

"Should we really . . . ?" I ask as she pushes the door. I brace myself for a pealing wail, but all I hear is Shay's gritty laugh.

"They disabled this thing years ago," she says, stepping into the sudden square of light. "It's the best thing about living here."

I follow her through the door and gasp. The entire world is spread out below us . . . miles of the Bronx's low brick buildings with Manhattan's skyline in the distance, silver spires gleaming against the last pastel streaks of a cotton-candy sunset. As I step onto the roof a breeze lifts my hair, making it dance in the air. To the north the apartment buildings peter out into suburban houses and low green hills. Coletown is up there somewhere, and way off in the distance are Crow and Nicky and Peter and Windham Music Camp. The wind plays a scale up my spine as I realize that Derek's out there somewhere too, planning his next warehouse party or just being gorgeous, doing whatever else it is that he does.

Shay plops down on the roof, and I take a seat next to her.

"There," she says, pointing to Manhattan. "That's where I'm going to make it." Her lips thin into a determined line. "I'm going to play every club on the west side. And someday I'll play Electri-City too."

"Electri-City?" I ask.

"Yeah, there, on Randall's Island." She turns until her finger lands on a speck of green in the East River. "It's like this giant, insane festival. It's totally my dream to spin there."

"I get it," I sigh, turning to Harlem and telling her about Fulton Jazz Conservatory—*my* dream.

"Hey." Shay sits down and crosses her ankles. "Play some more Miles Davis? I really liked his shit."

She doesn't have to ask me twice. "This," I say, pulling out my laptop and selecting *Kind of Blue*. "This album changed my life."

The first piano riffs float through the speakers, spare and searching and hopeful and sad. Shay gives a deep, contented sigh when the snare kicks in, and for a long time we sit there without saying anything, just listening to Miles and feeling the breeze on our necks and watching the sky grow dark.

Hearing this album now reminds me of Derek, of the way his eyes hit a bass chord inside me so low I never knew it was there. I want to ask Shay about him, to see if maybe they know each other from the party scene, but talking about it will make this feeling real in a way that maybe I'm not ready for yet. It still feels too raw, too personal. Private.

We stay on her roof, sometimes talking and sometimes just listening to Miles, until the sun has disappeared, leaving scraps of cloud hanging like laundry over the horizon. When the album is over I know it's time to go; I'm tired, and I have to work tomorrow. We descend the dark staircase and get on the elevator, Shay hitting *7* for her and *L* for me. She's just finished hugging me goodbye and is turning to leave when she stops the doors from closing with her foot.

"Hey," she says. "If you're not doing anything next Saturday, I'm spinning a daytime party out in Bushwick. I'll text you the info, k?"

Before I can agree—or not—she releases her foot and the door springs closed.

CHAPTER 9

As late May melts into early June I spend my days at The Gym Rat's front desk, frowning at half-written jazz compositions on my laptop in the long, empty stretches between swiping membership cards and washing threadbare towels. It's been a week since I hung out with Shay, and even though we've texted a few times we haven't had time to get together. She's been busy prepping for her next gig, and I've been obsessing over my audition, spending every moment I'm not at work holed up in my room with my trumpet. I've FaceTimed twice with Nicky and Crow, who swear that Windham isn't the same without me but somehow seem to be getting along just fine there regardless. I know I shouldn't resent them for it, but sometimes I still do.

The whine of a cheesy pop song slices through the gym. From the front desk I have a direct view of the dance studio, where Britt's teaching her Tuesday afternoon Cardio Jam class. She spins and her smile flashes, her teeth extra white in the room's harsh fluorescent glare.

Behind her, a half dozen Connecticut soccer moms shuffle along. They're the diehards who haven't defected to the new

Crunch across town, and my mom loves to point out that there are fewer of them every day.

"Lookin' great!" Britt calls over the music. "Now let's see some *attitude*!" She bonces, struts, pivots. She looks like a motivational poster, like the body you'd see beneath the word: *After.* She looks easy, confident, content.

But is she? Would a motivational poster really take drugs, even if she swears up and down they're perfectly safe?

Sighing, I drag my attention back to my laptop. I'm neck-deep in a new arrangement inspired by the warehouse party; I've spent the last hour adjusting the same six notes up and down and back again but nothing's working. That wild, poly-rhythmic energy feels stifled by my arrangement for trumpet, bass, and drums.

I need a break—just something to help me refocus so I can come back to this piece with a fresh ear. If I were at Windham I'd take a walk, run into friends, grab a soft serve from the dining hall, or just sit by the lake and let the quiet hum of nature clear my brain. But here I'm stuck. There's no escaping the whine of the treadmills, the bleat of overtaxed air condition-ers, and Britt shouting, "Kick, punch, spin!" from the dance studio.

I wish I could try DJing again. It's the only time in the past week I haven't been fixated on my Windham FOMO or my Fulton audition or my nagging worries about Britt. But I can't do it without Shay and her expensive equipment.

Or can I?

Shay may swear by her CDJs, but the DJ before her at the warehouse party—DJ Headspin—was using a laptop.

I have a laptop.

I pop open my browser and google "free DJ software." Suddenly I'm in in a tornado of options, swirling down a rabbit hole of features and reviews. As Britt leads her class in a mambo routine I select a program to download.

Then I need music. Google comes to my rescue again. Within seconds of searching "free dance music" I find myself sifting through hundreds of songs in dozens of genres: EDM, IDM, Big Room House, Mellow House, Beach House, Electro House, Dubstep, Crunkstep, Chillstep, 2-Step, Garage, Speed Garage, Breaks, Bass, Booty Bass, Future Bass, Jersey Club, Baltimore Club, Techno, Jungle, Psy-Trance, Drum and Bass, Hardstyle, Downtempo, Glitch. I don't know where to start so I just dive in, listening and downloading and filling my library with tracks from every genre, grabbing whatever sounds good. Some are forgettable, but others are so good it's hard to believe they're free.

I'm floating in a sea of beats, buoyed by the thrill of trying something new, when the door to the dance studio door flies open, releasing a cloud of perfumed sweat. I can't believe I didn't think of looking for free DJ software days ago. It's the perfect distraction, even better than playing mindless games on my phone.

Britt grabs a towel and blots her face, plopping onto the stool next to mine. "How's the front desk?" she asks.

"Front desk-y." I look up from my laptop, feeling disoriented in a dizzy, new-crush kind of way. I'd almost forgotten where I was. "How's teaching?"

"Tiring." She massages her temples.

"You looked like you were having fun."

"Yeah, well." Her hand moves up her head, rubbing the shaved part. "You're kind of supposed to."

Now that she's not leading a class anymore, Britt's lost some of her spark. She droops over the desk, elbows splayed, cheek resting against her palm. It makes sense that she's tired. She went out with Yelena again last night, and didn't come home until dawn.

"Hey, nice job in there." Dad jogs over and holds up his hand for a high five. Britt stares at it for a beat too long before offering a half-hearted slap.

Dad's grin falters. He doesn't lower his hand. "Once more with feeling?"

Britt forces a smile and tries again. The smack reverberates through the gym, making the lone guy on the treadmills miss a step and almost fall off.

"That's my girl!" Dad pretends to cradle his hand. "Hey, you talk to Coach Driggs yet?"

"Not yet." Britt looks down, kicking her heel against the stool's metal leg. A loud clang echoes through the gym.

"Better get on that." Dad pretends to elbow her in the ribs. "Time's a-wastin'."

"I know." Britt kicks the stool harder. *Clang.* "I will."

"Atta girl." Dad sprints across the gym to help one of the soccer moms adjust a stationary bike. I want to call after him that I'm here too—just because Britt's back doesn't mean I've ceased to exist. And yet, when it comes to my parents, it almost does.

Britt kicks the stool again, louder this time.

"You okay?" I ask.

Clang. "Yeah, why?" *Clang-clang. Clang.*

"You're kind of kicking the crap out of that stool."

"Am I?" *CLANG.* "Sorry."

"What's going on with you and Dad?" I ask. Normally she'd jump at the chance to kick soccer balls around with her old coach. Now she seems almost angry about it.

"Nothing. Are you going to that party on Saturday?" she asks, not-so-subtly changing the subject. "I saw your buddy Shay is spinning."

I consider pestering her more about Dad, but decide to let it go. "I think so," I say. The truth is, I'm actually looking forward to it. That's how lonely I've been.

Britt shakes her head. "It's crazy that you're friends with a DJ now."

I shrug. "Yeah, well . . . she was really nice to me after a certain *someone* ditched me to go be high."

"Shhhh!" Britt's gaze shoots over to Dad, and her voice drops to a whisper. "I've apologized like a million times. What'll it take to make you forgive me?"

"You could stop?" I suggest.

She laughs—a-*ha*-ha-ha-ha. "You worry too much," she says, elbowing me in the ribs.

I bat her arm away. "You give me too much to worry about."

"I'll be fine," she says, still whispering. "It's totally harmless, you can't get addicted, and you can't overdose. And it's not like I do it every day."

"But Miles Davis—"

"That was *heroin*." Britt shakes her head. "Seriously, I'm going to be fine. Unless I don't go take a shower right this second and literally die of my own stank."

She grabs a towel and starts toward the locker rooms. Halfway there she stops, pivots, and comes skipping back.

"But thank you for caring," she adds, planting a kiss on top of my head. "You're the sweetest."

Then she's gone again, leaving me alone with a laptop full of new music and a head still full of questions.

CHAPTER 10

"We are *painfully* early." Yelena fusses with her backpack as I pull the LeSabre up to a vacant lot surrounded by tall sheets of corrugated metal with the words *This Is A Lot* spray-painted across the front. We're in Brooklyn again, in a neighborhood that's all industrial buildings and street art and guys with beards riding bikes.

"Shay's performing first," I explain. "I told her I'd be here."

"Performing! God, you are so cute." Yelena pats my head. "You make it sound like a recital or something."

"That's 'cause recitals are what she's used to." Britt climbs out of the car and stretches. "We didn't need to come an *hour* early, though. Like, five minutes would have sufficed."

"We're not an hour early. Just forty-five minutes." I fetch my backpack from the trunk. "I told Shay I'd help her set up."

I don't tell them the real reason I wanted to come early: I have my laptop with me, and I want to ask Shay some questions about my DJ software. I've been playing around with it when audition prep gets too tough, watching tutorials and beat-matching the free tracks I downloaded, but I know I'm just skimming the surface. Shay said she'd give me a hand, but we haven't hung out since our DJ lesson and I'm pretty sure she'll be bombarded with admirers after her set. This might be the only chance I get.

"Such a Girl Scout," Yelena tuts, shouldering open the lot's plywood door. My feet slow as we enter, and my mouth goes slack. For a moment, I wonder if we're in the wrong place. Wooden pallets litter the ground, surrounded by thick bundles of cables. There are flats of water and beer next to a pair of folded card tables, and a half dozen people rush around carrying bundles of fabric and bags of ice that leave slime-trails in the dirt.

"Ugh, see?" Yelena groans. "If anyone finds out I showed up early, I'll lose all my cred."

"Why don't we go get a drink or something?" Britt suggests. "I saw a cute coffee bar like a block back."

"Brilliant!" Yelena throws her hands in the air, spinning in a circle. "Mimosas all around. Mira, you coming?"

"Nah." I bite my lip, hoping I'm making the right choice. "I'll wait for Shay."

"Suit yourself," Yelena says, taking Britt's arm and blowing me a kiss. They disappear through the plywood door and the world's longest minute ticks by as I wait for Shay, feeling more conspicuous with each second.

When five minutes have passed I start to worry. *Everything okay?* I message Shay. When she doesn't text back I sink onto one of the pallets and take in my surroundings: a hanging shoe rack filled with plants, rows of tables that look like they were scavenged from an old fast-food restaurant, and a decommissioned ice cream truck sitting on concrete blocks, flanked by massive speakers. A generator hums at its base, its throaty growl bouncing off the corrugated metal walls.

The setup crew is starting to give me funny looks, so I try to play it cool, sinking onto a pallet and pulling out my phone.

At another party, I text Nicky. *Think this one might be a mistake.*

So go home! he writes back. *Your trumpet probably misses you.*

No dice. I send him a sad-face emoji. *I'm Britt's ride.*

He messages back with a GIF of an elaborate shrug. Thanks, Nicky.

A guy struggling under an armload of Astroturf nearly trips over me. I leap up, spewing apologies, and move to a table where I'll be more out of the way. The party's supposed to start in fifteen minutes, but I'm still getting radio silence from Shay and the lot still looks like a garage sale.

Sighing, I pull out my laptop and start going through my new tracks. The longer Shay takes to get here, the less time I'll have with her, so I want to have all my questions ready to go.

"You can set up in there." I turn to find Astroturf Guy looking over my shoulder. He points to the ice cream truck.

It takes me a moment to realize what he means. "I'm not . . ." I start to say, but he's gone before I can explain. I go back to playing with the distortion effect and another few minutes tick by. Suddenly Astroturf Guy is back, this time carrying a bundle of tiki torches. "I thought I told you to set up," he says, a note of irritation in his voice.

"I'm not Shay," I explain.

He answers with a blank stare.

"The opening DJ?" I try again.

"Well, he's not here and we open in ten. Just play till he gets here, okay?"

"She!" I correct him.

He gives me a withering stare. "Huh?"

"DJ Shay is a *she*."

"Whatever. Just go play some shit." He hurries away, stabbing a tiki torch into the ground.

I open my mouth to call after him that I'm not a DJ, but something stops me. Maybe it's the way the generator's purring like a cat, or the empty window in the ice cream truck/DJ booth daring me to step inside. If Shay isn't here, and they need a DJ for a few minutes, is there any reason I *shouldn't* do it?

I gather my laptop and make my way to the ice cream truck. The inside has pink faux fur on the seats and old CDs covering the ceiling, making it look like a giant disco ball.

I hope you're okay!!! They want me to cover until you get here?! I text Shay before plugging in my laptop. I know how excited she was about this gig, but I also remember how close she cut it when I met her at the warehouse party. Maybe she's just the type of person who's always late to things.

My heartbeat picks up as I thumb through my tracklist, looking for the right song. Even though the party hasn't started yet and the fact that I'm even up here is a giant misunderstanding, I still want to put on a good show. Finally I pick a light, good-natured track that feels like summer sunshine and bunches of balloons. Maybe it'll put Astroturf Guy in a better mood.

I bring it in bright and strong, emphasizing the highs, and when the chorus starts I notice the staff outside pick up their pace. There's a new bounce to their step; a girl stringing fairy lights looks up from her ladder and nods in approval. A flush of pride tingles through me. This is different from spinning in Shay's basement or alone in my room, when all I cared about was getting the technical part right. This feels like a conversation with the people here, almost like I'm improvising with a jazz combo—except instead of responding with instruments they're giving me feedback with their faces and bodies.

I bleed the next track in and Shay still isn't here so I select another, rich with '60s-style psychedelic guitar riffs. From the ice cream truck's window I can watch the party slowly come together. The crew stacks pallets and plywood to form a dance floor; the sodas and card tables become a bar. I'm still worried about Shay and I itch to check my phone to see if she's texted, but between flipping through songs, matching beats, and tweaking levels, I don't have time. All I can do is hope she's okay.

I find a track with a gospel choir singing about universal love, then one that samples a rocket blasting into space. As I lose myself in the music I forget to worry about Shay, forget to wonder if Britt is going to take drugs again, forget to freak out about the fact that I'm DJing in front of real people for the first time. Track by track, I build a story with music: a story that takes place in a world where it's always the middle of summer and the sun is always shining, where there are no broke parents or greedy summer camps and my Grandpa Lou is still alive.

I'm in the middle of a mix when I feel the ice cream truck shift with new weight. Relief washes over me, combined with a tiny dash of disappointment: I'm glad that Shay is okay, but I was just starting to get in a groove. I finish mixing in the new track and spin around, ready to hand over my headphones.

But it's not Shay standing behind me.

It's Derek.

Derek, with the ice-blue eyes and rainbow tattoos. Derek, who's currently making me feel as warm and soupy as the first time we met.

Suddenly my heartbeat is the loudest thing in the lot.

"You didn't tell me you're a DJ," he says.

"I'm not." I'm way too aware of my knobby legs in jean shorts, my dorky blue pocket tee and makeup-free face and swollen, humid cloud of hair.

"Sure looks like it from here." He cocks his head, taking in my headphones, my laptop, the music coming through the speakers.

"Um. I'm just messing around. Filling in for a friend." My words tumble over each other. I can't tell if I'm saying too much or too little, talking too slow or too fast.

"Sounds like you're doing more than messing around."

My palms go slick. Derek's smile seems to distort the air around us, to make time move at a different rate.

"Who's your manager?" he asks. "Whoever it is got damn lucky."

"Manager?" I can't help laughing. "Are you kidding? I just learned how to do this last week."

"Reeeeeeeeally." He draws out the word: a slow, sexy drawl that hits below my stomach.

I shrug and he leans forward, a new intensity in his eyes. "You seriously just learned how to spin last week?"

His irises are blindingly blue. I turn back to my laptop so he can't see me trembling, and spend longer than I need to cueing up the next track. After the transition I can almost hear the music over my heartbeat again, and I sneak another glance his way.

He's inched closer. I feel dizzy.

"You really are new to this, huh?"

"Is it that obvious?"

"Only because of that." He points at my software. "Otherwise I'd swear you're a pro."

"Oh, well," I shrug, braving a smile. "Guess I'm busted."

His laugh is low and smooth, a sports car revving to action. "Next time you'll just have to cover your tracks."

My stomach spirals. "No pun intended."

He's just eased into a husky laugh when the ice cream truck heaves and Shay comes rushing in, her pink hair wild and her flight cases banging against her knees.

"Mira, I'm so sorry oh-my-god my ride broke down and I was on the phone with triple-A for an hour and I didn't see your texts and I can't believe you're actually covering for me and—"

She sees Derek and her stream of words freezes.

"Oh," she says, her voice suddenly flat. "*You're* here."

"Shay." He takes a step back, away from me. "Of all people."

"You guys know each other?" I choke.

"You could say that." Derek turns to me. "I gotta bounce. See you around."

He gives me a brief, bright smile. Then he's gone.

"Jesus, I'm sorry," Shay says again, heaving a flight case onto the table. "I can't believe they made you fill in for me. Did you tell them you've like literally never done this before?"

"I don't mind," I tell her. "This is fun."

"Well, thanks. I owe you. And look, they didn't even notice."

She gestures offhandedly at the ice cream truck's window. People have started trickling into the party, milling around the bar sharing hugs and cigarettes and leaning in close to talk over the music.

"I can take over now," she says, settling her pink rhinestone headphones over her head. "At least I'll get the last ten minutes of my own set."

I fade into the background and let her do her thing as she cues in her first track, only reappearing at her elbow when she unplugs my laptop. As she hands it to me she opens her mouth like she wants to say something, like it might be important.

Then she seems to change her mind, and instead we just stand there together, bouncing to the music and watching the party slowly fill through the ice cream truck's windows.

CHAPTER 11

Half the lot is in shadow when Britt and Yelena return, slurping up the dregs of iced lattes. I join them in one of the alcoves, now filled with a mattress and heaps of cheap, bright pillows. Yelena air-kisses both my cheeks and says Derek told her I saved the day with my DJ set. I fight the urge to grill her for details, and a moment later she sees someone she knows and goes screeching off, leaving me alone with Britt. My sister leans back against the pillows, releasing a soft puff of air. She seems a little spacey, kind of blissed out.

"Did you take drugs?" I ask.

She sighs. "I wish you'd stop saying 'take drugs' like I'm smoking crack or something."

"But . . . they're drugs," I remind her.

She shakes her head. "This is different."

"Fine." I roll my eyes. "Did you 'drop molly'?" I form air quotes around the words, borrowing a phrase I heard from Shay. "Are you 'rolling'?"

"I wish you'd stop judging." She settles back on her elbows, arching into a long stretch that shows off the muscles in her arms. She's wearing a purple terry-cloth romper, and the long side of her hair is twisted into dozens of tiny braids with baby barrettes on the ends.

"I'm not judging," I lie. "I just want to understand. Why . . . ?" I gesture at the party and her pupils, which are growing larger by the minute.

"Do you promise not to be all judgy if I tell you?"

I shrug. "I'll try."

She opens a pack of gum, sticks a piece in her mouth, and sighs as it hits her tongue.

"You know how I was always so competitive?" she says after a few contemplative chews.

I think of Britt on the soccer field, unstoppable until the ball nearly turned the goal inside out. I think of the hours I sat in her room watching her try on outfit after outfit before a party, nothing quite good enough until there was a pile of clothing up to my knees on the floor.

"I was trying so hard to be the best," she continues, still not looking at me. "And like, after a while I wasn't even sure I was happy anymore."

"But you always seemed happy," I say.

Her jaw works around the gum. "Sure. But then college happened."

She pauses and the music pauses with her, electric violins floating through the air like dust motes. I never knew any of this about Britt. Everything was always so easy for her. She was the girl who had it all.

"What do you mean?" I ask.

Britt takes a long breath. "So like, the coach was really mean. And so were the other girls on the team."

"Mean to *you*?" I can't keep the surprise out of my voice. Nobody has ever been mean to Britt. She's the golden girl, popular wherever she goes.

She nods. "They all hated me because I had a scholarship. Even Coach—he thought I should be trying twice as hard."

That sucks," I say, wondering why she never told me any of this before. Every time we talked online she said things were fine. Great, even. Was I just not asking the right questions?

She runs her hand over her romper, mussing the terry cloth. "So then Yelena came along and she was like the only person who'd been decent to me in forever. She invited me to my first party, and it was like this whole other world opened up. The people there were *nice*. It felt like one big happy family where everyone loved each other and nobody was a dick. And she said it was because of molly."

I remember the cluster of people in the warehouse who helped me to my feet when I fell, the girl who gave me her bandana and the guy who offered me a hug.

"So you tried it?" I ask, feeling fascinated and sick.

She shakes her head slowly. "Not right away. Yelena worked on me for a while. But then I finally did and I just *got* it. And it made everything so much better."

"Better how?" I'm leaning forward, watching her rub her hand more forcefully along her romper.

"Better like . . . I liked people again. And I could forgive them. Even those bitchy girls on the soccer team. You just, like, feel like you understand people, and people understand you. It's like, everything just seems to make sense in this really beautiful way."

I sit back, letting her words roll over me and wondering what it would be like to forgive Gabriella Lawson and the rest of the cretins at Coletown High who call me Sad Trombone. But when I think about them all I feel is anger, the same minor chords played long and low and loud. Could a pill really fix that? Would I take it if it could?

Britt shakes her head like she's clearing it, a smile playing across her face. "But enough with the philosophy already," she says, pushing herself up to standing. "Let's go dance."

This time, I don't even try to argue. I let her pull me to my feet and drag me onto the dance floor.

CHAPTER 12

The sky is the color of strawberry ice cream by the time the third DJ goes on. The fairy lights above the bar twinkle to life like colored sprinkles, and a wave of sound surges through the speakers. This DJ cranks the sound as loud as it'll go; my ears scream in protest, but nobody else seems to mind. The dance floor pulses, a mass of bodies with Britt and Yelena lost somewhere in its depths. I fumble in my pocket for the earplugs Derek gave me; I've felt silly carrying them around since the warehouse party, a slightly linty token of something I can't quite put into words, but now I feel like a genius. I'm about to pop them in when an arm swoops in, stopping my hand.

An arm covered in tattoos.

"Please tell me those aren't the same earplugs I gave you last week," Derek says.

"Maybe. But I washed them?" I struggle to keep my voice even. I need to keep my cool.

"Uh-uh. Still gross." He smiles, the corners of his eyes crinkling. "I have a ton back at my place. Take a walk with me?"

His place? I open my mouth to say yes, but all that comes out is a thin croak.

"You won't miss much." His eyes smile. "It's only three blocks away."

I nod, not trusting myself to speak, and follow him through packs of dancers and out the corrugated metal door. Once we're on the sidewalk Derek slows his pace, letting me fall into step beside him. I can't help noticing the wiry hair on his legs, so different from Peter's dark, downy fluff back at music camp. I gulp hard. Derek isn't a kid like Peter. He's a man, or almost one, and being near him makes my heart do laps and my stomach do flips and my hands want to fly away.

The rhythm of his walk is loose and easy, with a silvery jingle whenever his right foot hits the pavement. To soothe my nerves I work on a melody to go over it, something freeform and meandering to match the roll of his shoulders and swing of his arms.

"What're you humming?" he asks.

"Just something I made up."

I hadn't realized I was humming. We turn onto a side street lined with auto-repair shops and old one-story warehouse buildings, and I make a mental note to enter my new tune into Sibelius when I get home.

"Really?" Derek raises an eyebrow. "So you're a producer too?" He stops in front of one of the buildings and fishes a set of keys from his pocket.

"No. A composer. I write music."

"Right." He gives me a funny look and leads us up a narrow flight of stairs. "Like a producer."

I open my mouth to argue but then think that maybe this is more electronic music language, like "track" instead of "song" and "spin" instead of "perform." And then Derek opens the door to his apartment and I gasp.

Spread out in front of me is the loft I've always dreamed of. It's everything I picture when Crow and Nicky and I talk about getting a place off campus: huge windows, a makeshift stage and DJ booth, mismatched couches and piles of books, and kitchen cabinets painted bright, funky colors. A spiral staircase leads to a balcony that runs the length of the room.

"Nice, huh?" He closes the door with a satisfied click.

"It's . . . perfect." I can't help imagining Crow and Nicky up on that stage playing one of my pieces while I listen from a beanbag chair on the floor, surrounded by instrument cases and pizza boxes. "Do you have roommates?"

He laughs. "You think I could afford this place on my own?"

"I don't know." I shrug, feeling even younger than I am. "I'm not super knowledgeable about the rent situation in Brooklyn."

He shakes his head. "You're funny. Yeah, I have roommates. Four of them. They're all at the party right now."

"Oh." So we're alone here. Just the two of us in this big, empty loft, Derek loose and relaxed and me wound so tight my spine feels like it could shoot out the top of my head.

He brushes past me, sending sparks up my arm, and starts up the spiral staircase. "Let's get you those earplugs."

With each step my pulse drums louder, thundering in my ears as he opens a door off the balcony and ushers me into his room. For a moment everything is dark, and then he flips on a halogen lamp, revealing piles of plastic bins and cardboard boxes spilling clothes and party flyers and sound equipment. His bed rests on a double layer of milk crates, and there are posters of parties and DJs and festivals tacked to the wall two and three deep. I recognize a fresh one, directly over his bed, for Electric Wonderland.

"You threw all these parties?" I ask.

"Most, yeah." He perches on the edge of his bed and pats the place next to him. I pick my way through patches of bare floor until I'm next to him on the bed. Our thighs are three inches apart. Not that I notice.

"You go to NYU?" I ask, spotting a purple spiral notebook with the school's logo.

"Yeah." He rolls his eyes. "Not my idea."

"Why not? It's a good school."

"If you're into that kind of thing."

"You're not?"

"Hell no." He leans back on his arms, sending our thighs an inch closer. "I want to be throwing parties, not wasting time studying crap I'll never use."

"What about their music business program?" For a while Crow and Nicky and I were looking at NYU's Tisch School of the Arts, before we fell hard for Fulton and never looked back.

"Yeah, I did that for a year. But it's totally fake and corporate." He rubs a hand over his face. "It's all about contracts and record labels."

"Is that a bad thing?"

"Maybe not for some people. But I'm not about that."

"What are you about?" I let my eyes linger on the sharp line of his chin, the dark splash of eyelashes against his cheek.

He turns to me, his eyes lighting up. "The music, for one thing. And just the vibe, and creating something beautiful from almost nothing."

"That sounds cool," I sigh.

He grins. "It's what I love about throwing parties—you don't need a million dollars or a bunch of corporate guys in suits to do it. Just a good raw space and a sound system and some DJs. It's like we're all making it up as we go along, but that makes it so much better, you know?"

"Like you're improvising?"

"Exactly." He scratches his bicep, revealing a piece of tattoo I hadn't noticed before: a peacock with its tail turning to fire. "You get it."

I nod, even though I'm not sure I do. Improvising a warehouse party seems pretty different from improvising a jazz trio.

"So why not drop out?" I ask. "If it's not what you want to be doing."

His chin dips, his eyes drifting away for a moment. "Like I said, not my idea. Now it's *my* turn to ask *you* something."

My body tenses. Usually when someone's voice dips into that low, intimate register before asking me a question, it's about my skin or my hair. *What are you, anyway?* is a popular one, and even though it's nosy and invasive (if I want to tell you about my heritage, I will), it's still not as annoying as when people try to guess. I've gotten Italian, Mexican, Hawaiian, Brazilian, Israeli, and once a little kid even asked if I was Moana. I hate it when people try to categorize me, put me in a neat box and stick a label on me like I'm a dead insect in a glass case. Like they can't decide what they're going to think of me until they do.

"I'm biracial," I explain, before he can ask. "My dad is black and my mom is white."

Derek sits back, surprised. "That's not what I was going to ask. But thanks for letting me know, I guess?"

"You weren't?" A giddy relief seeps through me. Peter Singh assumed I was Latina the first time we met. I forgave him, but I never forgot it. "What were you going to ask?"

"Did you really just learn how to DJ last week?"

It's so different from what I was expecting, I laugh. "I *really* did. Is that so hard to believe?"

"Yeah, it is." He tilts his chin, giving me a look through half-slit eyes that turns my insides to pudding. "I've never seen a setup crew all into the music like that. Usually they're just running around like crazy, trying to get everything done. But you had this kind of power over them. Hell, you had this kind of power over *me*."

My hands start to sweat. "Me?" I squeak.

"Yes, you. You could really make a go of it, if you want."

"How?" I ask, genuinely curious. Shay never told me how she became a DJ. I always kind of pictured her emerging from the womb in her sparkly pink headphones.

"You know . . . play some parties, make some mixes, get your name out there. What's your Instagram?" he asks, taking out his phone.

The only pictures on my Instagram are dorky recital photos. "I don't have one," I say quickly.

He shakes his head. "You'll have to change that. It's all about image. You gotta promote, promote, promote."

"Oh." I deflate. "Image isn't really my thing."

"Why not? It could be. You have a great look."

My body ignites. Is he saying I'm pretty?

"So what is your thing, anyway?" Derek asks, leaning back on his elbows.

"You really want to know?"

"I really do."

"Fine." My breath catches in my throat. "I want to be a jazz composer."

He sits up suddenly, bringing our faces level and reminding me all over again that we're alone. In his bedroom. On his bed. "Jazz?"

"Yeah. You know: skiddly-bee-bop, lots of snare . . . that kind of thing?"

He gives me a lopsided smile. "So that tune you made up earlier: was that jazz?"

"Yeah. It was 3/4 time, probably for trumpet, bass, and drums. I actually based it off the way your keys jingled when you walked." I'm talking too fast. I tell myself to slow down, to keep my cool.

"And you just . . . do that? Write songs in your head while you're walking down the street?"

"Sure. There's music everywhere. You just have to listen for it."

"Interesting *and* talented." Derek shakes his head. "And cute. You really should try DJing for real. Maybe I could help you get some gigs."

"You think?" The word tickles something inside me: gigs. Was Shay serious when she said DJs can make serious money? Could that be me?

"I do." Derek's voice drops low, drawing me in. We're sitting closer now, our thighs officially touching. The soft cotton of his jeans feels like it's searing a hole in my flesh.

I can't think with his face this close to mine.

He smiles with only his eyes and tilts his head. Silence stretches around us until it feels like every sound in the world has been sucked away. I want to move closer but I'm paralyzed, scared I'm reading this wrong. Or that I'm reading it right.

His phone rings.

He moves away. The moment ends. He looks at his screen and groans before answering.

"Hi, Mom." He holds up a finger, rolling his eyes.

A soprano squall rises from the speaker.

"No, I said tomorrow."

The squall thickens.

"No, I *definitely* said tomorrow. There's no way I can make it out today, I'm in the middle of something important."

Important. Does he mean *me*?

"I'm sorry, Mom. I told you I'd come out and finish it Sunday. Not Saturday. Can you please wait one more day?"

The squall drops to an alto, the spaces between words expanding.

"Okay, then. I'll see you tomorrow. I love you, Mom."

A single squeak.

"Come on, don't be like that. We had a misunderstanding. I said I love you, okay?"

Three words, reluctantly.

"Okay. Bye."

He jams the phone back in his pocket.

"Don't ask," he says to me. His voice sounds like sawdust.

"I won't." I try not to let disappointment swell my voice. I rub my hands together, stretch my legs. "Well. Should we get back?"

His lip twitches. "I guess we should."

I ease myself off the bed and follow him through the neighborhood in silence, Derek jingling whenever his right foot hits cement. It isn't until we round a corner and the music from the party rises to greet us that I realize something.

Derek stops suddenly. "The earplugs," he says.

"I know. I just remembered."

Our eyes meet. I make a noise like a fountain bubbling over, and a chuckle rumbles low in Derek's throat. Suddenly we're laughing so hard we have to hold on to each other to stand up.

"I can't believe we forgot them," Derek gasps, his hands on my elbows.

"I know." I steady myself on his shoulders, our bodies inches apart.

"We should go back." He stops laughing and looks in my eyes, and my stomach flips hard. "Do you want to go back?"

"Ye—" I start to say.

"Derek!" The bouncer at the gate booms out his name, his face an angry block of concrete. "These kids tried to sneak in." He points to a trio of guys with baseball caps pulled low over their foreheads.

"Shit." Derek looks from me to the bouncer, and sighs. "You should probably give me your number," he tells me. "For earplug delivery purposes."

"Oh." My face goes hot. "Yeah, of course."

I give it to him, and he types it in his phone and then texts me a winky-face emoji so I'll have his number too. And then even though he has to stay with the bouncer while I go back into the party, even though the music is loud and boring and Shay is busy dancing with her friends and it takes me almost an hour to find Yelena and Britt, the rest of my night feels like hearing your favorite song on the radio—not just once but on repeat all night long.

CHAPTER 13

Derek doesn't text the next day, or the next. But even as a day turns into a week and my giddy anticipation peters out into disappointment his walk stays with me, and I can't forget the tune I started humming on the way to his loft.

I enter it into Sibelius so his foot hitting the pavement becomes a kick-drum, the shuffle of his jeans a snare and the jingle of keys a marimba, coppery and fleeting. The bass line is the easy roll of his shoulders, the way the sun glanced off his hair. And the trumpet is how I felt being with him, that dizzy airiness so full of possibilities.

When the arrangement is done I title it 'His Walk' and send it to Crow and Nicky, then FaceTime them to find out what they think. It's been six days, three hours, and twenty-seven minutes since I said goodbye to Derek, and by now I'm pretty sure I just imagined that moment in his bedroom, when the silence stretched around us for miles. I'm doing my best to forget him. I've even started thinking about hooking up with Peter again when I go to Windham over the Fourth of July, for Visitors' Weekend—Funyun breath be damned.

"What do you think?" I cut to the chase as soon as Crow answers. It's the end of the last free period of the day at Windham, when I know they'll be hanging out in the communal lounge. Familiar worn couches and framed portraits of great musicians swim into view as I balance my laptop on my lap in bed. I try to swallow the rush of FOMO.

"Nicky!" Crow turns and yells over her shoulder. "Stop flirting and get over here. It's Mira!"

Nicky? Flirting? The only other openly gay guy at camp last year was a sad-eyed bassoonist who wore the same holey Igor Stravinsky T-shirt every day. I wonder if Nicky decided to go for it anyway—or if there's someone new on the scene.

Nicky pops into the frame, his cheeks scarlet and his hair mussed.

"Who're you flirting with?" I ask.

"Nobody," he says quickly. "Crow's imagination has gotten the better of her, as usual."

I decide to let it go. We only have a few minutes until lights-out, and I *need* to hear what they think about my piece. "So what do you think of 'His Walk'?" I ask.

"Oh, it's okay." Nicky's face goes redder. "I mean he has those long legs, and . . ."

"*Nicky!*" Crow backhands him lightly on the shoulder. "She's talking about her piece."

"Right. I knew that." Nicky's face is the color of stewed tomatoes. "It's good!"

"It's *excellent*," Crow corrects him. "The bass is hot!"

"And the marimba," Nicky agrees, his eyes flitting past my shoulder, to someone in the lounge I can't see. "I like the marimba."

"Maybe we could play it for Visitors' Weekend?" I suggest. "At one of the recitals. They'd let me sit in for one piece, right?"

"Ugh, I *wish*," Crow sighs. "Between recitals and the ensemble concert I'm playing two different versions of 'Embraceable You.' *Two*! Can you believe it?"

A knot starts to form in my stomach. "They already finalized the program?" I was counting on Visitors' Weekend to debut this piece. It's the only chance I'll have this summer to play in front of a crowd.

"Yeah, last week." Crow squints at me from below the brim of her fedora. "You didn't know?"

"How would I know?" My stomach twists. "It's not like I'm there."

Crow scrunches up her forehead. "I thought we told you. Maybe you were so busy with all that raver stuff you missed it?"

"Raver stuff?" My voice goes flat. "Did you seriously just call it that?"

"Whatever." Crow takes off her glasses and cleans them on the tail of her men's dress shirt. "I'm almost positive we told you."

"Crow." I speak very calmly and evenly, because I know if I don't I'll scream. "You told me Regina started a food fight in the dining hall. You told me two string players got caught hooking up in a paddleboat. You did not tell me the deadline to submit pieces for Visitors' Weekend was coming, because I would have remembered that. I would have written this faster."

"We can still give it a couple run-throughs," Nicky jumps in. "Just like, informally, during free hours. I'll book a practice room."

"I don't *want* a practice room." The knot in my stomach squeezes tighter. "This piece is *good*. I want people to hear it."

"I'm sorry." Nicky shakes his head. "I don't know what to say."

"People will hear it someday," Crow adds. "We'll play it all the time at Fulton. Every night!"

I stay silent. All the disappointment of the last few days comes crashing over me: Not hearing from Derek, which matters even though I keep telling myself it doesn't. Feeling like a third wheel when I hung out with Britt and Yelena and they gabbed endlessly about clubs in the city I can't get into and people at Pepperdine I don't know. And now losing my only chance to perform at Windham this summer, my only chance to play for a real, live audience before my audition.

Nicky reads the disappointment on my face. "I'm sorry," he murmurs, the pink draining from his cheeks and making him look sallow in the fluorescent light. "We'll figure out a way to make it up to you."

A counselor calls for lights-out, and Crow and Nicky give me apologetic air-kisses before signing off, swearing again that they'll make up for it somehow when I see them on the Fourth of July. I pick up my trumpet and play a long, angry blast that echoes through the empty house. Britt went into the city with Yelena and my parents are still at the gym, trying to fix a leaky pipe in the basement so they can save money on a plumber.

I play the melody from my new piece, first to tempo and then with a slow, bluesy swing. I try it in a minor key, echoing the way I feel. But it sounds lonely all by itself. That's the thing about jazz: it's not the kind of music you play alone. Jazz is improvisational, collaborative, built in the moment. You can practice on your own, but when it comes to really feeling the music in your blood you need other people; you need your combo.

But you don't need other people to DJ.

I open my laptop and click into my DJ software, my fingers suddenly itching to get at the controls. As I slip into a noise-scape of drum-machine beats and fat, juicy bass, I'm transported back to the party last weekend, the connection I created with the crew as they set up. If I can't perform my jazz pieces this summer, maybe I can find a crowd to DJ for instead.

My mind flicks back to my conversation with Derek in his bedroom. *Play some parties*, he said. *Make some mixes. Get your name out there. Maybe I can help get you some gigs.*

I haven't been invited to play any parties and have no idea how to get my name out there, but I bet I can figure out how to make a mix.

As I begin selecting tracks and layering them together so they blend like my favorite flavors of ice cream, some of the sting of the past week melts away. I may not be able to control the program for Visitors' Weekend; I can't control Britt's partying or Derek's lack of texts or my family's finances.

But I can control this. When it comes to this, I have all the control in the world.

CHAPTER 14

I text Shay as soon as my mix is finished. She's meeting up with some friends in a park and invites me to come along, so I scrunch some moisturizer into my hair and dig out my least nerdy top, a plain black tank that's a hand-me-down from Britt.

Shay's friends have staked out the area near a skateboard half-pipe, marking their territory with a patchwork of blankets and beach towels and a Bluetooth speaker blasting upbeat house music. As I squeeze in next to Shay they take turns falling off a pair of skateboards and alighting on the blankets like a flock of pigeons.

I've seen these people before, surrounding Shay after her set in the warehouse and swallowing her into their crowd at *This Is A Lot*. Shay tells me they've all been going to parties together since her freshman year, and I can tell by the way they act. They're friendly enough when Shay introduces me, but they talk mostly to each other, in a patter so thick with shared history and in-jokes it may as well be another language.

My throat constricts as I realize that this is how Crow and Nicky and I must sound. I can almost picture them in the dining hall right now, probably dumping Froot Loops and Cap'n Crunch on bowls full of soft serve. FOMO strikes hard, leaving a searing emptiness in my chest.

"So you made a mix?" Shay asks, turning to me. She has a plastic tackle box open next to her and is giving herself a manicure, complete with tiny jewels she attaches to her nails with tweezers.

I nod. "Is it okay if I play it?" I ask, gesturing to the speaker.

"Go for it," her friend Ty says, grabbing his iPhone and silencing the house track. "Shay says you're really good!"

"Thanks." My hands go clammy as I connect to the speaker and hit "play" on my mix. I've been obsessing over it for the past three days, tinkering with the order and smoothing out my transitions. Now I'm nervous to be debuting it not just for Shay, but also her entire crew.

A third of the way through, I can't take the suspense anymore. "What do you think?" I ask Shay.

"It's dope!" She reaches for a lavender rhinestone. "Definitely high energy. And your transitions are tight."

"I'd dance to this," Ty adds, giving me a shy half smile from under shaggy bangs.

"Anything you'd do different?" I ask. I'm used to Crow and Nicky's brutal honesty, but with this they wouldn't even know where to start.

Shay scrunches up her nose. "I didn't love that third track. With all the whooshing sounds?"

"Agreed," Ty says. "Too slow."

"Like that set at that party in Baltimore," their friend Lin giggles. "With the rain?"

"Oh man." Ty shakes his head. "That was a crazy night."

I try not to squirm as they launch into a memory I'll never be a part of, then another and another. As soon as the mix is over, I pounce on Shay.

"So?" I ask impatiently.

"Like I said, it's dope." She turns to her friends. "Right, guys?" Lin and Ty nod.

"Okay." I drum my fingers on my leg. "So once I fix that third track—then what?"

"What do you mean?" Shay asks, blowing on her nails.

"What do I do with it after that?"

"Why?" Shay fans her fingers through the air. "You change your mind about wanting gigs?"

"Maybe," I mumble, looking down at my feet.

"Hah." She gives me a triumphant grin. "Told you—everyone wants to be a DJ. 'Cause it's dope as shit."

"Dope as shit," Lin choruses, laughing.

I feel like I've been caught with my hand in the candy jar. "So let's just say, hypothetically, that I did want gigs." I try to look casual as I wipe my hands on my shorts. "What would I do?"

Shay shrugs. "Post it online. Send it out to your followers. Ask people to share it. Send it to promoters and see if they'll book you."

"Right," I say, like I knew it all along. Like I have any followers. "That makes sense."

"I know—it's a hustle." She pats me gingerly on the knee, careful not to mess up her manicure. "DJing is like ten percent making music and ninety percent figuring out whose ass to kiss."

I laugh, even though I'm groaning on the inside. "I feel like I should embroider that on a pillow," I say, disconnecting my phone and putting it in my pocket.

"Make it pink and I'll buy it off you," Shay jokes. "You heading out?"

I nod. "It's a long drive home."

She stands and kisses me on the cheek. "Text me if you want to hang again," she says. "We come here a lot."

I wave goodbye to her friends and spend the drive home wondering if I should really take her advice and post my mix online. Is there a possibility it could get me gigs—and that, eventually, I could start making money?

At home I swap out the third track and export the mix to mp3 format. Then I sit staring at the green waveform for a long time. Up until now I've just been messing around: downloading tracks, beat-matching alone in my room, playing a slot I wasn't booked for at a party that hadn't started yet. But now it's starting to feel different. It's starting to feel real.

I shake my head. I'm being ridiculous; posting this mix won't change anything. It won't make me a DJ. Electronic music is just a stopgap to fill the void that Windham left in my life. As soon as Crow and Nicky come home I'll have my combo back. I can start really playing jazz again, not just practicing alone in my room, and my real life as a musician and composer will resume.

Until then, it doesn't hurt to experiment.

I go to the website Shay recommended and create a profile. It asks for a photo and my DJ name, so I snap a quick selfie standing in front of my egg-crate-foam wall and type *Mira Mira* into the name bar. It's the best I can come up with, and in a way it's a tribute to Shay, the way she always says my name.

Then, before I can chicken out, I upload my mix and push it live. My breathing is the loudest thing in the room as I sit there waiting for something to happen.

But, of course, nothing does.

I think about how I don't have any followers or know any promoters.

And then I think about how that's not, strictly, true.

I promised myself I wouldn't text Derek if he didn't text me first. I don't want to seem too eager, or like I see something between us that isn't there. I'm not one of those girls who goes chasing guys who aren't interested. I'm like Miles Davis: I play it cool.

But if I'm texting Derek as a promoter, not a guy I like . . . that's different, right? That's not being desperate. That's just hustling. And according to Shay, I have to hustle if I want to get gigs.

So I text him: just a link to the mix, and nothing else.

It's not like I have anything else to say.

It's not like I have anything left to lose.

CHAPTER 15

Two days, thirteen hours, and eight minutes after I text Derek the link to my mix, my phone rings.

At first I ignore it. I'm finishing up my shift at the gym, and ever since Grandpa Lou died, the only calls I've gotten are wrong numbers. But then I glance at the screen and a bomb goes off in my chest.

"Mira." Derek's voice turns me liquid. "We have to talk about your mix."

My throat goes dry. "Is it bad?"

"No. Mira, *no*. It's *good*."

My body starts to vibrate. "Oh. Wow. Thanks."

"Don't thank me. Can you come to Brooklyn? I'm taking you to dinner tonight."

I almost drop the phone. Ten days of silence, and now this?

"Mira? Are you still there?"

"Tonight?" I croak.

"Yeah, as soon as possible. You already have plans?"

Play it cool, I tell myself. *Tell him you already have plans.*

"Not really," I hear myself say.

"Great." He gives me the name of the pizza place. "See you soon," he says, and hangs up without saying goodbye.

I leap up, run to the locker room, and stare at myself in the mirror. The girl gazing back at me does not look ready to go have dinner in Brooklyn with a guy who looks like Derek. Her Gym Rat polo hangs like forgotten laundry from her shoulders, her hair's an oversized cumulus cloud, and her face looks bare and surprised.

I can't meet up with Derek looking like this. I weave through the rows of weight machines, knocking on the door to the rear office.

"Mir-Bear!" Mom looks up from her computer and rubs the creases from her forehead. "Is everything okay?"

I nod, and my voice comes out very small. "I kind of have this thing tonight and I was wondering if maybe, if you have time, you could do my makeup?"

Her face brightens. "Really? Oh, how fun!"

Within seconds she's unloading pounds of cosmetics from her locker, spreading them across the vanity before taking my chin in her hand and turning my face one way and then another, examining it in the light.

"So tell me about this 'thing' you have." She can't stop smiling. "Is it formal? Trendy? Boho?"

"Not formal. You really don't need to go crazy. I just want to look a little more . . ." my voice ebbs.

"A little more what?" She opens an eye shadow palette, frowns, and closes it with a plasticky snap.

"Pretty, I guess." I twist the edge of my tank top.

"Oh, Mir-Bear. You're *always* pretty." Mom's eyes narrow, and a sly grin creeps across her face. "Wait a minute. Is this 'thing' a *date?*"

"That's none of your business," I mutter.

"Of course it's my business. I'm your mother!" She reaches for an eye pencil, her voice brimming with delight. "Who is he? Do we know him? Is he cute?"

"*Mom*," I say. "It's not a date. We're just getting pizza. That's all."

"Sounds like a date to *me*," she chirps, pressing me onto a stool and going at my face with an assortment of pencils, tubes, and brushes. "Can you at least tell me his name? Does he go to your school?"

"Derek," I say, eyes still shut. "And . . . no."

"Well, we'd love to meet him." Mom brushes something cool along my lids. "Maybe you can bring him by?"

I squirm under the feathery touch of her brush. "Maybe sometime," I say, meaning never. Dad would have a heart attack if the first-ever boy I brought home was a tattooed college student.

She finishes my lids and tells me to open my eyes.

"What do you think?" she asks, spinning me so I face the mirror.

I look at my reflection and gasp. Mom lined my eyes in subtle shades of brown and curled my lashes. I barely look like I'm wearing makeup; instead I just look older, more sophisticated. Almost like I belong with Derek.

"It's perfect," I breathe.

"You should let me do this more often." Mom smoothes styling gel into my hair, gathering it into a thick French braid that circles the back of my head—one of the styles Aunt Shonda taught her when Britt and I were little. "So pretty," she sighs, and I have to agree. Now I look older *and* almost elegant.

"Thanks," I say, scooting off of the stool and grabbing my bag.

"My pleasure." Mom gives me her biggest, toothiest grin. "Have fun tonight. And be safe!"

"I will," I promise. But my heart is already beating dangerously fast, and safety is the last thing on my mind.

CHAPTER 16

The pizza place where I meet Derek isn't like the ones in Coletown. A waitress with huge black spirals in her ears leads me through a dimly lit room and into a multilevel backyard, where Derek's waiting for me at a wrought iron table under an arbor dripping with vines. He's even better looking than I remembered, his multi-colored arms loose and sinewy in a black T-shirt, his face all sharp lines and ice-blue eyes.

As soon as he sees me he leaps to his feet, comes around the side of the table, and kisses me lightly on the cheek. Goose bumps rise on my skin and I force myself not to melt into a giant puddle of girl on the floor.

I remind myself to play it cool. I just need to pretend I go out to dinner with handsome older guys every night of the week; that my experience with them doesn't begin and end with awkwardly groping Peter Singh in a practice room at summer camp.

"You look nice," he says, resting his hand on the small of my back and setting off a tiny fire there. "I like your hair."

"Thanks." I touch the braid self-consciously.

"So your mix." Derek leans forward as I open my menu, his fingernails drumming in 7/8 time on the tabletop.

"Yes?" My pulse thumps along.

"It's really good." His smile is quick and light. I lean into his words, barely conscious of the waitress setting a glass of water by my elbow. "You know how to set a mood with music. It built kind of slow but once it did—damn!"

I reach for my water, grateful to have something to do with my hands. I take a long sip.

"Plus you have this look. . . ."

He trails off. I raise an eyebrow.

"I mean, I hope it's okay for me to say this, but you're fucking hot."

I choke. Not figuratively. Literally. Water shoots from my nose and dribbles down my chin; my eyes burn as I double over, spluttering and hacking. The waitress hands me a stack of napkins, rolls her eyes, and flounces off again. Derek comes around the side of the table and pats me gently on the back as I dab at the wet spot on the front of my T-shirt. So much for playing it cool.

"It went down the wrong pipe," I explain, my voice strained. Nobody has ever called me "hot" before—not even Peter. Britt has always been the hot one: the one with the looks, the style, the cool clothes.

The waitress returns and looks at me like I'm a drowned cat as Derek places our order. "You don't have dietary restrictions, do you?" he asks me as she's walking away.

I shake my head.

"A girl after my own heart." He smiles, leaning back in his chair. "Half the people I know are vegan or gluten-free or can't even look at a peanut without bursting into flames."

"My parents are paleo," I volunteer. "So I basically live off carbs and cheese."

"You rebel, you." His eyes crease at the corners when he smiles. I notice myself noticing this, reach for my water again, and then think better of it. I don't trust my body to do what I tell it to.

"So I found something I think you might like," he says, raising an eyebrow.

"Found something? That *I* might like?" Derek barely knows me. How can he guess what I'll like?

"I do some work with this crew, the Pax Collective," he says. "They're putting on this festival in a couple weeks, the Pax Summerfest. . . ."

"Wait." The name jogs something. "Shay was talking about that. I think she's playing there?"

Derek shrugs. "I thought you might be interested."

"Interested?" My tongue feels thick.

"In DJing," he explains. "For the silent disco. It pays a hundred dollars, plus a ticket and a plus-one."

"A hundred dollars?" I nearly choke again.

"Pretty sweet, right?" Derek's eyes twinkle.

"To DJ? In front of people? At a festival?"

"That's the general idea." He cocks his head, smiling. "You down?"

"Seriously?" A volcano of excitement builds inside me. Even without Windham, I'll get to play music in front of people this summer. Sure, it's not the music I imagined, but it's better than nothing—and I'll make money too. I can't wait to tell Crow and Nicky I landed an actual paying gig. "I mean, yes."

"Good," he sits back, smiling. "So I'll tell them you're in." He gets out his phone and I watch, my jaw hanging open, as he punches words into the screen.

"So what *is* the silent disco, anyway?" I ask when he's done.

He puts his phone back in his pocket. "Exactly what it sounds like. They broadcast your set through headphones instead of speakers. It means two DJs can go on at the same time and they can put it closer to a big sound system without worrying about noise bleed. Plus it's hilarious—everyone looks like they're dancing to nothing."

He continues to describe the silent disco and the festival with its multiple stages and forests and campgrounds, until our waitress sets a thin-crust pizza between us. It looks like a piece of modern art with swirls of mozzarella, shavings of ham, and artichokes that brown and curl at the edges.

"Do you really think I'm ready?" I ask.

"Absolutely." He reaches out and puts a hand on my wrist, sending little lightning bolts up my arm. "I wouldn't recommend you if I didn't."

"But you've only heard me play once."

He shrugs. "I heard your mix. You know what you're doing. Besides, it's the silent disco at like five in the afternoon on the first day. It's not like you're headlining the main stage."

"And they really pay a hundred dollars?" I've never been paid for a jazz gig before. The competitions cost money to enter; Grandpa Lou was usually the one who picked up the tab.

"Really." Derek grabs a slice of pizza and closes his eyes. "Damn, this stuff is the best."

A hundred dollars is more than I make in a whole day at The Gym Rat. It's enough to put gas in the LeSabre for a month, as long as I don't drive too far from Coletown.

A smile bubbles out of me, growing slow but giddy across my face as I reach for a slice of pizza. Sweetness, salt, and grease explode in my mouth.

"So good, right?" Derek looks up, smiling.

"So good," I say. I don't know if it's the ham or the artichokes or the festival or the fact that Derek called me hot, but it tastes like the best pizza I've ever had.

"So when is this festival, anyway?" I ask, taking another bite.

"Over the long weekend." Derek grins at me across the table, his eyes sparkling. "The Fourth of July."

CHAPTER 17

"No." The slice drops from my hand, splattering cheese-side-down on my plate. The Fourth of July is Visitors' Weekend—the only time this summer I can see Crow and Nicky, and visit camp.

Derek looks up, startled. "What's wrong?"

"I can't do it." Disappointment floods my stomach, sticky and rank.

"Why not?" His face darkens. "I just told them you can."

"I have . . . a thing." I don't know how to tell him about Visitors' Weekend. Being into jazz is one thing; being into summer camp is a whole other.

"So cancel it." His voice is matter-of-fact.

"I don't know if I can." My fingers curl around my napkin, crumpling it into a ball. Suddenly I'm angry at Windham Music Camp all over again. First they wouldn't let me come this summer; now they're taking away my first-ever paying gig, too. "I didn't realize when this was. I should have asked."

I watch the darkness concentrate in his face, then disappear as suddenly as a summer storm cloud.

"No, Mira." He reaches across the table and puts his hand over mine, his voice as soft with concern as it was cold and matter-of-fact just moments before. "*I'm* sorry. I should have told you when it was." He shakes his head sadly. "This is all my fault. I was just so excited you said yes." His hand stays on mine, squeezing gently. "I mean, is there any way you can change your plans? It's going to make both of us look bad if you cancel now."

His eyes meet mine, and for a moment my resolve wavers. I want to say yes to him more than anything. Would it really be so bad if I took this gig instead of going to Visitors' Weekend?

"I don't want to make you look bad," I admit.

"I don't want you to make me look bad." He flashes a playful smile. "Especially since I think you could make me look so good."

The compliment sends a slice of light through my anger and frustration. Desire tugs at me. It's not just that I want to make Derek happy. It's that I think this gig would make *me* happy, too.

But it would mean going eight whole weeks without seeing Crow and Nicky . . . and my camp friends, and my teachers, and the amphitheater, and the lake. I don't know if my heart could handle that. And I don't know if Crow and Nicky would forgive me.

"Can I sleep on it?" I ask finally.

Derek grins. "Sure. But wait'll you hear who else is spinning . . ."

He spends the rest of our meal naming DJs, making my mouth water as much for the festival as it does for the food—and for him.

"Come on," he says when we're done. "Let's get out of here."

He flags down the waitress and insists on paying the check, even though I try to hand him money twice. Does that make this a date, I wonder as we leave the restaurant?

Outside, the air feels like hot silk and the sky is purple with the last gasp of sunset. We walk without any destination, shoulder to shoulder, his keys jangling in his pocket just like the marimba in my piece. We pass my car, the corrugated metal doors to *This Is A Lot*, a two-story mural of hands taking flight like birds, and a girl walking a peacock on a leash. A clutch of motorcycles idles outside a VFW clubhouse, their leonine growls stirring the lazy air.

Derek ducks into a narrow alley between buildings and beckons for me to follow.

"Where are you taking me?" I ask.

He smiles over his shoulder. "Can't you just trust me?"

"I don't know. Can I?"

"Yes." He grabs my hands and pulls me in. "Come."

I follow, laughing as he slowly shuffles backward. There's a hazy light where the alley ends, and a smell like wet wool and ocean brine.

"This," Derek says as we emerge. "This is my favorite place in the city. And it's a secret, so don't go telling everyone."

"This?" I wrinkle my nose. We're standing on the banks of a canal lined with gray, water-stained buildings. The water is inky green and slow-moving; a crumpled coffee cup drifts by like a small, sad sailboat.

"This." He leads me down a crumbling concrete stairway and onto a tiny platform just above the water's edge: a dock, I guess. The smell is stronger here, laced with gasoline.

Derek sits on the stairs, his feet on the dock. After a moment, I join him. The stairs are narrow, pressing us together. I can feel the touch of his arm against mine; it burrows beneath my skin, strong and insistent as a song.

"Why is this your favorite place in the city?" I ask.

His eyes slide sideways, into mine. "See if you can guess."

I look around, trying to see it. The canal isn't beautiful, and neither is the way it smells. The stairs are cold and damp, with pieces of crumbling concrete that dig into my back and legs. It's hard to see why anyone would want to come here. Unless that's the point.

"Because it's a secret?" I finally venture.

"Bingo." He reaches over and taps me on the tip of the nose. "I knew you'd get it."

"It *is* pretty peaceful," I concede. The gentle lap of waves against the concrete banks is almost hypnotic, and lights from the buildings' windows dance across the canal's dark surface. The city noise is muted here: there are no trucks idling, no engines revving, no voices calling across the night. Derek's arm rubs against mine, a rainbow of colors and intricate, swirling designs.

He catches me looking. "Go ahead," he says. "You can ask about them. Everyone does."

"Okay." I lick my lips, my throat dry. "What's the deal with your tattoos?"

"Funny you should ask." He rolls up the sleeve of his T-shirt, pointing to a pink lotus flower on his shoulder. "I got this one first, mostly to piss off my mom."

"Did it work?" I ask. If I were trying to piss off a parent, a pretty pink flower isn't exactly what I'd choose.

"Oh yeah." He sits back, rubbing his hand over the ink. "She always wanted me to be the man of the house, so when I was seventeen I went out and got the most feminine design I could find."

"Wow." I long to touch him, to run my fingers over the pink petals. "And she hated it?"

"So much," he says, grinning. "She gave me the silent treatment for a week."

I think of my mom's reaction to Britt's hair. "She must really love you, though," I say.

"Oh yeah." He shakes his head. "There's no doubt about that. She loves me *too* much. It's stifling."

I bite the inside of my lip. Is it possible for a parent to love you too much, I wonder?

"What about the rest?" I ask, indicating his sleeves. "Why'd you get those?"

He shrugs. "More of the same. I just wanted them to be beautiful. There's so much ugliness in the world. I wanted people to look at my arms and experience beauty and feel peace."

"Like you feel here?"

"Yes." He sighs, deep and long. "You get it. I knew you would." Then he stretches his arm across my shoulders, slow and languid, pulling me close.

My heart starts to pound. This was a date. I wasn't imagining that moment in his bedroom. Something is going to happen. I can feel it all over my body, from the ends of my hair to the tips of my toes.

I rest my head on his shoulder and we stay that way for a moment, watching the lights on the water break apart, scatter, and come together again. I can feel his ribs move as he breathes, and my breath syncs to his, slow at first and then faster, shallow. He takes my other hand and pulls me around until we're facing each other on the narrow stairs. I can't stop looking at his hand in mine, at our legs stretched side by side down the stairs. The tension that's been building inside me unravels, the place below my stomach turning liquid and sweet.

"Mira," he whispers. "Look at me."

I raise my eyes. He's the same height as me, I realize, but I've never thought of him as short. He's always been larger than life.

That's the last thought I have before he kisses me, and every cell in my body turns to gold.

CHAPTER 18

Derek's scent sticks to me as I drive home, Miles Davis on the stereo and my body still singing from his kisses. My parents are asleep when I tiptoe into the house, but Britt is home for once, curled up on the couch with the TV on low and her hand dangling in a bowl of popcorn. I've never been so glad to see her in my life. I feel like I'll explode if I don't share what just happened with someone, and it's well past lights-out at Windham, so I can't tell Nicky and Crow.

Britt grabs the remote and hits PAUSE as soon as I walk in. "Hey, you." She gives me a devilish smile. "Mom said you were out on a date."

"I guess you could call it that." I try to keep my cool, but I can't keep a grin from spreading across my face.

"Sit," Britt commands, patting the spot next to her. "Tell me everything. Who is he? Mom didn't remember his name, but she said he doesn't go to your school."

"Word travels fast, huh?" I climb onto the couch next to her and help myself to a handful of popcorn, secretly glad she already knows.

"Don't pretend it wasn't a big deal. You even let Mom do your makeup!" Britt tosses a piece of popcorn at my head. "You look nice, by the way."

"Thanks." I take my time chewing as Britt fidgets on the couch. All through high school it was the other way around: me draped across her bed begging her to tell me who she had a crush on, who she'd hooked up with, whether they were going out. Now the tables are turned, and I can't say I'm not enjoying it.

"So who *is* he?" Britt insists, tossing more popcorn at my head.

"Stop!" I catch a piece and throw it back at her. "It was Derek, okay?"

"Derek?" She pauses, a kernel falling into her lap. "Like, Yelena's friend?"

My face reddens as I nod. "We were kind of hanging out at that party on Saturday, and I sent him this mix, and then he texted me today and wanted to talk about it, and he got me a gig at Pax Summerfest but I guess it was also kind of a date, and . . . I mean, he's really cute, right?"

I'm expecting Britt to shriek and throw her arms around me, to congratulate me for finally going out with someone who isn't a giant dork. Instead she frowns. "Did you guys hook up?" she asks.

I bite back a smile. "A little, yeah."

"Mira . . ." She stops, shakes her head.

"What?" I toss popcorn into my mouth. "You're the one who's always saying I need to get out more."

"Yeah but . . . he's older."

I turn to her, my mouth hanging open. Judgment is the last thing I was expecting from Britt right now, and I'd be lying if I said it didn't sting. "You dated a senior when you were a sophomore," I point out.

"I know." She tucks her leg under her and sighs. "But that was different."

"Different how?" My golden mood is dissipating, replaced with irritation at Britt. Hooking up with Derek is the best thing that's happened to me all summer. Why does she have to act like it's some kind of crime?

"Fifteen-to-seventeen is different from seventeen-to-twenty-one," she says, like that explains everything.

"Okay, whatever." I toss the rest of my popcorn back in the bowl and stand. I wanted Britt to be excited for me—happy, even. I wanted to tell her everything and have her hug me and squeal like Crow and Nicky would if they were here. "You're being weird. I'm going to bed."

"Mira." She reaches across the couch and rests her fingers on my arm. "I'm not trying to be a jerk. I just want you to be careful, okay?"

"I *am* being careful," I insist. I don't understand why Britt is acting this way, and I don't like it. I thought telling her about Derek would make us closer; that we could giggle and commiserate about our boy problems just like the kinds of sisters you see on TV. "You're the one sneaking out to do drugs every night," I add.

She recoils a little, hurt flashing across her face. I feel bad, even though I shouldn't. All I did was tell the truth.

"Mir-Bear . . ." she tries again, a note of pleading in her voice. But I'm done with Britt. She has no right to judge my decisions, not with the way she's been acting.

"It's late," I say, my voice cold. "I'm going to bed."

"I love you," she calls after me. And, even though I'm still mad at her and she's acting completely weird, I find myself turning around and saying it back.

Big hookup news, I text Crow and Nicky first thing the next morning. They send back multiple exclamation points and FaceTime me from the lounge the second they have a free period, while I'm working the front desk at the gym. In the background I can see the blurry shapes of campers hanging around the lounge, dangly legs and musical instrument cases draped over the faded couches.

This time Nicky isn't distracted. He gasps, whoops, blushes, and pretends to faint as I launch into a blow-by-blow of my date with Derek and our make-out session on the dock. His reaction is everything I didn't get from Britt, and my smile stretches until my cheeks hurt.

"So you're going to perform at a festival?" Crow says after we've fully analyzed every tongue-wrenching detail. "Like, as a DJ?"

"Um, actually." I twist my hands in my lap. There's one tiny detail I left out: the fact that Pax Summerfest happens to coincide with Visitors' Weekend. "I wanted to ask you guys about that."

"I think you should do it!" Nicky whoops.

"As long as you can still get enough practice time in for your audition," Crow adds. "You don't have to practice a lot to be a DJ, right? It's just, like, playing other people's tunes?"

I bristle at her words—even though, just a few short weeks ago, I would have said the same thing. "So, about this festival." I take a deep breath. "It's over Fourth of July weekend."

I watch their smiles go from major to minor. "But that's Visitors' Weekend," Crow says.

"I know." I bite my lip.

"You're coming here," Nicky says. "Right?"

"Well." I twist my hands until my fingertips start to tingle. "I mean—I want to, don't get me wrong. But would you guys be really mad if I didn't?"

They look from me to each other and then back again.

"What do *you* want to do?" Nicky asks slowly. His voice is measured, but I can sense disappointment behind his words.

"I mean, I really want to see you guys," I say. "But this gig pays money, and you know how broke I am. . . ."

"Sure." Nicky says flatly.

"And the fact that Derek and all your cool new friends are going to be there has nothing to do with it?" Crow asks suspiciously.

"It's not about who's going to be there," I try to explain. "It's about getting paid, and playing in front of people, and . . ."

"Is this because we're not playing your piece?" Nicky asks suddenly. "Like, if we got your piece into the recital you'd definitely be coming here, right?"

"I don't know," I sigh. "I guess so. But you didn't, so . . ."

"So you're ditching us because something better came along," Crow finishes for me.

"You guys ditched me to go to camp," I blurt out.

I regret it as soon as it's out of my mouth. My hands fly to my lips, like I can push the words back in. But it's too late.

"Oh, now you're going to bring *that* up?" Nicky shakes his head. "We did everything we could to help you. Sorry I wasn't going to give up my whole summer just because your folks couldn't get their shit together."

His words tear into me, making me burn. He doesn't have to bring my parents into it. That's hitting below the belt.

"Yeah, well, sorry I'm not going to give up an actual paying gig to spare your feelings," I bite back.

"But it's not even a real gig," Crow points out. "You're not even playing an instrument."

"It *is* a real gig!" I yell. An elderly woman on a nearby elliptical looks up, the loose flesh of her arms jiggling in shock. I lower my voice. "You don't know what you're talking about."

"Yeah, and I don't want to." Crow's eyes narrow behind her glasses. "The Mira I know would never choose techno over jazz."

The way she calls it techno makes my blood boil.

"I don't play techno," I hiss.

"Whatever." Crow rolls her eyes. "All I know is, it's not real music."

"God, Crow." My voice comes out thin and venomous. "I was still trying to figure out what I should do about Visitors' Weekend, but if you're going to be like this I guess I have my answer."

I slam my laptop shut, silencing them before they can reply. Then I pick up my phone.

"Mira!" Derek's voice on the other end is the opposite of Crow's. It's like raw honey, thick and grainy and sweet. "What's up?"

"I'll do it," I tell him, and even though my hands are still shaking my voice is firm and clear. "See you on the Fourth of July."

CHAPTER 19

A bead of sweat rolls down my back as I raise the mallet, pounding the final tent stake into the ground. It connects with a perfect D-flat, blending into the mosaic of sound as the Dream campground goes up all around us. Through the woods we can hear the distant thump of music starting up from the stages. A Ferris wheel peeks out over the treetops, crowned with a banner reading *Welcome to Pax Summerfest!*

I check my watch for the gazillionth time since we left this morning, our parents shouting final warnings about tick checks and bug spray. Britt told them we were going on "a camping trip with friends," which I guess is true as long as "a camping trip" means "staying in a tent at a music festival" and "friends" means "three thousand strangers." My first real DJ set—my first-ever paying gig—starts in an hour, and I keep wishing time would either stop or fast-forward to the moment it's over. The last week has been a whirlwind of downloading music, texting with Shay about tracks and tents, and practicing beat-matching. Derek called almost every day to see how my set was coming, which more often than not led to me driving down to Brooklyn after work to play him my new tracks, which then led to long, blissful make-out sessions on his bed. Each time our hands explored a little further, and I'm starting to think that after this weekend I won't be a virgin anymore.

Between work, Derek, and prepping for my set I've barely had time to think about my Fulton audition, but I tell myself I'll make up for it by practicing twice as hard once this weekend is over. I'll still have six weeks to get ready, and it should be more than enough time—not just to get my jazz chops back up, but also to smooth things over with Nicky and Crow. We haven't spoken since our argument last week and I need some time to cool down before I'm ready to talk it out.

"You remember how this goes?" Britt holds up a wrinkled rainfly. We haven't used the tent since we were kids, back when our mom's parents used to take us camping. It felt larger then, a flashlight-illuminated palace for two giggling little girls. Now it's barely big enough for Britt, Yelena, Yelena's two giant suitcases, and me.

A cell phone chimes inside the tent next to ours, which Shay is sharing with a half dozen of her friends.

"Crap!" Her voice cuts through the flimsy fabric.

"Are you okay?" I ask.

There's the dull percussion of cell-phone typing, the whine of a zipper, and her pink-tipped head pokes through the flap. "One of the other DJs is running late." Her voice is sour. "They want me to swap set times."

"Is that bad?" I ask.

"It's not good." She squints up at me, blocking her eyes to shield the sun. "I wanted a later time so more people would be there. And I bet this guy did too, and that's why he's suddenly having 'unavoidable delays.'" Her fingers make unhappy air quotes around the words.

"What time are you on now?" I ask. Shay is also booked in the Silent Disco.

"Five." She wrinkles her nose. "This is so shitty. I told all my followers I'd be on at ten!"

I shake my head, nerves suddenly jangling. "That has to be wrong. *I'm* on at five."

"Right." Shay settles a pair of pink-framed sunglasses over her eyes. "We're going head-to-head."

The jangling intensifies. "What does that mean?"

"Derek didn't tell you?" Shay rolls her eyes. "That's so typical. We're both on at the same time. People can choose who they want to listen to in the headphones."

"So we're competing?" I remember what Derek said about the headphones letting more than one DJ play at once, but he never mentioned that it would be a competition. The last thing I want is to compete with Shay.

"It's not a big deal." She runs a hand through her hair, fluffing it. "Most people bounce back and forth between channels anyway."

"So they'll hear both of us?" I ask.

"Sure. If there's even anyone there."

"People will be there." Yelena pokes her head out of our tent, one false eyelash glued to her face and another in her hand. "You're on at the same time as Mira now? I sent out an invite to like two hundred people."

My jaw drops. "Seriously?"

"Of course." Yelena waves the eyelash to dry it, then presses it to her bare lid.

"Two *hundred?*" I can't imagine having two hundred friends. Until I met Shay, I only had two.

"What?" Yelena shrugs. "I'm popular."

Tension spreads through me, making my muscles ache. Now my first-ever DJ gig will not only involve going up against Shay, but also performing for two hundred of Yelena's closest friends.

"We should probably get going," I say, trying to shake off my nerves. "I don't want to be late."

Yelena's eyes widen behind her lashes. "You're not going in *that*." She eyes my plain black tank top and denim shorts and makes a face.

"I'm not?"

"Oh, no-no-no. You're a DJ now. You have to think about your image!" Yelena dives backward into the tent, and I hear frantic rustling.

I blink in the sunlight. Over the past week I've spent hours looking for the perfect tracks, practicing my transitions, and trying out new effects. But in all the time I've put into this set, I never once thought about clothes.

"Here." Yelena tosses me a bundle of green fabric.

"Uh-uh." I toss it back. "We're not playing this game again."

"This is different." Britt's head appears next to Yelena's. Even though it's at least eighty degrees out, she's wearing a knitted cap that looks like a panda head. "We got it just for you."

Yelena unfolds the fabric and holds it up. It's a dress made of soft green cotton, sprinkled with tiny silver stars.

"Try it on!" Yelena urges.

I sneak another glance at my watch. I know how persuasive Yelena can be, and I don't have time to argue. Sighing, I push past them into the tent and yank off my shorts and tank top, pulling the dress over my head. The fabric swirls around my knees, loose and comfy and buttery soft. I've never been much of a dress person, but if I were, this is what I'd wear.

"Okay, you guys win." I emerge to a round of applause from Britt, Yelena, and Shay.

"I knew you'd like it." Britt finishes lacing up her sneaker. In addition to the panda hat, she's wearing a white crop top, black-and-white-striped knee socks, and a pair of black shorts so tiny they may as well be underwear. Her eyes soften as she looks me up and down. "You look so pretty," she says.

"Like a princess," Yelena adds.

"Totally dope," Shay agrees.

Something inside me cracks, like an egg breaking and the gooey yolk spilling out. Britt and Yelena didn't have to do anything for my first DJ gig, but they went out and spent time and money to find an outfit I'd actually like. And Shay . . . well, without her I wouldn't even be here in the first place. This isn't the summer I wanted, but maybe, in its own way, it's just as good.

"Thank you." My voice is muffled with emotion. I look from them to the dress, then back again, and I don't know what else to say but they seem to get it.

"Come on." Shay takes my arm. "Let's go destroy this silent disco."

I grab my headphones and we take a curving path through the woods. Two girls dressed as harlequins pass us on stilts, smiling down at me. My heart is racing again, willing my feet to move faster until we break through the other side of the forest and into the open fields where the stages have been set up.

"This way." Shay leads us past a row of concessions and down a gentle slope to a blue-and-yellow circus tent with a revolving sign that says *Silent Disco*. I clutch my headphones closer, my palms going damp.

The only noise in the tent comes from a trio of whirring ceiling fans. A handful of people dance lazily in the center, their footfalls silent on foam flooring. They each wear a pair of wireless headphones with a small light by the right ear, some blue and some green. There's a station at the entrance where visitors leave their IDs in exchange for borrowing the headphones, and a pair of DJ booths face each other from opposite ends of the tent.

I look around for Derek, but he isn't here yet. Shay marches up to one of the booths and consults with the DJ, then motions for me to take the other. My hands tremble as I climb the stairs, standing off to the side until the DJ makes his transition and turns to me.

"You're Mira Mira?"

I nod. Hearing my new DJ name from a stranger's lips feels strange and not altogether bad.

"Cool, so you can mix in after this track," he says. "We're green, by the way."

He returns to the rig before I have a chance to ask what that means. My heartbeat rises in my throat, nearly choking me. For a moment I want to turn around and run out of this tent and all the way to the parking lot, to jump in the LeSabre and not stop driving until I hit Windham Music Camp where everything is familiar and safe. If I leave now I could still make it for the recitals. My life could almost go back to the way it was before.

But it's too late. The DJ is bringing in his last track, wishing me luck as he jogs down the stairs. At Shay's suggestion I left my laptop at home and brought my music on thumb drives—she said they'd have CDJs like hers here, and she was right. But now I'm missing my laptop, the familiar glow and pulse of my DJ software and the comfort of the keyboard beneath my fingers. My hands are shaking so hard it takes me two attempts to plug in my thumb drives. I slide on my headphones and check the levels on the CDJs and mixer, noticing that the split-cue function is on so I'll hear what the audience hears through one ear and my upcoming track in the other.

I scroll through my music library, scanning for my first track. I want something lighthearted and easy, as much to calm my own fraying nerves as to get people dancing. From the corner of my eye I catch Britt and Yelena down on the dance floor, pretending to jostle each other out of the way so they can get the best spot in the vast swatch of empty space in front of my booth. They grin up at me, their headphones glowing green.

Green. That must be what the other DJ meant. Which means that Shay, looking cool and confident in the booth across from me, is blue. She catches my eye and shoots me an encouraging smile, which only makes my heart pound faster. Why, of all the DJs in the world, do I have to be up against her?

But then I can't think about it anymore, because it's go time. I let my first track enter quietly, tiptoeing in behind the one that's fading out. But, like an impish child, it can't stay quiet for long. It's whispering, then giggling, then letting out a belly laugh of rich, rumbling bass as the old track beats a retreat. The music takes my hand and won't let go—it wants me to roll down hills and play in giant piles of leaves and not let up until I'm covered in grass stains and my face hurts from laughing. As the beat fills my ears and the melody takes over I feel my stomach unclench and the sweat dry on my palms. My face relaxes into a smile. My hips start to move.

I cue up the next track and sneak a peek at the dance floor. Yelena's chatting with a half dozen people who are clearly her friends; to my surprise, there's a small line forming at table where they hand out headphones. Britt's still dancing, gazing up at me with an unmistakable sparkle of pride in her eye. Warmth spreads through my stomach, soupy and rich. Britt has always come to my recitals, always clapped and cheered and told me I did a great job. But I've never seen her look at me quite like this before: like I'm finally doing something she not only understands, but loves.

Buoyed by her smile, I choose a track with a complex Afro-Brazilian beat and a female MC rapping in Afrikaans. I love the organic sound of the drumbeats, the rooster crows that have been warped and distorted until they're barely recognizable as animal sounds. But when I look up, three quarters of the growing crowd has their headphones set to blue. I glance at Shay, who is grooving hard to the beat in her ears, pumping her fist in the air as the audience dances along.

A hot blast of adrenaline streaks through me. I don't know what Shay is playing, only that I need to top it. It has nothing to do with her and everything to do with the feeling that this crowd belongs to me, that there's nothing more important than winning them back. I scroll through my tracks until I find the perfect banger, a remix of a pop song that must be in the Top 40 because it plays on The Gym Rat's Pandora station at least five times a day. I hate the song itself—it's the musical equivalent of saltines, dry and bland—but the remix strips its boring beat and replaces it with a frenetic mix of wood block and snare, distorts the vocals until they're a cartoon parody of the original, and wraps the whole thing up in bass that feels like electric shocks to my hips.

I'm still playing with levels when the chorus kicks in—so I feel, rather than see, the crowd respond. Suddenly there's a surge in the air, an energy that rises like heat into the DJ booth. More than half the audience is tuned to green now, all dancing like tiny hurricanes. The tent's filling quickly, the line at the headphone station snaking out the door, and as people make their way to the dance floor I watch them switch from green to blue and then back to green. A few tracks later, three-quarters of the dance floor are stuck on green. I'm determined to keep them there.

My fingers feel like tiny electric transmitters as I select my next track. It's another high-energy blaster with a sense of humor, full of musical jokes and sound effects like creaking bedsprings and cowbell. As I ratchet up the volume I feel my smile spread from my face to my hands, from my hands to the CDJs to the audience's ears. And then, like magic, I see the same smile break out on faces around the tent.

As the crowd pounds the dance floor I feel like I'm full of helium, like all I'd have to do is jump and I'd be airborne, floating above the silent disco tent and the festival and the whole state of Pennsylvania, a human hot-air balloon. This is better than the quiet, expectant faces and polite applause I would have gotten at Visitors' Weekend. Here the audience is visceral and immediate, responding to every note like I'm Fred Astaire and they're Ginger Rogers. This isn't a one-way transmission like a jazz concert; this is a dance between me and the crowd, a constant feedback loop.

The crowd stays with me through the next track, and the next. The tent is full, the bodies below me a blur of colored hair and smiles and sweat illuminated in green.

Sometimes one of the faces swims into focus: Yelena with her eyes closed and a blissful smile stretching her face. Britt looking like she just scored the winning goal for the state championship–clinching game. A stranger gazing up at me like I'm the first person to ever bring music to his world. Shay, her lips set into a thin, hard line, her eyes firmly on her rig. Derek with an all-access lanyard around his neck, standing off to the side with the headphones half on his head, approval sparkling in his eyes.

The helium inside me warms, expands. I'm too in-control to be nervous, too tuned in to the crowd to second-guess how I'm doing. Even Derek's perfect face and older-guy cool can't throw me off right now, not when the music is so good and the dance floor is so clearly mine. Our eyes meet, and he gives me the kind of smile that can melt icebergs. I smile back.

My next track is for him and him alone. It's my heartbeat when I'm around him and my breath when he touches me: fast and fluttery, shallow and staccato. It's the agonizing buildup before he kisses me, my breath and the bass and the world a swirl of anticipation and whispers and longing. The crowd stops dancing and suspends in time, swaying like saplings in a barely there breeze. They turn their faces up to me, waiting. Their stillness expands until it fills the tent, until it fills us all like a collective breath just waiting to be released.

And then the beat drops.

The beat drops, and the bass envelops us in a tidal wave.

The beat drops, and the crowd explodes.

The beat drops, and Derek pushes his way to the center of the dance floor.

The beat drops and the Silent Disco is the only place at the festival, the only place in the world. And I'm the one who made it that way.

For a few moments I lose myself in the music. I let my hips move and my eyes close, and when I feel a tap on my shoulder I know it's the next DJ ready to go on and I tell him he can mix in right away because I know there's no track I own right now that could ever possibly top this.

I unplug my headphones and the sudden silence is like dumping a bucket of ice water over my head. In the heat of the music I'd forgotten we were in a Silent Disco; the music was so real and so close, it seemed impossible that only the people with headphones could hear. The mass of moving bodies, so graceful when there was music blasting in my ears, looks clumsy and comical dancing to nothing but the far-off thump of bass and the whirring of ceiling fans.

I sneak a glance at Shay. She's also handing off to the next DJ, her back an angry ripple as she shoves headphones into her bag. A worm of guilt slithers through my joy. She said earlier that it was just friendly competition, nothing to get bent out of shape about. But I know how seriously Shay takes DJing. I saw how many people were dancing to my channel, and I know that means they weren't listening to hers.

I hurry down the stairs. I don't know what I can say to make it better, only that I have to find her and say *something*. But I've barely touched the floor when a hand on my arm stops me, and a girl with a flushed face and violet eyes is gushing about my set, telling me she hasn't danced like that in ages, and before I know it she's hugging me and other people are pressing in close, wanting to touch me and talk to me and take selfies with me. They smell like sweat and peppermint gum and feel like they're standing too close, robbing the tent of air. They were so beautiful from up in the DJ booth, but now I feel like they're a hungry monster, trying to swallow me whole.

"Thank you," I say again and again, because I can't think of anything else to say. "Thank you so much." I'm shaking hands and accepting hugs, learning names I'll never remember, thinking this is what it must be like to be famous and I'm not entirely sure I like it, when a familiar pair of arms wraps around me, covered from shoulder to wrist in tattoos.

"That was incredible," Derek breathes, kissing me on the lips. "You were made for this."

The crowd falls away and it's just the two of us, his warm metallic smell and the softness of his breath. I melt into his kiss, letting it take me to places even music can't. When he pulls away he introduces me to a guy standing next to him with thinning blue-dyed hair and horn-rimmed glasses. From the way Derek says his name, I can tell he thinks this guy is important.

"Jake Melville," he introduces himself, reaching for my hand. "I loved your set."

"Jake does booking for Electri-City," Derek explains, his voice heavy with meaning. "They're looking for fresh talent."

My jaw drops. Electri-City is the festival Shay told me about—the one it's always been her dream to play.

Jake hands me a card. It has his name in white against a black background, and a logo for Freaknic Productions. "Shoot me an email," he says. "Link, headshot, bio—you know how it goes."

I nod, too dumbstruck to tell him I actually have no idea how it goes.

"Thanks, man." Derek intercepts the card. "I'll take care of the deets. I'm her manager."

"Right on," Jake says, patting him on the shoulder. "Hey, I was supposed to be over at the Bass Sector stage twenty minutes ago. Nice meeting you, Mira."

He pumps my hand again before disappearing into the crowd. I'm left with Derek's arm around me and my mouth hanging open, still trying to process what I just heard. A booking manager. From Electri-City. One of the biggest festivals in the world.

"Come on," Derek urges, turning us around. "We have to celebrate!"

It's then that I see Shay. She's looking at me with wide, wounded eyes, her mouth hanging open. She must have been standing right behind us the whole time. Without headphones in the quiet of the Silent Disco tent, she would have heard everything.

"Shay . . ." I say, taking a step toward her. But just as I'm about to touch her sleeve another cluster of well-wishers floods between us, asking if I have mixes up and when I'm playing next, swallowing me in a cloud of praise. Derek answers for me, giving them the URL to my DJ page and saying they can catch me at Electri-City.

By the time I manage to fight my way past them, Shay is gone.

CHAPTER 20

Derek escorts me out of the Silent Disco, his hand on the small of my back. The festival grounds are more crowded now and late afternoon sunlight slants over the hills, bathing the tents and stages and revelers in liquid bronze.

"You killed it in there!" Yelena bursts from the tent behind us, Britt at her side. "My friends loved you. *I* love you!"

"Thanks." I give them quick hugs. "Have you seen Shay?"

Britt's brow furrows. "Not since she got off the decks."

I frown and pull out my phone. *You okay?* I text Shay as Derek wraps his arms around my waist from behind.

"Wait'll you hear Mira's big news," he tells Britt and Yelena. "They want her to play Electri-City."

"Electri-City!?" Yelena squeals. "Oh my god, that is the *best* festival. It's freakin' huge. We have to go," she says, turning to Britt. "We should start planning our outfits *now*."

"When is it, anyway?" I ask.

"Third weekend in August," Derek and Yelena say at the same time.

"Seriously?" My stomach drops. "That's right after my audition."

"What is with you and other commitments?" Derek kisses my shoulder. "You need to start clearing your schedule. You're a big-time DJ now."

"I don't think I can do it," I mutter, bitterness rising in my throat. I can't believe this is happening again. I need to spend the next six weeks laser-focused on my audition, but this seems like too good an opportunity to pass up. Plus, if Pax Summerfest pays a hundred dollars for a DJ set, I bet Electri-City pays even more.

"Hey." Derek rubs my shoulders. "You can *totally* do it. You'll be fine."

"You can't *not* play Electri-City," Yelena adds. "Nobody in their right mind would turn that down."

"Even the smallest stage is like five times the size of this," Derek adds, gesturing to the Silent Disco tent. My eyes follow his hand and I think about the crowd in there, how good it felt to make them dance. How good it would feel to do that again.

"What do you think?" I ask Britt.

"If you can dream it, you can do it," she says, quoting one of the motivational posters Mom tacked up in The Gym Rat.

"Thanks, Mom," I say, rolling my eyes. "Can you hold off on emailing Jake?" I ask Derek. "I'm honestly too hungry to even think right now."

I don't mention that I've been too nervous to eat all day. Now that my set is over, my appetite has come rushing back.

"Sure thing," Derek says, putting his arm around my waist and kissing my cheek. "Let's get you some food."

"Have fun, you two." Yelena twirls in a circle. "We're going to dance!"

Britt shoots me a reluctant glance. "I could maybe get food. . . ." she says.

"Come on!" Yelena tugs at her hand. "We already housed those cheeseburgers at the rest stop."

Britt stands between us, looking torn.

"Just go." I wave her off. "I'll catch up with you later."

Britt looks back at me as Yelena starts skipping off to the main stage.

"Come on," Derek says, pulling me tighter. "They have these fries here that'll blow your mind."

I nod and snuggle into his embrace, but I can't help checking my phone again as we make our way to the vendors. I still haven't heard from Shay.

"You okay?" Derek asks.

"Yeah." I sigh. "I'm just worried about Shay."

"Her?" His eyes crinkle. "Why?"

"She always wanted to play Electri-City," I tell him.

"So?"

"I feel bad that I got it instead," I explain. I watch a giant toadstool on wheels drift by, with bass pumping from hidden speakers and a cluster of people dressed as gnomes dancing on top. "It's not even *my* dream. It's hers."

"Hey." Derek stops in the middle of the path, his eyes slicing into mine. "You can't let Shay hold you back. You owned it in there, fair and square. That's why Jake noticed you. You should be fucking pumped right now."

"I am," I insist. "But she's been doing this forever and I just started. I barely know what I'm doing."

"You *clearly* know what you're doing." He tucks a curl behind my ear and kisses me: gently at first, then less so. I sigh into him as people stream around us, trying to forget about Shay and the hurt in her eyes. I run my hands up his back and into his hair, and after a long time he pulls away.

"We should get going," he says, breathing hard. "Before I drag you back to my camp and we miss the whole festival."

I raise an eyebrow. "That doesn't sound so bad."

"*You're* bad," he laughs. "It's your first festival. You should enjoy it."

He takes my hand and we find a food vendor selling burgers and Belgian fries in paper cones. Derek nibbles at his as I rip into mine, a trickle of grease and ketchup escaping down my arm. Before I can catch it, he leans over and licks it up.

"Who's bad now?" I tease.

He winks and pulls me toward the Lip Smacker stage. It's decorated with dozens of giant lips, made from slick plastic and pink mirrors and LED lights. An enormous, magenta mouth mounted over the DJ booth opens to emit a cloud of colored smoke.

"I have to pop backstage for a sec," Derek says, dangling his all-access lanyard. "Think you'll be okay here?"

"I'll be fine," I assure him. The DJ is playing a track that sounds like rubber balls bouncing down a highway, and the crowd is going nuts. I'm full of fries, still riding high from my set and Derek's kisses. "Just promise me you'll come back."

"You won't even have a chance to miss me." He gives me a ketchup-y kiss before disappearing into the throngs.

As soon as he's gone I check my phone again, but there's still no message from Shay. I hesitate, then quickly type *Text me?* before standing back to watch the festival come to life.

The sun is almost gone now, and lights are beginning to blink on. The crowd in front of the Lip Smacker stage is a mass of glowsticks and blinking buttons, hairpieces that look like tiny fiber-optic waterfalls. The DJ whips the music into a spiral of sound that drops down suddenly into a single primal beat. "Everybody drop it now!" he yells into a microphone, over and over until the crowd is screaming along with him. I can't help picturing myself in his place, wondering what would happen if I had a microphone, if I'd ever have the guts to use it.

Could I get one for Electri-City, I wonder? Could I use it for the crowd that's five times the size of the one in the Silent Disco?

I shake my head. I'm being crazy. As soon as Derek comes back I'll tell him I made a mistake; I can't play Electri-City, not when my audition is the same weekend. I'll ask if Jake can book Shay in my place. Then everybody wins, right?

"Miss me?" Derek cuts through the mass of bodies. He has an open bottle of champagne in one hand and a mischievous grin on his face. Just seeing him floods my body with longing.

"Derek . . ." I start to say.

"Cheers!" he interrupts me, raising the bottle in the air. "To your killer set today—and your next one, at Electri-City!"

He hands me the bottle. I can't tell him now, not when he's smiling this big and the night feels so full of possibility. I grasp the bottle and promise myself I'll do it tomorrow.

"What, no flutes?" I joke. The last time I had champagne was at my cousin's wedding two years ago. Mom told me the tall, thin champagne glasses were called flutes, and I dimly remember thinking this was hilarious after my first glass, and doing the Electric Slide after my second. I haven't done much drinking since; Britt did enough for both of us in high school. But like Derek said, tonight we're celebrating, and champagne feels absolutely right.

"Glasses are for snobs." Derek raises the bottle to his lips and drinks. "This is more fun."

He hands me the bottle and I take a swig, filling my throat with tart, tickling bubbles. I come away spluttering and laughing.

"Easy there!" Derek puts his lips over the rim, catching the overflow while patting me on the back.

"Let me try again." I sip more slowly this time. "Wow. That's actually really good."

"Damn right." Derek kisses the side of my neck. "Nothing but the best for my girl."

My girl. He called me his girl. I glow on the inside, lit up with happiness and bubbles as Derek pulls a pack of gum from his pocket. He pops a piece in his mouth and closes his eyes as he starts to chew.

"Want one?" he asks, offering me the pack.

"With champagne? Doesn't it taste funny?"

He shrugs. "So?"

I shake my head, grinning. "You're weird."

"*You're* weird." He takes my hand. "Want to dance?"

I nod, too happy to be self-conscious about my dancing, and we melt into the mass of bodies, pushing forward until we're almost to the stage. The music is so loud here it feels like we've crawled into its mouth and let it swallow us whole, but for once I don't care. I want to be in the very center of the action, to feel what people were feeling when they danced to my set.

"Hey!" Derek presses something into my hand. I look down and my face cracks into a smile. It's a brand-new set of earplugs, orange and pristine in their cellophane packaging.

"You remembered!" I pull him to me and plant a big, sticky kiss on his lips. His mouth tastes like bubbles and peppermint and he says something back but it gets lost in the noise, and even with the earplugs the music is so loud it feels like it's inside my body, a million decibels pouring through my veins.

Derek and I lose ourselves in the beat, passing the champagne back and forth as the DJ gives way to two lanky Swedish guys and then a tattooed Asian girl wearing a dress that looks like a disco ball. I swing my hips and Derek presses against them and spins me away, our bodies meeting and parting as the beat swells and skips and slows. Sweat soaks my dress. Derek's hand inches down my back and his leg is between my thighs and I'm arched so far back I meet another girl's eye upside down and she gives me the thumbs-up and mouths something that looks like: *he's hot!*

I reach for the champagne and tilt the bottle to my lips, but all I find is air.

"It's gone," Derek tells me, popping another piece of gum into his mouth. In the flashing stage lights his eyes are wide and almost black.

I pout, my hips against his. "But I'm thirsty," I say, my voice high-pitched and breathy and not my own.

"Then let's get you some water."

We push away from the stage, through thrashing, close-packed bodies, until we're free of the throngs. The cool night air hits my face and post-dancing tingles race through me, making me feel like I'm made of stars.

"That was so fun!" I gush as we weave down one of the curved paths, night revelers brushing by us like moths. We stop at a concession stand and buy two bottles of water, the plastic so cool I press it to the back of my neck.

"Hey, you're supposed to drink that," Derek teases.

"Right." I unscrew the cap and arch my neck as I drink, looking up past the lights to where a few brave stars twinkle in the sky. He drapes an arm over my shoulders and mine goes effortlessly around his waist, my hand slipping into his back pocket. I give his butt a playful squeeze.

"Hey!" He wriggles under my touch. "You really *are* bad."

"So bad." My voice feels thick and full. "And you like it."

"Can't say I don't." He nuzzles my neck and we wander through the festival, flowing like liquid as beats and lights compete for our attention from every stage. We wait in line to take a turn on the Ferris wheel, Derek's hand warm in mine, his pulse flickering against my wrist like a butterfly.

"Isn't it beautiful?" he asks when we reach the top. The festival spreads out below us, an electric patchwork quilt.

"It's gorgeous," I sigh. Our car swings gently in the breeze.

"You know this could be your life." He traces my palm with his fingertip. "Playing festivals. Dancing all night. Drinking champagne."

"You make it sound so glamorous," I laugh, kicking my legs like a kid on a swing.

"It *is* glamorous," he says. "All you have to do is say yes."

"To what?" I ask, even though I know what.

"Electri-City." He turns to me, his eyes dark and serious in the glittering night.

The question swirls around us. I want to drink in his eyes, the lights, the night. I want this to be my life. I want everything to feel just like this moment.

"You promise it won't conflict with my audition?" I ask.

"I promise," he says. "I'll make sure they give you a later set."

"And it's just an hour?"

"Just an hour." His thumb traces circles on my palm. "You know you can do this, Mira. You totally can."

"Okay," I say.

"Okay?" He turns to me, a laugh bubbling from his mouth.

"Okay!" The laugh leaps to me and ignites. "I'll do it!" I yell out over the treetops, pumping my legs to swing our car higher, my face flushing as I grasp his hand.

Derek's smile is champagne-sweet. He tilts in to me, and just as his lips brush mine the Ferris wheel lurches forward and we throw our hands in the air, shouting and kissing and laughing as we zoom back to earth.

CHAPTER 21

When our feet touch grass again I find myself stifling a yawn.

"Sleepy?" Derek asks, rubbing my back in lazy circles.

"A little," I admit.

His mouth twists into a reluctant half-grin. "I should let you go to bed."

"Or you could come with me." The words are out before I have time to think, my tongue loose from the champagne.

His eyes widen. "Are you sure?"

Am I? I look at Derek, his eyes dark and twinkling in the Ferris wheel's lights, and think that I've never wanted anything more. All those nights in his bedroom this past week, kissing until my lips hurt and touching just a little bit more of him each time, left me aching for this moment, wanting more. My pulse picks up, takes off, and I put my arms around his neck. I give him a slow, deliberate kiss and feel the erratic patter of his heart.

"I'm sure," I say.

He takes my hand and leads me past the stages and vendors and blurs of people like friendly ghosts. The Vision campground is full of vans and RVs, teardrop-shaped trailers and tents pitched in the back of pickup trucks. Derek stops in front of a blue-and-tan Chevy Astro van that looks like it drove here straight from the 1990s. He fumbles in his pocket and drops his keys twice before finally unlocking it. The champagne must have hit him harder than I realized.

"You sleep in here?" I ask.

"Oh, wait till you see. This thing was made for festivals."

He opens the door and a string of soft Christmas lights blinks on, revealing a shag rug and mattress covered in silky pillows. Gauzy fabric hangs from the van's sides, covering the windows. There's even a small cooler and a plastic chest of drawers.

"Welcome to the VIP lounge," Derek jokes, helping me inside.

"You weren't kidding." I kick off my shoes and sprawl out on the bed. "This is way better than our crappy old tent."

"Damn right." He shuts the doors and joins me, propping up on one elbow so his head is level with mine. For a long time we just lie there, close but not touching. Someone is playing a guitar outside and a small group sings along, off-beat and off-key but impossibly sweet. I try to memorize Derek's face the way it looks right now: his eyes just a thin line of blue around wide, black pupils, lips working lazily over a wad of gum. His fingertip grazes my cheek, making me shiver.

"You're different," he says finally. "You know that?"

"How?" Tufts of hair stick up on both sides of his head, making him look like an owl. I reach over and smooth one out.

"You don't want things from me all the time." He takes my hand and kisses it, turning my insides to liquid. "You're just cool."

Cool. Just like I've always tried to be. Someone finally noticed.

"Are most people not cool?" I ask.

"Most people are a goddamn pain in my ass." His eyes crinkle into a smile, and we both crack up.

"Like who?" I ask once our laughter subsides.

"Other promoters, DJs, ex-girlfriends . . . even my mom. *Especially* my mom."

I think back to that afternoon in his bedroom, the accusing squawk on the other line. "What about your dad?" I ask tentatively.

"Out of the picture. Since I was five."

His voice is matter-of-fact, but I can feel the bitterness beneath.

"I'm sorry," I breathe.

"It's fine. He's a jerk." He blinks hard. "Or at least, that's what my mom says."

"Do you remember him?" I ask.

He sighs. "Not from when I was little. But there was this one time . . ." He trails off. "It's a weird, fucked-up story. You probably don't want to hear it."

"I do," I tell him. I want to know everything about him, no matter how strange or painful or twisted.

"Okay." He takes a deep breath. "So one day, I was like ten years old, the phone rings and I go to pick it up and . . . hold on, I need to get comfortable."

He lies back on the mattress and pulls me into him, so my head is resting against his chest and I can feel the flutter of his heart against my cheek.

"Anyway," he continues, "I pick up and this older guy with a kind of twangy voice says my name. And I'm like, 'Who is this?' because we were getting a lot of calls from telemarketers but how would they know *my* name, y'know? And he's like, 'Derek, it's your dad.'"

His heartbeat speeds up as he says the words. "Whoa," I say quietly.

"Right? At first I was like, 'I don't have a dad, my dad hates us'—all this stuff my mom had always told me for as long as I could remember. And he goes—I'll seriously never forget the way he said it—'Didn't you get my letters?'"

I can feel his voice vibrate in his throat, so close and full of pain. "So he was sending you letters?" I ask.

"Yeah, like the whole time. For years. And my mom was throwing them away."

"That's messed up."

"Right?" He looks down so his eyes meet mine, blurring into one from the nearness of our faces. "No wonder I have trust issues."

"Did you ever talk to him again?" I ask.

His eyes go sad. "Not really. I always thought it would happen when I moved out on my own. But I never ended up calling him. I kept telling myself it wasn't a good time or whatever." His laugh is bitter. "I guess my mom got to me more than I thought."

"You know it's not too late," I say quietly. "You could still call him if you want."

"Yeah." He rolls onto his side so I'm looking up at the curve of his neck. "That's the thing: I don't even know if I want to.

My mom never wanted me to get close to anyone but her. She was worried I'd get hurt. But instead I got trust issues."

I kiss his neck. "I'm glad you can trust me," I say.

"Mmmm. Me too." He closes his eyes as I kiss my way up to his jaw, his cheek, his mouth.

"So tell me about you," he says after we've made out for a while. "What's your damage?"

I laugh softly. "I'm not damaged," I say.

"Sure you aren't." He pulls back so he can look me in the eyes. "Everyone's damaged. Even people with the greatest families in the world are messed up. Is your family the greatest family in the world?"

Outside there's the flick of a lighter and a long inhale, followed by a bout of hacking coughs and muffled laughter. The smell of pot smoke seeps into the van, sleepy and sweet.

"Well," I say finally. "You've met Britt."

"Right," he shrugs. "She seems okay."

"Just okay?" I search his face for signs that he's joking, but his eyes are wide and serious. "Everyone else thinks she's amazing."

"Aha." His mouth curls into a sardonic half smile. "There's the damage."

I open my mouth to tell him he's wrong. I'm not damaged; everything is cool. What comes out instead is my life story: how I've always been Britt's little sister first and Mira second, how my parents dote on her and don't know what to make of me, how Grandpa Lou was the only person in our family who took me seriously and now he's gone and I miss him more than words can say.

Derek strokes my hand and takes it all in. It's the first time I've told this story the way it really is, not the watered-down way I tell it to Crow and Nicky and Peter and everyone at camp so I can still sound cool, like I'm way past caring. It's the first time I've ever told someone exactly how it is and exactly how it makes me feel.

Derek stays silent, but from the way he's nodding I can tell he understands. Tears tickle my eyes by the time I finish, and he leans in and kisses them away. Then his mouth moves down the side of my face, inflaming every patch of skin it meets. He kisses my neck, and the moth-wing touches of his lips leave me trembling. By the time he lowers them onto mine I feel like an electric wire, taut and conductive.

I kiss him back hard, wrapping my legs around his waist like I did on the dance floor. Except there's no dance floor this time, there's nobody watching and it's just the two of us horizontal behind the closed doors of his van. I kiss the side of his neck, tasting salt-sweat and skin, pulling him closer. My dress rides up and I feel his hands on it, under it. I arch my back and there's the skim of fabric over my face and then I'm in just my bra and underwear, goose bumps flashing across my skin.

"Damn." Derek's eyes go wide and I wonder if he sees me the way I see myself in the mirror, right breast obviously larger than the left even in Britt's hand-me-down Victoria's Secret Pink polka-dotted bra. "You're beautiful," he breathes. He lowers his mouth to my chest, hands on my shoulders pushing me gently back and down until I'm staring up at the Christmas lights twinkling green and blue and gold.

I pull him on top of me and we roll around for a long time, until my bra is off and he's down to his boxers and I know we're getting to the point of no return.

"I want you," he breathes, his voice twilight-blue.

"I want you too," I whisper back.

"Should I get a condom?" he asks.

I hesitate, just for a moment. Because I want this, I know I do. But I also know that once we go there, we can't ever go back again.

He feels my hesitation and pulls away a little, resting on his elbows so he can look me in the eyes.

"Mira," he asks softly. "Is this your first time?"

"Yes," I whisper. I can't lie to him, not after what we just shared.

"Then I'll be gentle," he says.

And he is.

CHAPTER 22

I'm not a virgin anymore.

It's my first thought when I wake up, pushing through the layers of memory in my aching head. The van is hot and my stomach feels uncertain and sour from the champagne, but this thought gives me a new feeling of solidity, like I was just floating through life before but now I'm really here. I toss off the blanket and stretch, sending a new chorus of cymbals pounding through my skull. The space between my legs feels sticky and humid.

Outside there's the sizzle of bacon frying, a Big Room House track gone small and reedy through someone's portable speaker. A sudden cascade of laughter punctuates the morning. Next to me, Derek's eyes drift open.

For a moment he looks surprised to see me, and my heart tightens. Is he second-guessing what we did last night? Because even now, sober and hungry and hungover, I wouldn't change a single second.

Then his eyes soften. "Morning, you," he says, voice mossy from sleep.

"Hi." I feel like I need to whisper, even though the voices outside are going full-throttle, recounting stories from last night like they're the exploits of medieval heroes.

"What time is it?" His eyes are still half-closed, hair sticking up in every direction. I smooth it down, and he smiles drowsily at my touch.

I shrug. I have no idea when we went to bed, or how long we slept. Last night existed outside of time. Now I'm reluctant to go back to the orderly progression of hours, afraid it will break the spell of what we had.

He sits up slowly and feels around for his shorts, digging in the pocket for his phone.

"Shit," he says. "It's past one. I'm late to meet someone."

"Oh." I try not to let my disappointment show. I thought we could have a lazy morning, recover from our hangovers and maybe have sex again, talk about our families and music and everything huge and small in the world.

"Sorry, babe." He gives me a quick peck on the lips. "We can meet up later if you want."

"Okay." I try not to let my voice sound small.

Derek opens a plastic drawer and digs out a fresh pair of boxer briefs, and I rummage in the pile of blankets for my underwear. There's a smell in his van like the trees in Coletown that bloom white in spring. I guess it's the smell of sex. I wonder if Britt will be able to tell when I get back to the tent.

Outside the air is moist and heavy, fat gray clouds masking the sun. Derek locks his van and starts down the hill, a backpack slung over one shoulder. His pace is purposeful, not the syncopated amble with keys jingling on the downbeat that I've come to think of as his. I hurry to keep up, worrying that maybe he's trying to get rid of me; maybe now that he's had me, he doesn't want me anymore. I've heard of that happening, through whispers in the cafeteria and tear-streaked confessions on the terrible teen-vampire shows Crow likes to watch. But last night felt so real, so close. How he told me I was different, the way he opened up to me about his mom.

The path widens and forks where the vendor stalls begin. He stops, waiting for me to catch up.

"I wish I could spend all day with you," he says. "But I'm late to meet this guy." The tenderness in his voice makes me angry with myself for doubting him. Of course he meant what he said last night. Of course what we had was real.

"It's fine." I hesitate, wanting to put my arms around him, to kiss him. Waiting for some sign that things feel as different now for him as they do for me. But even now, after everything we've done together, I don't think I can say these things out loud. He doesn't like it when people are clingy or demanding. He appreciates that I can play it cool.

"Hey," he says, stepping closer. His eyes dig into mine. "Last night was really . . ." He pauses.

"Cool?" I suggest.

"Yeah." He nods. "Definitely cool."

He draws me into a hug and I rest my head on his shoulder, smelling the muted sex scent coming off his skin.

"I'll text you later," he says as we break apart, and then I'm watching his back disappear down the path, feeling like part of me is going with him. Is this what it's like to not be a virgin anymore? Is this how it feels to be in love?

I watch until he rounds a bend, then head toward the vendors. My stomach moans at the smell of frying food and I stop to buy a breakfast sandwich, wolfing it down in a few bites. I can't remember the last time I was this hungry, or that food tasted so good. It seems like all my appetites are stronger now: for food and sex, for music and dancing. As the last greasy morsel slides down my throat I find my strides growing longer, propelling me toward the Dream campground and, I hope, Britt and Yelena and Shay.

I cut through the woods, swatting at clouds of gnats that weren't there yesterday, and find our tent.

"Whoozere?" Britt's voice is slushy as she raises her head, squinting up at me. She and Yelena are sprawled on top of their sleeping bags, still wearing the same clothes from yesterday.

"Me," I whisper. "Were you sleeping?"

"Not sleeping." Yelena giggles, staring at the tent's ceiling. "Sleep is for losers."

The air inside is warm and stale. I note a pile of empty energy-drink cans in the corner, and a half-full bottle of vodka. Just looking at it makes my stomach somersault.

"Were you guys up all night?" I ask.

Britt takes a long beat to answer. When she does her vowels sound stretchy and spaced out. "We caught the sunrise set at the main stage," she says. "It was . . . magic."

"Then we came back here," Yelena adds. "Or, wait, did we stop in that dome thingy first?"

Britt laughs, but it's not her usual up-the-scale chime. It sounds like a car engine turning over, trying to start. "That dome thingy," she repeats. "That was fun."

They don't ask about my night, about why I didn't come back until now. I open my duffel bag and pull out a change of clothes, wishing the festival had showers. I don't know what

I was expecting from Britt this morning, but it wasn't this. Maybe I just wanted her to be my big sister so I could tell her about my night with Derek and have her reassure me that it's normal and he'll still like me later on today. Maybe I was hoping she'd notice that I'm different (and that I'm wearing the same clothes as last night) and coax it out of me. Already it feels too big to keep inside.

I long to call Crow and Nicky and tell them the big news, even though we haven't spoken since I slammed out of our chat last week. I find my phone and hit the power button, but the screen stays blank. Dead. Of course.

My head throbs. "Do you guys have any Advil?" I ask.

"Oh yes!" Yelena sits up suddenly. Her hands fly to her head and she rocks in a wobbly circle, her face tinged with green.

"Are you okay?" I ask.

"Fine. Just a head rush." She tries to steady herself against the wall of the tent, shivering the thin fabric.

"Maybe you should get some sleep," I suggest. The skin under her eyes is raw and blue, like a bruise.

"Nope." She shakes her head firmly. "We'll sleep when we're dead. Right, Britt?"

"Right," Britt agrees, struggling to sit.

You already look dead, I want to tell them. Britt's hair is frizzy and misshapen, and Yelena's so pale she may as well be a ghost.

"And you need Advil, and we should all go dance," Yelena announces. She burrows into her suitcase and comes up several minutes later, giggling.

"Here." She hands me two tablets. I look around for water, but all I can see is vodka.

"You know what *else* I have?" Yelena says to Britt.

Britt yawns. "Too much energy?"

"Nope." Yelena laughs a witchy laugh. "More molly."

"Ugh, I don't know." Britt frowns. "Didn't we do enough last night?"

"Britt!" Yelena looks aghast. "Who are you and what did you do with my best friend?"

"It's just early," Britt protests. "Maybe later."

"Suit yourself." Yelena pops a pill into her mouth and washes it down with vodka. "Phew!" she says, shaking her head like a wet dog. "Breakfast of champions!"

"Can we go now?" I plead. The Advil is melting in my hand.

"Woo!" Yelena says, which I take as a yes.

I grab my dead phone and a charger and unzip the tent, the rip of fresh air like a warm washcloth being squeezed onto my face. All around me people are moving in slow motion, struggling through the heat. I find the vendor who sold me the breakfast sandwich and order a large iced coffee.

"How 'bout some water for those two?" He points behind me at Britt and Yelena, who are sagging against each other like a pair of wilting plants.

I nod. "I'll take two."

I pay for our drinks and gulp down the Advil, the coffee sending a welcome surge of energy through my blood.

"Drink this." I command, handing water to Yelena and Britt.

"Good call." Britt takes a long swig.

"So responsible. Like den mother." Yelena takes a small sip and re-caps the bottle, shoving it in her backpack. "Where to? I want to dance!"

"The Bass Sector stage?" I suggest, thinking maybe Shay will be there.

"Brilliant," Yelena pronounces. "Lead the way, young DJ."

I start toward the sound of bass, keeping an eye out for Derek, Shay, or a place to charge my phone. But all I see are limp groups of people dragging themselves across tired-looking grass. Everyone's hiding behind oversized sunglasses, and the glitter that made them twinkle like fairies last night looks strange and crusty in the daylight, like a disease.

There's a small crowd down by the Bass Sector stage, dancing to a tech-house set that's all regimented bass lines and industrial thuds.

"DJ Skizm!" Yelena exclaims, pointing at the man behind the decks and doing her happy dance, hopping in a circle with her hands above her head. She leads us into the crowd and I try to relax into the music, a spare four-by-four beat splintered by bright, ringing chimes. I close my eyes, remembering how good it felt to dance with Derek last night. We still have twenty-four hours left at this festival. Maybe tonight we can do it all again.

The next track is harder, harsh synth chords crashing around us like lightning. There's a thud that isn't part of the music, and the ground trembles under my feet. My eyes fly open just as a scream splits the air, a high and terrifying A-sharp. I whirl around and see a snarl of limbs convulsing on the ground, a web of messy dark hair.

The scream comes again, and now I recognize it and my stomach turns to stone and everything goes cold. I push past arms and legs, into the center of the close-packed bodies. I don't want to look at what's on the ground, but I can't help it.

The scream comes again, directly below me. It's all too familiar and all too real.

Britt is at my feet, crouched over Yelena's body. She grasps Yelena's hand but Yelena jerks away, her eyes rolling back in her head until there's nothing there but white. She writhes and twitches, her face chalky and slick with sweat, hair tangling in the dirt. Next to her, the doll head on her backpack stares pleadingly up at me from the ground.

I crouch next to Britt and grab her by the shoulders.

"Call 9-1-1!" I beg. "Now!"

Britt looks past me, her mouth frozen in a new scream. Her eyes are wild, dazed, like she doesn't know who I am.

"You!" I point at the closest bystander, a guy with a pierced lip and a cowed, frightened gaze. "Do you have a phone?"

Mutely, he pulls it out.

"Call 9-1-1," I repeat, my voice shaking. "Tell them where we are and to come quick. Make sure he does it," I say to the girl standing next to him. She nods silently, her nose ring trembling.

Then I turn and run. I remember seeing a tent with a red cross somewhere near the vendors; help has to be closer than the nearest hospital. I nearly fall over my own feet as I dodge slow-moving clumps of revelers, my breath coming in labored bursts. The paths and vendors blur with tears.

I never should have let Yelena take more drugs, never should have trusted her when she said she was fine. I saw her face, the bruise-dark circles under her eyes, the tinge of green. I should have made her drink more water, should have forced her to sleep instead of dancing. I should have made her eat something.

Instead I'm here, running, while Yelena seizes like a hurt animal in the dirt.

Finally the medical tent looms into view. I duck inside, gasping and sobbing. A man and woman in matching EMT polo shirts leap to their feet.

"Let's get you sitting," the woman says, guiding me toward a chair while the man reaches for my pulse.

I shake my head, my nose wet with snot. "It's not me. It's my friend . . . by the Bass Sector. . . . She's having a seizure or something."

They exchange glances, and for a minute everything feels like it's in slow motion. "Hurry!" I beg.

Then the world leaps into action and they're gathering duffel bags and an oxygen tank and a stretcher, racing out of the tent and loading everything onto a golf cart with a revolving red light on the top.

"The Bass Sector stage?" the woman confirms.

I nod, crying too hard to speak, and they pull me onto the cart and take off down the path, the red light flashing and the siren far too quiet, lost in the clash of sound from three different stages. It's not nearly loud enough to scatter the clumps of people milling in the path, dumb and slow-moving as cows.

"Did she take anything?" the woman asks as she navigates past the Lip Smacker stage.

A sob freezes halfway up my throat.

"We need to know," she insists. "So we can treat her."

"You won't get in trouble for telling us," the man adds. "Pennsylvania has Good Samaritan laws."

"Molly." The word rips past my lips. "She took molly. MDMA."

They exchange glances. "And she's having *seizures?*" the woman confirms.

"I don't know." I'm choking on my own spit. "It looks like it. But I don't know."

We pull up to the Bass Sector stage and the crowd parts to let us through. I see Britt kneeling by Yelena's side, her face blank with shock.

"She's barely breathing," she states, robotic as if she's reading off a cue card.

The EMTs descend, swarming around her. They sweep Yelena onto the stretcher, slide an oxygen mask over her face, and lift her onto the golf cart, the pathetic little siren chirping away the whole time.

"Does she have ID?" the woman asks me. "She'll need it for the hospital."

I stiffen, the mention of the hospital making this nightmare all the more real. I find Yelena's baby doll backpack and hand it over, a limp and silent offering.

"Which of you is coming with her?" the EMT asks. "There's an ambulance waiting outside." I take a deep breath, ready to volunteer, but Britt steps forward.

"I will," she blurts. "I'm her best friend."

The EMT tells me the name of the hospital as Britt climbs onto the golf cart, her gaze focused straight ahead. "You two stay in touch," he says to me. "But your best bet is to pack up everyone's stuff and meet them there."

I nod, shaking. Then they're gone, the golf cart's small, sad siren fading into nothingness before they disappear around the bend.

CHAPTER 23

I find Britt in the waiting room of the ER. Her skimpy festival outfit looks out of place in the sterile, fluorescent-lit room, and she's hugging Yelena's backpack to her chest and staring at the wall, her eyes blank and unfocused.

"How is she?" I whisper, sinking into the chair next to hers. The air-conditioning in the hospital is on full blast, and I rub my hands over my arms, trying to smooth away the goose pimples.

"She's fine." There's mascara caked around Britt's eyes, a nightmare reflection of the panda hat perched on her head. She clutches the backpack tighter. "I mean . . . of course she's fine, right?"

I swallow. The last time I saw Yelena, she definitely didn't look fine.

"Is she with the doctors?" I ask.

Britt nods, holding the backpack tighter.

"Did they say anything? Did anyone come talk to you?"

Britt shakes her head. "They won't tell me anything," she says, more to the backpack's empty, staring eyes than to me. "But she's okay. She's definitely going to be okay."

"I'm sure she will be," I say, because I can't imagine the alternative. I put my hand on her knee. Her skin is icy under my touch.

"You want a sweatshirt or something?" I ask.

She looks at me blankly. "Why?"

"You're cold." I pat her bare knee. "It's freezing in here."

"Is it?" she asks lightly. Her tone turns my blood even colder. It's creepy the way she's acting like everything is fine, when everything is clearly not fine. I tell myself to ignore it, that she's probably just in shock.

"Yeah." I start to get up. "I'll get us sweatshirts. And maybe some coffee. They have a cafeteria here, right?"

"Don't." Britt clamps a hand onto my arm, her fingers frigid. "We should both be here when she comes out."

Unease snakes through me, but I sit back down. Britt needs me here now, and that's more important than sweatshirts or coffee.

"Did you call her parents?" I ask.

"Nah." She snuggles the backpack closer. "They don't need to know."

"Britt!" I pull back, alarm bells clanging in my head. "Of course they do."

"No, they don't. We said we were going camping. If they find out about this, they'll kill her."

My gut lurches at her choice of words. "Britt," I say, trying to keep my voice even. "Their daughter's in the emergency room."

"But she's going to be fine." Britt draws her knees in around the backpack, sinking deeper into the chair.

We don't know that, a voice rumbles in the back of my head. I screw my eyes shut, but I can't make it stop.

"Give me her phone," I say, opening my eyes.

"Huh?" Britt has one arm on the doll's head, absentmindedly stroking its hair.

"Yelena's phone. Is it in her backpack?"

Britt narrows her eyes. "This is *Emma*," she says, wrapping a protective hand around the doll.

"Okay, fine." I swallow, the half-digested breakfast sandwich doing backflips in my stomach. "Is Yelena's phone in *Emma*? Can I look?"

Britt wrinkles her nose. "I *guess*," she sighs, unzipping the backpack. She takes out the full water bottle I bought for Yelena earlier, a sparkly wallet with a star on the front and a packet of watermelon gum before eventually finding Yelena's cell phone. I reach for it, but she holds it out of reach.

"You're making this into a bigger deal than it needs to be," she says.

"Just give it to me."

She rolls her eyes, but hands it over. "If her parents ground her for the rest of the summer, we're blaming you."

I ignore her and turn on the phone. My stomach contracts as I flip through the contacts, my fingers clumsy on the keyboard. I find *Mom* and press CALL before I can think too hard about how awful this is going to be.

"*Yelena, zdravstvuy.*" A woman's voice answers in Russian on the third ring. It's even gruffer than Yelena's, deep and smoky, and it makes my heart plummet.

"Mrs. Andreyev?" My voice feels thin and forced.

"Hello, yes. Yelena? Who is this?"

"I'm Mira. Yelena's friend. Britt's sister?" I look over at Britt but she's placing Yelena's items back in the doll's belly, as precisely as if she were doing surgery.

"Yes. What is it? Where is Yelena?"

"Um, that's why I'm calling." I feel like my throat is closing up. "I'm so sorry, but Yelena's in the hospital. You need to get here as soon as you can."

"What?" Panic rises in the woman's voice like a startled flock of birds. "Who is this? Is this a prank?"

"I'm sorry. It isn't a prank." I fight back tears as I give her the name and address of the hospital. "I'm with Britt right now. We think she'll be okay, but we don't know."

There's a scrape and static on the other end of the line, and I hear Mrs. Andreyev conversing with a man in rapid Russian. A few minutes later she's back.

"You're a friend?" she asks again. "From the camping trip?"

"A friend." I dig my fingernails into my leg.

"Something happened?" She sounds lost. "Did she break a leg? Was it a bear?"

Every word out of her mouth makes this worse. "She collapsed," I say, just above a whisper. "We don't know why. She's with the doctors now. But you should come. Soon."

There's more static, more muffled Russian conversation.

"Fine," she says brusquely. "This better not be a joke." She confirms the hospital's address one more time, tells me they'll be here as soon as they can, and hangs up. I slump over and rest my elbows on my knees, staring at a patch of pale green tile on the waiting room floor.

We sit like that for another hour before Britt caves and lets me go get us warmer clothes. I charge my phone and flip aimlessly through Shay's Instagram, which is filled with filter-heavy festival pics of her and her friends in front of the stages. I text Derek to tell him what happened.

OMG, he texts back. *Is she ok? Are YOU ok??*

I text back that I hope so. That I don't know. That I'll keep him posted.

A couple of times I try to talk to the nurse at the check-in station, but since we're not family nobody will tell us what's going on. We're practically frozen with boredom and fear by the time the hospital doors swing open and an older couple rushes in. The woman is stout, with bleach-blond curls piled on top of her head, but I recognize the curve of her mouth and her huge, dark eyes—Yelena's eyes. I nudge Britt as they hurry to the check-in window.

The nurse asks them to wait. A moment later a doctor comes out. Britt and I leap to attention, straining at the edges of our seats. The doctor says something to Yelena's parents and the three of them disappear down a hall.

I jump up. The doctor knows something; it's obvious. Britt grasps my hand and we rush through the waiting room and into the hall. I keep expecting someone to stop us: a nurse, an orderly, anyone. But nobody's paying attention.

The doctor ushers Yelena's parents into an office and shuts the door. We stare helplessly at the bland, pale wood as his voice rumbles unintelligibly behind it. I'm about to press my ear against the door when a high-pitched wail pierces the air, stopping my blood in its veins. It sounds inhuman, like a wolf chewing off its own leg.

"I'm sorry," the doctor says, louder now. His voice is like petrified wood. "I'm so sorry."

The wail rises again, turning my blood to ice.

"Mrs. Andreyev . . ." the doctor begins. The door in front of me swims out of focus. Blood roars in my ears.

"You're lying!" Mrs. Andreyev gasps, despair and venom spitting through her Russian accent. "She's only twenty-one years old! She's strong as an ox!"

"I'm sorry," the doctor says for a third time. My knees buckle, and I sink to the floor. "I know how difficult this must be."

"She can't be," Mrs. Andreyev chokes.

Britt's face turns to ashes.

"This must be a mistake," Mr. Andreyev says.

Britt collapses next to me, her hand flailing for mine.

"I'm sorry," the doctor sounds helpless. "We did everything we could."

The roar in my head drowns out his words, Mrs. Andreyev's wails, everything. I grope for Britt's hand and find it, and it's the coldest thing I've ever touched.

CHAPTER 24

It's raining when we leave the hospital, drops hitting the pavement in warm, angry bursts that send steam spiraling into the humid air. Britt stops once we're through the doors, tilting her face to the sky so the water streams down her cheeks and turns her hair to sodden ribbons.

"Come on." I take her arm, guiding her to the car. "We're getting wet."

"Mmmmm," she says, letting me lead her like a child. She's humming a tune that sounds familiar, although I can't quite place it, and she's wearing Yelena's backpack on her chest so the doll bounces against her as she walks. She doesn't seem to notice where we're going, or to care.

But I notice everything: the rain seeping through my sneakers and wrinkling the skin of my toes, the protesting squeak of windshield wipers as I pull out of the hospital parking lot, the specter of Yelena's two giant suitcases rising from the back seat. The world seems too close and too real, too sharp around the edges. I keep waiting for it to take on the blurred quality of a dream, soft and surreal, so I can wake up all over again in the warmth of Derek's van and none of today would have happened.

But there's the back seat in my rearview mirror, the spot where Yelena laughed and chattered all the way from Connecticut to Pennsylvania, now silent and empty. There's my sister staring through the windshield at nothing, her face closed and gray.

The drive home takes hours, the rain and holiday traffic turning the highway into miles of red brake lights and frustrated sighs. Somewhere around Scranton, Britt leans her head against the window, but her fingers never loosen their grip around the doll's plastic arm so I know she's not asleep. I want to put on music, long for the comfort of one of Grandpa Lou's jazz tapes to soothe away this hurt, but even the most mournful blues aren't sad enough for this. Instead I hunch my shoulders against the erratic whine of the LeSabre's windshield wipers, hit the brake in time to the patter of rain on the windshield.

I can feel Britt's shock rising off of her like steam, my grief a lump that won't leave my throat. I want to say something that will bring us together again and make this all right. But nothing will make this all right.

The sky is dark and I've just crossed the town border into Coletown when Britt turns to me, her eyes suddenly focused and sharp.

"Mira," she says, and to my surprise her voice has the bossy quality of the old Britt, the one who hid animal crackers under her pillow when we were kids and made me promise to cover for her when she snuck out to parties in high school. "We can't tell Mom and Dad."

"What?" The LeSabre swishes through a puddle, splattering water on the side of the car.

"About Yelena." She sounds impatient.

"Why?" I can't imagine not telling Mom and Dad. It would be like trying to hide an elephant under my bed.

"Don't you know how stressed they've been?" She puts a hand on my arm, her fingers bitter cold. "All they ever talk about is the gym going under."

"Yeah, but—"

"If they find out about this, it'll break them." Britt speaks clearly and calmly, enunciating every word. "Dad's still sad about Grandpa Lou and Mom's freaking out about our finances. They're barely holding it together as it is."

"I know," I sigh, squinting into the rain. "But don't you think they'd *want* us to tell them? Don't you think they'd want to be there for us, no matter what?"

"Like they were there for you when Grandpa Lou died?"

Her words land like lead. Grandpa Lou's death happened to coincide with the new Crunch opening across town and Britt going off to college. Our parents managed to organize the funeral, empty out his apartment, and sell off his possessions, but they didn't have a lot of time or energy left over to comfort me as I drifted through the house like a tear-swollen ghost.

Britt was the one who was there for me instead, messaging every day to ask if I was okay and sending me goofy GIFs to cheer me up. If it hadn't been for her and Crow and Nicky, I don't know if I would have survived those first few months.

"Look, this is already bad," Britt says. "Listening to Mom and Dad freak out about it will just make everything worse."

I sigh, sinking back against the seat. "I don't know, Britt. I'll try, okay? But if they ask—I can't make any promises."

"Fine." Britt turns away, resting her head on the window. She keeps it there until we're parked and our engine is off. The house is dark; our parents must still be at the gym, although I can't imagine anyone is working out at this time of night on a holiday weekend.

"Do you want the first shower?" I ask, grabbing my duffel bag from the trunk.

"No." She drags one of Yelena's oversized suitcases from the car. "I just want to go to bed."

"Okay," I pause at the foot of the stairs, put the bags down, and hug her cold, stooped shoulders. "Knock on my door if you need anything. I love you, okay?"

"Mrrrrmph," she replies, dragging the suitcase up the stairs. I'm too tired to ask why she grabbed Yelena's suitcase instead of her own. All I want is to get under a stream of water so hot my skin can hardly stand it, then put on fresh pajamas and crawl into bed.

But even after I've scrubbed my skin until it's raw and steaming, even after I've put on my favorite oversized Windham T-shirt and green plaid boxers and pulled the covers over my head, today's memories crash and burn in my mind. Yelena seizing in the dirt. The sad siren on the EMT golf cart. Yelena's mother's inhuman wail.

I've held it together all day, keeping my cool for Derek and the paramedics and Yelena's parents and, most of all, for Britt. But now I can't anymore. A plume of grief wells up and catches in my throat, erupting in a ragged sob. Grandpa Lou dying was hard enough, but at least I understood it: he was old, and he kept smoking even after his doctor and everyone else begged him to stop. But Yelena wasn't old, and she wasn't sick. I can't believe she's just *gone*.

Suddenly I want my mom more than anything in the world: just to hear her voice, to know she's still here. I won't say anything about what happened unless she asks me. I promised my sister that, and I keep my promises.

I call Mom's cell first, but she doesn't pick up. When it goes to voice mail I try the gym's landline. She never ignores that, not when it could be someone wanting to join. She picks up on the third ring, sounding frazzled and out of breath.

"Mom." I struggle to steady my voice. "It's me. Mira."

"Mira! Can this wait? That pipe in the basement burst again; I'm up to my knees in water."

My voice catches. "I guess. . . . "

"Great! Love you, Mir-Bear!" She hangs up, leaving the dial tone buzzing in my ears.

Slowly, tears still streaming down my cheeks, I bring the phone to my side. I want to call back and tell her to hire a plumber and stop trying to fix everything with hope and duct tape. But I know they don't have the money and I realize now that Britt was right; Mom and Dad really do have a lot on their minds. Telling them about Yelena, and expecting them to fix a problem that can't be fixed, would only make things worse.

It's not just the pipe in the basement. Our whole world is falling apart.

CHAPTER 25

I call Nicky, my face a mess of tears. I don't care anymore about our petty argument; I'll apologize a thousand times just to hear one of his acerbic cracks. When it goes to voice mail I dial him again.

Pick up, I text him. *Emergency. SOS.*

On the fourth ring of my fourth call, he answers.

"Jesus, Mira." I hear music and laughter in the background, and realize he must be at the Visitors' Weekend dance. I long to be there with him, so much it makes my lungs ache. "What do you *want?*"

"Nicky . . ." My voice catches. I can't move on to whatever comes next.

"Yes, that's me. Glad you remembered."

"Don't be like that. Please." The words come out as a gasp. "I need you."

"Oh, *now* you need me?" I picture his cheeks flaring pink the way they always do when he's upset. "You sure didn't need me this weekend."

"I'm sorry. I fucked up," I sob into the speaker. "And now everything's broken, and I can't . . . there's nothing . . ." My words tumble over each other, cracked and leaking tears.

"Mira. Jesus. It's not that bad." I hear a door shut, and the background noise dies away. "That was some serious drama, but I was going to forgive you eventually."

I choke on a sob. "I'm sorry," I say again. "It's not just that. It's . . . Nicky, it's really bad."

"How bad?" Another door shuts in the background, and there's a chorus of crickets. He must be outside now, standing on the porch overlooking the lake. "It's not like anyone died."

A wail tears past my lips before I can stop it. I clamp my hand to my mouth, hoping Britt didn't hear.

"Jesus," Nicky says for the third time. There's a long pause, and then, very quietly: "*Did* someone die?"

Through choking sobs, I tell him about Yelena, about my set and Derek and Electri-City, about the weekend that started out like heaven and then turned to hell. "Oh, and I lost my virginity," I finish. "Not that it even matters, now."

"Whoa." Nicky exhales slowly, his breath releasing static into the line. "And I thought my weekend was crazy 'cause Crow's parents brought éclairs."

I laugh a little in relief. That's exactly the Nicky I was craving. "I don't know what to do," I say. "This is like a nightmare."

"Sounds like it." Nicky's voice is soft and soothing. "I wish I was there to give you a hug."

I sniffle. "Me too. I miss you guys so much. Both of you."

"Yeah." There's a pause on the other line. "We miss you too. Even though Crow refuses to admit it."

I curl up with my head under my covers, the glow from my phone turning the space into a small green cave. "Is there anything I can do?"

He sighs. "I can try to run damage control. I'll tell her what happened to you this weekend. But eventually, you have to talk to her yourself."

"I know." I rearrange the covers over my head. "I will."

There's a comfortable silence as I struggle to control my breathing. Gently, almost like a lullaby, Nicky tells me about Visitors' Weekend, about Crow's anti-"Embraceable You" rant and the cocktail wieners they served in the dining hall and meeting the parents of Sidney, the boy he has a crush on. I close my eyes and half listen, letting the cadence of his voice lull me into a place where it almost seems like everything is okay.

Then I hear another voice in the background, calling Nicky's name. A male voice.

"Mira . . ." he begins, his voice tinged with pleading.

"It's okay," I say, realizing he's been missing the dance—his first-ever dance with a boy he likes, one who likes him back—to stand outside and talk me off a ledge. "You should go."

"Okay," he sighs. "Take care of yourself, okay?"

"You too," I say. "And thank you. For everything."

We hang up and I drop my phone onto my mattress, plunging my blanket cave into darkness. But as soon as I close my eyes I see Yelena's face again, pasty and slick with sweat. I hear the thud of her body hitting the ground and the growl of DJ Skizm's track and Britt's agonized shrieking. And then I think of Grandpa Lou wheezing in a hospital bed, his body skinny as a spider and covered in tubes and wires.

My eyes fly open and I reach for the light. This is too much death for one year; too much death for one lifetime. And even though I'm exhausted, I know it's going to be a long, long time before I can sleep.

CHAPTER 26

All I want is an iced coffee. It's been a week since Yelena died and I haven't had a good night's sleep since. Now, as I knock on Britt's door, exhaustion makes the world shimmer around me like a desert mirage.

"Come in!" Britt calls. I turn the knob with one hand and yank at my recital dress with the other. It's made of black polyester that sticks to my skin in the heat, but it's the only thing I own that can pass for funeral attire.

Britt's reflection smiles at me from her mirror. She's wearing a backless shirt and shiny silver leggings.

"You can't wear that!" I exclaim.

"Why not?" Britt turns, a mascara wand in her hand. Her computer speakers vibrate with a familiar tech-house track.

"To a funeral?" I march to her desk and turn the music down. "It's totally inappropriate."

"Oh." She flicks her hand dismissively. "I'm not going to the funeral."

"Seriously?" I don't have time for this. If we don't leave now, we won't have time to stop for coffee. "Come on. Yelena was your best friend."

"Exactly." She bats her eyes at the mirror, reminding me of Yelena in the Dream campground right before my set. A rush of grief blocks my throat. "I knew her better than anyone. She'd want everyone to go out dancing, and have fun. She hates when people are sad."

Britt grabs a sparkly cosmetics bag from her desktop and rummages through it. My stomach twists as I realize the bag, and all the makeup inside, is Yelena's.

Was Yelena's.

"But you still have to go to her funeral." The words are slow and sticky on my tongue. I'm sure, on some level, Britt is right—Yelena probably *would* prefer for everyone to go out dancing. But Yelena's not here anymore, and funerals aren't really for the dead. They're for the living.

"Says who?" Britt swoops silver shadow across her lid. "There's another party at the lot today, and DJ Headspin is spinning, and I'm going to *that*."

"Britt, you can't." Even as I say it, I know I'm fighting a losing battle. There's no arguing with Britt when her mind is made up. But this feels too important to let go. Britt needs to go to the funeral if she's going to start processing Yelena's death—and I need her to come with me, because I don't want to have to do this alone.

"I can!" Britt insists. "You should come. We'll dance till we drop." She spins in a circle with her hands waving over her head, just like Yelena always did when she first hit the dance floor.

"I'm going to the funeral," I choke. "And you should too. You'll regret it if you don't."

"Too bad." Britt grabs Yelena's backpack from her bed, swinging it over her shoulder so the doll's empty eyes meet mine. The sick feeling churns in my stomach. That backpack was creepy even before Yelena died.

"Gotta go!" Britt chirps, bouncing past me into the hall. "Have fun. Tell people I say hi," she calls back over her shoulder as she thunders down the stairs.

"Britt, wait!" I turn to chase her but she's already slamming the front door, her patent leather Doc Martens thundering down the sidewalk. I'm left standing alone in her room, my mouth hanging open and my hands balled into fists.

I know, rationally, that Britt is still in denial, the first of the five stages of grief. Nicky got me a book about grieving when Grandpa Lou died, so I'm aware that eventually she'll move into anger, bargaining, depression, and finally acceptance. According to the book everyone goes through the stages at their own pace— so, really, I should be more patient with Britt. But it's hard when she's running around pretending nothing happened, as if Yelena had just taken a weekend trip. She even went clubbing in the city the other night, and didn't come home until dawn.

"At least turn off your music," I mutter, stalking to her computer. I jiggle her mouse and her iTunes pops up. *DJ Skizm*, the track reads. *Pax Summerfest Live Set.*

A wave of nausea sweeps through me as I hit PAUSE. This is the tune Britt was humming in the car, the one I recognized but couldn't quite place. It's the track that was playing when Yelena collapsed.

For the millionth time I wonder if I should tell Mom and Dad. But then I remember again how they were after Grandpa Lou passed, and how stressed Mom has been about the gym. Telling them might not make anything better, and I'm not sure it's worth risking Britt's trust to find out.

Still feeling sick, I lock up the house and text Derek one more time before driving to the funeral. I haven't seen him since the festival last weekend—I've been trying to play catch-up with audition practice, and worried about leaving Britt alone—but his sweet, flirty text messages have been the one bright spot in an otherwise very dark week. He says he's been in touch with Jake from Electri-City and is working on getting me a good slot . . . and a good rate. And even though I know I should probably back out, walk away from this music and this world and never look back, I can't bear to disappoint Derek after what we've shared. Plus there's the money, and the siren song of spinning for a giant crowd.

I'm almost late and buzzing with fatigue by the time I pull into the funeral home's crowded parking lot. I tiptoe into the hall and find a seat in the back, behind weepy Russian families and college students with sunken, tear-streaked faces. As the priest approaches the podium I scan the crowd for Derek; in his last text, he said he was on his way.

I don't see him, but I do notice Shay sitting with a few of her friends, her pink hair tucked beneath a black velvet cap. She turns and I duck my head, hiding my eyes. She still hasn't returned my texts from Summerfest; I've picked up the phone to contact her so many times this past week, but then I'd look at the seven unanswered messages from last weekend and darken my screen. Shay knows I want to talk to her. It's up to her to make the next move.

A priest approaches the podium and begins a hushed soliloquy about a Yelena I never knew: an honor-roll student who loved tennis and books about dragons, who went to college for psychology because she wanted to help people who were hurting. Then her best friend from high school, a girl named Hannah with a fake tan and hair the color of bread, reads a speech off of index cards about the time Yelena volunteered at an animal shelter and tried to adopt all the dogs. Sniffles echo through the hall and I swipe at my own eyes, wishing I'd thought to bring tissues. This is a side of Yelena I never saw, one I wish I'd had the chance to get to know.

Yelena's mother is next. My heart constricts as she shuffles to the podium, supported by her husband. Even now, as she speaks in a halting Russian accent, I'm haunted by her wail in the hospital, the moment she learned her daughter was gone forever. I've been hearing it when I try to sleep at night, jolting me upright just before I sink into dreams.

As Mrs. Andreyev describes a young girl who loved dolls and animals, she dissolves into big, hacking sobs, weeping until makeup pools in the lines above her lips and she's no longer able to speak. Then there's sad organ music and a receiving line, the choking scent of lilies and a reception with platters of mayonnaise-y sandwiches that everyone's too sad to touch.

Snippets of conversation brush my ears as I move slowly through the crowd, looking for Derek: *her poor mother . . . camping trip . . . beautiful service . . . autopsy report . . .*

I stop moving.

Autopsy report.

I still don't know exactly how Yelena died: whether it was drugs or dehydration or a preexisting condition. But it sounds like someone here does.

"So shocked," the voice—young, female, bland—continues. "Like, what *happened* to her in college?"

Very slowly, I turn my head and see Hannah, the girl who gave the speech about the animal shelter. She's talking to a trio of people who look like they could be Britt's high-school buddies: clean-cut, preppy, athletic-looking. Their eyes are wide with shock.

"So what did it say?" asks a girl with a face like pizza dough and watery green eyes.

"They found drugs in her system," Hannah whispers. Her voice curls around the words, cupping them like a secret. "*Crazy* drugs."

The trio gasps. I freeze next to them, hoping they won't notice me lingering too close. I take out my phone and hit random buttons, trying to look like I'm absorbed in whatever's on the screen.

"Like what?" someone asks.

"Like *meth*," Hannah hisses.

My phone tumbles from my hand.

"Yelena was on *meth*?" someone repeats as I crouch to retrieve it. I sneak a glance at the group, but they're too absorbed in their conversation to notice me scrambling around on the floor.

I stand, my heart pounding. The air in the room feels hot and close. I grip my phone harder, my palms slippery with sweat.

"Uh-uh," says a guy with acne scars. "That's got to be wrong. Do they have, like, false positives? Or maybe it got mixed up with someone else's or something?"

I fight the urge to nod. Those results can't be right. There's no way Yelena could have been taking meth at that festival, not without us noticing. Sure, Yelena was manic and full of energy, but that was just because she was *Yelena*. It couldn't be from meth. Could it?

"That's what her parents said," Hannah's voice is coiled tight. "They made them go back and check again. So they did, and . . ." She trails off, but I can almost feel her nodding.

The tiny logos on my screen swim in front of my eyes. How could Yelena have kept something like that from us? She wasn't shy about telling people she did molly—but maybe she had other vices, hidden addictions she never let anyone see.

"Man," a reedy male voice pipes in. "I mean, she got weird in college, but meth?"

"They found other stuff, too," Hannah's voice dips low. "Like, MDMA—which is like molly, I guess?—and this stuff butylone that I'd never heard of, but I googled it and it's *nasty*."

I still have my phone in my hand. I google *butylone*, my fingers shaky and unsure on the screen. A page full of dense scientific language dances in front of my eyes: *Entactogen. Cathinone. Methylenedioxyphenethylamine.* Somewhere in all of that, I find the only phrase I need: *psychoactive drug.*

My dress feels claustrophobic. I tug at the too-heavy fabric as I dig through my memories of Yelena, looking for clues. When she claimed to be gulping down molly, was she really swallowing other stuff, too? Was she sneaking more pills in the porta potties, crushing and snorting and smoking and huffing things when we weren't looking?

"That just can't be true," Hannah's friend says again, her voice quivering.

The air quivers along with it. It presses in on me until I feel like lilies are crawling down my throat. Did Britt know about any of this, I wonder? Did Derek?

"Shhh, her mom's coming," Hannah spits. "She'd kill me if she knew I was telling you this."

Behind me I feel the group shift. I turn in time to see Hannah rearrange her face into a blank wall of sympathy for Mrs. Andreyev. The sight of Yelena's mother's grief-deep eyes is more than I can bear. I start toward the exit, needing air. I'm almost there when I spot Shay.

She's signing the guest book. When she puts down the pen, our eyes meet and I'm glued to the spot, all the things I just heard and everything from the past week roaring in my head.

Yelena died before I even got to know her: before I knew that she volunteered with rescue animals or was into books about dragons. She died before I could thank her for buying me a dress and inviting two hundred people to my first set.

But Shay's standing right here. It's not too late to really get to know *her*. And life is too short to lose another friend.

She must be thinking the same thing because suddenly we're rushing toward each other, not stopping until we're crushed in a big, weepy hug.

"I'm sorry," I say into her ear as she squeezes back, her cheeks leaving damp spots on my dress.

"No, *I'm* sorry," she replies, her voice muffled. We pull apart and look at each other, trying to smile through our tears.

"That thing with Electri-City . . ." I start.

"No." Shay cuts me off. "That's my own bullshit. I shouldn't have taken it out on you."

"It should have been you," I confess. "You deserve it more."

"Yeah, well . . . like I said, DJing is ten percent music and ninety percent knowing whose ass to kiss." She reaches for a paper cup of lemonade. "I just . . . I don't know. I would've stayed with him longer if I knew he could get gigs like that."

"Who?" I ask, confused.

"Never mind." She shakes her head. "It doesn't matter."

"Wait." It dawns on me slowly. "You mean Derek? He was your manager?"

Shay gives a short, dry laugh. "I guess you could call it that."

Suddenly, everything I've noticed about Derek and Shay starts to make sense. The strange chill between them. The way he changed the subject every time I mentioned her name.

"You used to go out," I say slowly. "Didn't you?"

Her cheeks turn pink. "Just for a few months, like a year ago. It's not a big deal. I'm over him. It's just—"

My mind skips back to everything Derek said about Shay, everything Shay said about Derek. There isn't much, because Shay and I never talked about boys that much—we were usually too busy talking about music. Except for one time . . .

"Hold on." I flash back to our conversation on her rooftop, the very first time we hung out. "When you said you used to sell molly for your ex. Did you mean Derek?"

"Uh, yeah." Shay draws back. "How many dealers do you think I've hooked up with?"

My stomach drops as everything I thought I knew about Derek comes into sharp, sudden focus. How he was always ducking off to "meet someone." The fact that he always seemed to have money, even though he told me he didn't have a job. How weird and cagey Britt got when she learned I was hooking up with him—she must have known. And how he was always the first person Yelena looked for when she went to a party, and then suddenly she'd have a palm full of molly that she'd want to take *right that second*.

And then it hits me even harder: Derek's not just a dealer. He was *Yelena's* dealer.

Yelena, who died from taking a cocktail of drugs I can't pronounce.

Yelena, who will never dance in a circle with her arms above her head again.

Yelena, whose body is in a casket about to be lowered into the ground.

"Derek sells drugs?" I ask, my voice tiny.

Shay raises an eyebrow. "You didn't know?"

My heart plummets. The air attacks me with the smell of egg salad and lilies.

"I'm sorry," she says. "I mean, everyone knows."

Everyone. Even Britt. No wonder she didn't want me going out with him. I wouldn't want my sister dating a drug dealer, either.

"I didn't." My throat is raw and my eyes sting. I can't stand to be here anymore, standing in front of Shay, feeling like the world's biggest fool. I turn and start through the crowd, gagging on the scent of too many bodies pressed together, too much heat and food and flowers.

"Text me?" Shay says to my back as I stumble out of the funeral home.

CHAPTER 27

Sweat soaks my dress as I drive to Brooklyn. Even with the windows open and the air conditioner wheezing away I can't seem to cool down or catch my breath. All I can think about is Yelena convulsing in the dirt, her mother's agonized cry in the hospital. Could Derek have done that to her—*my* Derek, the guy I lost my virginity to? The guy with whom I was maybe, possibly starting to fall in love?

I don't want to believe it. I can't imagine my sweet, gentle Derek slipping meth into Yelena's hand. But I also couldn't imagine Shay selling molly, or Yelena taking meth. I'm starting to think that nobody I've met this summer is who they seem to be.

My hands shake as I buzz Derek's loft. My heart races with unanswered questions.

"Mira." He answers the door in an undershirt and track pants, his eyes dark and sad. "Damn, it's good to see you."

He opens his arms and I long to pitch forward into them, to bury my face in his neck and let him kiss all this confusion away. But that's not why I'm here.

"We need to talk." I march past him into the loft.

"Um, okay." His eyes widen in surprise, but leads me past a girl making smoothies in the kitchen, three guys playing video games on a couch, and a couple in leotards practicing a dance routine. In the cramped quiet of his room he sits on his bed and pats the spot next to him. I tuck my dress around my thighs and leave a few inches between us, but Derek doesn't seem to notice. He takes my hand and runs his thumb along my palm, sending electrical currents up my arm. I want to melt into his touch, but I can't. I yank my hand away.

Hurt flickers across his face. "What's wrong?" he asks.

"Why weren't you at the funeral?" I demand.

The hurt flares. "You think I didn't *want* to be there? Yelena was one of my best friends."

"So why weren't you?"

He sighs and drops his head into his hands. "My fucking mom," he says. "She ruined everything. Again."

I train my eyes on him, tucking my head to one side.

"I *told* her I was going to a funeral," he continues. "But she said it was an emergency and I needed to come right away. When I got there, it turned out she just needed someone to drive her home from a dentist appointment." He laughs a sharp, tuneless laugh. "They didn't even use general anesthetic."

I shake my head slowly. "That's messed up."

"It's totally messed up. I missed her funeral for nothing. One of my best friends, and now I'll never get to say goodbye." He turns and punches a pillow, his back heaving. Then he pulls back and punches it again.

"Dammit!" he screams.

His back is coiled with tension, and it takes everything I have not to put my hands there and try to melt it away. But I can't. Not now.

"I need to ask you something," I say quietly.

"What?" He turns to me, still breathing hard. I notice a rim of red around his eyes, tiny blood vessels crossing the white.

"Did you sell her drugs?" The question stings my throat.

"Whoa." Derek pulls back, his jaw hanging open. "Is *that* why you're being like this?"

"Did you?" Now that it's out it feels urgent, filling my head with pressure.

He shakes his head. "It doesn't matter if I did or not. Nobody dies on molly."

The pressure pops, the truth leaking through my body until I feel like going limp. Shay was right. The guy I lost my virginity to is a drug dealer.

"What about meth?" I ask.

"What?" He gives a sudden, harsh laugh.

"They found meth in her system," I tell him. "I heard at the funeral."

He shakes his head. "Yelena wasn't on *meth*."

"Did you sell it to her?" I ask.

He drops my wrists, his face creased with sudden distrust. "How can you even *ask* me that?"

"You just told me you sell drugs." A tear cuts loose from the corner of my eye. "How am I supposed to know what to think?"

A slow, sad smile crosses his face as he sits back on the bed. "You're really innocent, aren't you?"

I squirm under his gaze. "What does that have to do with it?"

"Mira." He sighs and reaches for me, his fingertips grazing my face and filling me with tingly longing before I can push his hand away. "There's a huge difference between molly and meth. Molly isn't addictive. It doesn't ruin lives. You can't *die* from it."

Gently, he wipes a tear from my cheek. I know I should stop him. But I don't.

"I would never sell meth," he continues, his eyes holding mine. "I care about these people—why do you think I bust my ass throwing parties for them?"

"But you still sell them drugs," I sniffle.

He sighs and takes my hand. "It's different," he says. "Maybe if you tried it you'd understand."

I shake my head. Now more than ever, I have zero interest in trying molly. Still, I can't help remembering how Britt said she stopped hating the girls on her soccer team, how molly opened up her world in a really beautiful way.

"Mira, you have to understand," he says. "Molly is part of what makes this scene what it is. It breaks down people's barriers—it makes them more open and accepting. It lets them show the world who they really are."

I remember the wide-eyed kids who helped me up when I face planted in the warehouse, the gum-chewing fairy-girls who hugged me after my Silent Disco set. I have to admit, the people I've met who were obviously on molly are nicer than anyone at Coletown High.

"And people are going to do it anyway," Derek continues. "They're going to seek it out. All I'm doing is providing a service. If they didn't get it from me, they'd just get it from someone else."

I swipe at my eyes. I know what he's saying is true. But I still feel blindsided—and hopelessly young and naïve.

"And you swear you only sell molly?" I ask. "No meth? Ever?"

"Hey." He slides his hand under my chin and raises my face until we're eye to eye. "I swear. Just molly. That's all. Ever."

"Why didn't you tell me?" I ask, my voice cracking.

"I thought you knew." His finger traces my cheek. "It's hardly a secret."

"I guess there's a lot I didn't know," I say quietly.

"Yeah, me too." Derek shakes his head sadly. "She was on *meth*?" he repeats, disbelieving.

"That's what I heard." I swipe at my eyes. "And some other stuff too. Have you heard of butylone?"

"Damn." His thumb traces my palm. "I just wish I knew . . ."

He trails off, looking at an empty point somewhere beyond my head.

"What?" I ask.

"I just wish I knew she was into that kind of shit." His voice cracks. "I could have talked to her. I could have . . ." He breaks off and looks away, drawing a long, jagged breath.

"Derek . . ." I start to say.

He holds up a hand. "Just give me a minute."

I try not to watch as he struggles to gain control of himself, but it's impossible to look away. He gasps a little and his shoulders shake. His eyes go glossy. He blinks a few times. And in that moment the last little jagged piece of distrust melts inside of me and I know he can't possibly be the one who sold Yelena meth.

He's not lying; he adored Yelena. He would never want to hurt her. He only sells molly, which everyone keeps telling me is perfectly safe.

Yelena was his *friend*.

"I'm sorry," I say softly, reaching out and touching his cheek. "I believe you."

"Thank god." His eyes return to mine, brimming with tears. "I don't think I could handle it if you didn't."

He leans forward and plants the lightest, softest kiss on my lips, letting it linger until I feel like I'm full of helium, about to float away. Then he kisses me harder and I'm kissing him back, our lips mashing into each other as if they can erase all the misery of the past few days, can crowd out the thought of Yelena's coffin going into the ground.

My mind goes blank and we fall back on his bed, grappling with our clothes, and it feels like we're screaming to the world that we're still here, we're alive. Soon we're down to our underwear and he's reaching for a condom and we're not talking, not looking at each other, not thinking about anything except what's happening right here and right now.

CHAPTER 28

It's nearly dark when I leave Derek's place. I swing by *This Is A Lot,* hoping to run into Britt, but the doors are padlocked and there's only silence behind the metal walls. I send a text asking where she is and if she needs a ride home, and she replies with a single heart emoji. It's not the answer I was looking for, but at least I know she's okay.

When I pull into the driveway there's a light on in the living room, and Mom is on the couch in her magenta bathrobe, some kind of gray gunk spread over her face. It's almost pathetic how happy I am to see her. Normally she's at the gym this time of night, going over the day's attendance reports and wiping down equipment.

"Why aren't you at work?" I ask, plopping down next to her and pulling the afghan over my lap.

"I can't take a night off every now and then?" She tries to smile, but her features are frozen from the mask. I'm immediately suspicious.

"You could, but you don't," I say. "What's going on?"

She looks down, rearranging her robe on her lap. "It's nothing to worry about—just that leak again. We had to shut down a little early and call a plumber. Your dad said he'd stay there and deal with it while I came home and took a load off, which is *very* sweet of him." She toys with the edge of her robe, picking at a loose thread. "So I get a night off and a little R and R, and now I get *you*. Isn't that nice?"

She's trying to sound positive, but her voice is stretched thin. I wonder what the plumber is costing us, and how my parents are going to pay for it.

"And where were you tonight?" She takes in my recital dress and raises her eyebrows. "Another date?"

I think of the darkness in Derek's room, his hands on my skin. "Sort of," I say.

Mom beams, making the gray gunk crease and crack. "Sounds like it's getting serious. When are you going to bring him by?"

You mean the drug dealer who took my virginity? Good question, Mom.

"Maybe sometime," I murmur.

"We'd love to meet him," she says. "It's nice to see you branching out a little this summer. I love Crow and Nicky, but . . ."

I know. They're weird. Not like Britt's bland, preppy high school friends who Mom loved.

"And what about Britt?" Mom leans forward. A chunk of clay falls off her face and lands in her lap. "What's she up to tonight?"

My throat constricts. For a moment, I want more than anything to tell her the truth: that I don't know, and I'm worried. That she should be worried too. That there's more going on with Britt than she realizes.

On the coffee table, Mom's phone begins to shriek and vibrate. She lunges forward, silencing it. "That's my alarm—gotta wash this goop off. Be right back, Mir-Bear."

The truth about Britt hovers on my tongue as I watch her pad down the hall, listen to the rush of water coming from the downstairs bathroom. Would it be so wrong if I told her what was going on? What if she and Dad could help?

Mom emerges from the bathroom blinking droplets from her eyelashes.

"Wow, I needed that." She gives me a warm smile—a real one, no longer restricted by her mask. "Nothing like a little R and R when the chips are down, huh?"

She sighs onto the couch and puts her feet up on the coffee table. In the lamplight I notice the tiny web of wrinkles around her eyes, the skin below them purplish and delicate.

Those wrinkles weren't there a year ago. Our family's finances must be getting to her more than she lets on. The last thing Mom needs is more to worry about—and there's no guarantee that telling her will actually help Britt.

"Maybe you should take a bath or something," I suggest. "Make the most of it."

"Now *there's* an idea," she says as I stand. "I like the way you think."

"Enjoy it." I kiss her cheek. "Love you, Mom."

"Love you, Mir-Bear," she says as I climb the stairs to my room.

I shut the door and sink into my desk chair. I'm exhausted, but I know if I try to sleep I'll just keep hearing Mrs. Andreyev's scream in my head, and picturing Yelena gray-faced and seizing in front of the Bass Sector stage. I can't stomach another night of that. I can't keep revisiting the ghost of Yelena the last time I saw her, jerking and twitching on the ground.

That isn't how I want to remember her. I want a different picture in my mind: Yelena the first time I met her, rushing toward me in her huge patent leather boots and silver belly chain. Yelena dancing with her hands in the air, reaching for the beat like it's the string of a balloon that'll ferry her away to a magical land.

A bass line starts to weave through my head, powered by the memory of Yelena's dancing and the funny, happy hop she always did when she got excited.

Quickly, before it can disappear, I open Sibelius on my laptop. Maybe this is a way I can keep her memory alive. Music can't make this pain go away, but maybe it can turn it into something different, something beautiful. Maybe it can help me make sense of what happened.

I transcribe the line in my head into a bass solo, the notes practically shoving each other aside to get onto the staff. But when I've entered them into Sibelius and hit "play" I realize I've written it for the wrong kind of bass. This isn't meant to be acoustic: it's the deep, pounding kind of bass that sounds best fattened by a synthesizer and played too loud on giant speakers, the kind that made Yelena shriek and throw her head back, spin in a circle, and shake her manic curls.

My piece for Yelena isn't meant to be jazz. It's meant to be dance music: the kind of music Yelena loved.

Chapter 29

I'm up for most of the night working on Yelena's piece. When I finish I fall into a deep sleep, and, for the first time since she died, I'm not plagued by dreams.

I text Shay the next day.

What do people use to write dance music? I ask. *Like from scratch?*

I watch the three dots appear on my screen start, pause, then start up again.

Just come over, she finally replies. *I'll show you.*

After work I drive to the Bronx and take the rickety elevator down to her studio. As I pick my way through the maze of storage rooms I try not to get spooked by their hulking shadows, try not to imagine Yelena's ghost lurking in every corner. It's a relief when I find Shay hunched over her DJ rig, bathed in the peachy glow of her lamp. Behind her I see a sleek black rectangle covered in LED buttons that glow orange, green, and violet.

"What is that?" I ask.

She grins. "My new baby. I got it cheap from some yuppie in the Financial District who finally figured out he's too busy making money to ever be a producer."

"That's how you write music?" The box looks warm and tactile, the opposite of the sterile black-and-white staffs in Sibelius. A few of the squares blink under my gaze.

"Uh-huh. This thing is everything: drums, bass, synth, effects—you name it." She taps a button and it lights up, making a sound like a kick-drum.

"Can I try?" I feel like the box is calling to me.

"Sure." She moves aside. "Maybe you'll have better luck coming up with something that actually sounds good."

"It does bass?" I stretch out my fingers, hypnotized by the blinking squares.

"Sure." Shay shows me how to switch into bass mode, how to choose a style and manipulate it until it sounds the way I want. "I guess you're supposed to play chords or whatever, but I never had, like, formal music training. So it's tough going."

"I can show you." I rest my fingers on the box and play the bass line I came up with last night. The buttons light up under my fingers, yellow and blue, as the notes boom clear and mellow through Shay's speakers. Warmth sweeps through me, sinking into my hips. This is the way I wanted that bass to sound. This is the first thing that's felt right in days.

"Damn." Shay nods along to the music, a sliver of tongue wedged between her teeth. "That's tight."

I show her a few basic chord progressions and we tweak the bass line together, stretching the sound until Shay's head-nod is a full-on dance. "It sounds so *good*!" she exclaims. "Now all we need is a beat, and a melody, and some effects, and . . ."

"And we can take over the world," I laugh. For the first time since Pax Summerfest I feel like myself again, like all I need is music and everything will be okay. "Let's try some drums."

We spend the next hour playing with kicks, claps, and snare, then move on to structure and effects. As Shay shows me how to use the equipment, I teach her about meter, tonality, song structure, and all the other music-theory-nerd things I could talk about forever, if anyone besides Crow and Nicky ever wanted to listen.

"I think we might have something here," Shay says when we're finished adding effects.

"We definitely have *something*." I cock my head. "I don't know. It's good, but I feel like it's missing something."

"Like what?" Shay rests her chin in her palm and looks up at me, her eyeliner smudged from sweat and excitement.

"I don't know." I can't quite put my finger on it, because the song has everything it should need: a tight beat, fun effects, and a rock-solid structure with an intro and outro, verses and chorus and a bridge. But it still feels somehow incomplete. "Vocals, maybe?"

"Hmmm." Shay blows a stray piece of hair away from her face. "We could look for samples. Or, I dunno—you know anyone with a microphone? Maybe we could record something."

"Yeah, maybe." I drum my fingers on the tabletop. "I'll think about it more at home."

"Oh!" Shay brightens. "I could play it at my gig next weekend! Maybe we just need to hear it over a real sound system."

The idea of a track I wrote being played over a real system, for a real dance floor, sends an inadvertent zing through my chest. Maybe if it works I can play it at Electri-City, I think, although of course I don't say that to Shay. I know it will always be a sore spot between us, and the last thing I want is to rub it in.

"You have a gig this weekend?" I ask.

"Yeah, in the Pine Barrens. I'll put you on the list."

"Oh, Shay. I don't know." I wilt against the metal wall. "My Fulton audition is in a month."

"And you're going to practice on Saturday night?" She rolls her eyes. "C'mon—I want you to hear my set! It'll be fun."

I want to tell her that I'm out—there's no way I can come. But there's so much hope in Shay's voice. I don't know how to tell her no.

"I'll think about it," I say, gathering my bag.

"Sure you will." She gives me a knowing smile. "I'll see you there."

CHAPTER 30

I keep waiting for Britt to move on from denial, but a week after the funeral it only seems to be getting worse. I watch her from the front desk at The Gym Rat as she drags herself through teaching a Cardio Blast routine, her feet not leaving the ground. Her hair has started to grow out where she buzzed it, and the other side is dry and damaged.

If I didn't know better I'd assume she's moved on to depression, but I know better. She went out dancing again last night even after I begged her not to, sneaking down the stairs in a red vinyl romper that used to be Yelena's.

In high school Britt could go out and get hammered and still be bright-eyed and bushy-tailed the next day, but now all her partying is starting to show. She's barely keeping time to the music, and she winces whenever it hits a high note. There's no applause when the class finishes. Britt just turns off the music and leaves, picking up Yelena's backpack and slinging it over her shoulder. She stares down at the floor as she trudges through the gym, so she doesn't see Mom coming.

"Britt, honey!" Mom grabs her shoulder, her overbite flashing. "Great news! I just got off the phone with Coach Driggs. He wants to start up your training tomorrow."

"Um." Britt tries to plaster on a smile. Can Mom not see how wrecked she is, I wonder? Or does she just not want to look?

"You're free then, right?" Mom purses her lips. "Because I told him you were, and he's going out of his way."

"Yeah." Britt's smile falters. "I'm free then."

"Great! So it's a date." Mom squeezes Britt's bicep. "Let's get your strength back so you can kick some butt this fall, huh?"

Britt nods weakly. The doll's head bobs with her.

"What *is* that thing, anyway?" Mom asks, pursing her lips and pointing at Yelena's backpack.

"This?" Britt looks over her shoulder like she's surprised to see it perched there. "Just a backpack."

"Well it's kind of gross," Mom says, wrinkling her nose. "Can you maybe leave it at home tomorrow? It might freak out our customers."

Britt looks crestfallen. "Sure," she says quietly. I expect Mom to ask what's wrong, but she's distracted by a motivational poster that's coming off the wall. As she jogs off to fix it, Britt wanders to the exit.

"Hey," I call as she passes the desk. "Are you okay?"

She stops, startled. "I'm fine," she says.

"Britt. Come on."

"No, everything's cool." She leans against the desk, the doll backpack's dirty plastic feet trailing on my keyboard. "I mean, I could skip this soccer business. But everything else is fine."

I frown. "But you love soccer."

"Yeah . . ." her voice trails off. "But I'm out of practice. Coach will know."

"So practice," I suggest. "You're not seeing him until tomorrow. You could go right now."

"Yeah, no." She rests her hands on the desk, the nails painted bloodred and embedded with black sparkles. "I'm too beat."

Of course she is, I think. She keeps skipping sleep to go out dancing.

I take a deep breath. "What if I go with you?" I suggest. Maybe playing soccer will help refocus Britt on what matters: doing what she loves. Maybe it will help her confront Yelena's death and convince her there's more to life than partying.

"Are you serious?" Britt's laugh is broken and dry, not the usual peal of silver that climbs one note before descending the scale. "You hate sports."

"Yeah, but I love *you*."

Britt rolls her eyes. "Whatever, weirdo."

"Well, my shift is over." I secede the front desk to Dad's work-study, a college student determined to lose fifty pounds despite the fact that he never actually works out. "Let's go kick some balls around."

Britt tries to protest but I'm already scrounging a soccer ball from the equipment closet. From the corner of my eye I see Dad watching me. We make eye contact and his face breaks into a smile of pure joy as I palm the ball. My gut twists. The only time I've seen him smile like that is when he watched Britt on the soccer field. I've never gotten quite that look from him, not even when I won the regional music competition and took home a trophy too big to fit in my bedroom.

Britt doesn't notice. She's staring emptily into space, twisting a strand of the doll's hair around her thumb. Seeing her like that makes me clutch the ball tighter. I want the old Britt back, even if it means I have to do sports to help her get there.

"Can't we just go home?" she complains as I drive us to the high school soccer field. "I'm really tired."

"I'll bet," I say. "You've been out a lot."

I expect her to argue, but she just nods and looks out the window. I pull into the parking lot, batting away thoughts of my three lousy years in this awful building and the one ahead. Our feet crunch on grass that's gone brown with summer neglect as I lead the way to the soccer field, Britt trailing behind.

"So I guess I'll be goalie," I say. "And you can work on your footwork or whatever."

Britt takes a long time getting ready, carefully arranging Yelena's backpack on the bleachers. When she's done it looks like the doll is watching us, and I shiver in spite of the July heat. Britt slowly returns to the field, the toes of her sneakers dragging behind her and kicking up clumps of dirt.

"Do your thing," I tell her, trying to find a good spot in the goal. I haven't played soccer since middle school gym and I'd forgotten how big the net feels. "Get it past me—it shouldn't be hard."

I roll the ball to Britt and she nicks it with her toe, sending it skittering. The blur of black and white seems to uncoil something inside her and she goes after it like a cat chasing a toy mouse, dribbling from foot to foot and then kicking it high into the air, bouncing it off her knees.

I relax into the sight of Britt being Britt again, her limbs unspooling like a skein of silk. She flows down the field in the dying light, all the grace and poise I remember from her high school days finding itself in the way the ball meets her body, the magnetic pull as it returns to her every time. Britt's back in control again: the rising star, the Alden Family MVP.

Watching her I'm flooded with the same admiration and envy I felt all through high school, the sense that I could never be like that and the fleeting wish that sometimes, just to see what it was like, I could.

Finally, Britt draws back her leg and sends the ball hurtling into the air. I stand transfixed in the goal, hypnotized as the black and white hexagons spiral closer and closer, growing larger until . . .

"Duck!" Britt screams, a second too late.

The ball connects with my face and pain explodes across my cheek. I stumble backward and watch my legs rise into the air and fall back to the earth. Through the ringing in my ears I hear Britt call my name. A moment later she's crouched next to me, her face swimming in and out of focus. "Are you okay?" she asks.

"Ouch." I sit up slowly, cupping my cheek. "I feel dizzy."

"I'm sorry." Britt sits down hard next to me. "I'm so sorry."

"It's okay." I rub my face. "Am I bleeding? Is there a bruise?"

Britt looks at me, and her face collapses.

"Fuck!" she screams at the sky. "Why do I fuck up everything I love?"

She crumples to the ground, sobbing.

"Whoa, hey, it's okay." I get to my knees and crawl over to her, my cheek still throbbing. "It's not that bad. I'm fine."

"I hurt you," Britt whimpers. Tears leak from between her fingers.

"No you didn't." I pull my hand away. "See? No blood."

Britt just cries harder.

"Hey, it's okay." I reach over and rub her back in circles, the way Mom used to do when we were little. "You were amazing out there. Let's just try again. This time I'll duck."

"No!" The word pierces the air, teakettle-sharp. "Why doesn't anyone get it? I don't want to do this anymore."

My hand stops moving on her back.

"What do you mean?" I ask.

"This." Britt gestures at the ball, the net, the field. "Soccer. All of it."

"You don't want to play soccer anymore?" Soccer is Britt's whole world. I can't imagine who she'd be without it; it would be like me without music, an outline of a person still waiting to be colored in.

She shakes her head. "It's just so fucking pointless. All this competition for no reason. To get a ball into a net? Why bother?"

"Hey." A piece of hair is sticking to her cheek. I brush it away. "I get it. You're grieving. You probably feel like nothing has any point right now."

"You *don't* get it." She sits up and draws her knees to her chest, tucking herself into a ball. "I've felt this way for a long time."

"Since when?" I pluck a blade of grass by the root and run my finger along the edge.

"I don't know. Months? Years?" She nuzzles her chin into her knees. "Yelena was the only one who understood. She was, like, the only person in the world who didn't care whether or not I was some soccer star." Her eyes gloss over with tears. "She was the only one who liked me for *me*."

"That's not true." I run my finger harder along the blade of grass. "Everyone likes you for you. *I* like you for you."

"Then why are you making me do this?" she explodes, tears streaming down her cheeks.

My stomach churns. All I wanted was to make things better for Britt, to bring her back to normal. Instead I've made everything worse. "I thought it would make you feel better," I admit after a while. "Like, to do something you're really good at. Like what writing music does for me."

"That's the *thing*." Britt sniffles loudly. "Everyone thinks soccer is the only thing I'm good at. Nobody sees past the trophies. Nobody sees *me*."

"Britt." I take her hands and hold them tight. "You know you can stop after college. You don't have to play soccer forever."

"Huh?" she says, wiping her eyes with the bottom of her shirt.

"I mean, you still have to play now, for your scholarship," I continue. "But if it's not really what you want—like, there's no law saying you have to be a professional soccer player when you grow up."

Britt blinks. "You didn't know?"

"Know what?" I yank a new piece of grass from the ground.

She sighs. "I can't believe Mom and Dad didn't tell you. I lost my scholarship. I almost got kicked off the team."

"What?" Blood rushes to my ears, flooding the world with white noise.

"I lost my scholarship," Britt repeats. "Mom and Dad think I just wasn't playing well, but it was more than that. The coach called it poor sportsmanship."

"Poor sportsmanship." I roll the words over my tongue. Suddenly my parents' obsession with getting Britt to train this summer makes sense. This whole time, I was the only person in our family who didn't know. "What does that even mean?"

She shrugs, not looking at me. "Showing up late for practice. Not giving it a hundred and ten percent. Just generally . . . I don't know, not caring enough?"

A timeline starts to form in my head. Britt meeting Yelena. Britt taking molly. Britt losing her scholarship.

"Because you were partying," I say.

"It wasn't just that." Britt sniffles and wipes her eyes. "I just . . . I don't know. I stopped caring."

"So how are you paying for college?" The white noise grows stronger, drowning out the hum of a far-off airplane and Britt's close, ragged breaths.

"We took out a loan," she says. "Which covered part of it. But a lot's coming out of savings."

The rush in my ears is deafening, drowning me. Those savings were supposed to be for *me*. To help pay for Fulton. And to send me to camp.

"So that's why . . ." I start, and then stop. I can't finish the sentence. I don't want to believe it's true.

But there it is, big and ugly and loud. So that's why our parents couldn't afford to send me to camp this year. It wasn't because business was worse than usual, wasn't because the money just wasn't there.

It was because of Britt.

CHAPTER 31

I'm stunned into silence. We sit there for a long time, Britt weeping quietly into her hands as I rip up more grass, first by the blade and then by the handful. Finally I can't take it anymore. I stand and stalk to the car, my sneakers grinding angrily against the gravel. Britt follows slowly. The soccer ball stays on the field.

I keep my eyes trained on the road as I drive home. If I even look at Britt I'll explode, sending a hailstorm of curses echoing through the car. I can't believe my own sister is the reason I'm not at camp this summer. I can't believe our whole family has been lying to me. I can't believe our parents put Britt first again: ahead of the gym, ahead of Windham, ahead of *me*. But most of all I can't believe Britt kept partying, even after losing her scholarship.

Not only that, but she dragged me into it with her.

When we get home I don't wait for her to get out of the car. I run upstairs and slam my door, pacing my tiny bedroom until it feels like a cage. Finally I grab my trumpet and start blasting scales, warming up my lungs as I attempt to cool down my heart.

It's not like this is the first time our parents have put Britt first. Britt always got more presents for her birthday: soccer balls and jerseys and trendy clothes and makeup. I know she was easier to shop for, but that didn't make it hurt any less.

I segue into an easy Scott Joplin rag. Our parents have more pictures of Britt on the walls. They closed the gym the day of the state soccer championship so the whole family could attend her game, even though Grandpa Lou was the one who went with me to all my music competitions, even the one where I took home the trophy that now lives in the garage. Grandpa always said he enjoyed it; he loved being around all that music and it took his mind off missing my Gram. But there was always the unspoken question: if he hadn't been the one driving me around, who would have?

I finish the rag and start in on a tricky Dizzy Gillespie riff that's all speed and fingerwork. A muted thump comes from Britt's room, throwing me off. I grit my teeth, set my metronome, and try again. But just as I hit the apex of the solo the thuds come louder, breaking what little concentration I have left. She's listening to tech-house again; I can't quite tell through the egg crate on my walls but I'm almost sure it's that DJ Skizm set.

The fury I've been struggling to tamp down bursts to the surface. She's already ruined everything else for me, and now she's ruining this too. Still clutching my trumpet I storm into the hall. If she had to take away summer camp and any money left to send me to college, the least she can do is turn her goddamn music down. I need to ace this audition now more than ever—if I don't get a scholarship, I may as well not even get in.

And if I *do* get a scholarship, I'm not going to blow it. Not like Britt.

I barge into her room without knocking, my cheeks burning and a million accusations ready on my tongue. The music pulses around me, curt and angry: definitely DJ Skizm.

Britt's room is a mess. There are clothes everywhere, makeup smeared on her dresser, club and party flyers scattered on the floor. She's curled on the bed, still wearing her clothes from before: bike shorts and a Gym Rat tank top and cleats that leave little clumps of dirt on her yellow comforter. She's cradling Yelena's backpack like it's a child, with the doll's head up against her cheek and a piece of its hair wrapped around her finger. Her eyes are closed and her mouth is open, slack . . . asleep.

I sag against her wall. Britt always kept her room immaculate. Now it's clear she's not even trying. She's given up, our parents are completely oblivious, and I don't know if I can keep doing this anymore. Since Yelena died I've gone out of my way to keep it a secret from Mom and Dad, to be there for Britt if she wants to talk, to try to help her grieve. I even played soccer for her. But the more I've tried, the less she has.

Britt doesn't want to get her life together, I realize as I look around her room, and our parents don't want to see the truth. If they did, they'd notice that she can't keep her hair or her room clean, that she can barely teach an easy cardio class and is carrying a creepy, grubby baby doll wherever she goes. But they're still too blinded by the old Britt, the golden girl who could do no wrong. I bet if I tried to tell them that girl is gone, they wouldn't even believe me.

As I stomp across her room and turn off her music I tell myself I'm done with this family and all its lies. If Britt wants to throw her future away that's fine, but I need to focus on *my* future: on Fulton, on getting in. And on paying for it.

I return to my room and start sifting through my new tracks, the ones I've been setting aside for Electri-City. I play them loud enough to jiggle the egg-crate foam on my walls, not caring anymore whether I wake Britt or bother the neighbors. If my family isn't going to help me pay for Fulton, I'll just have to find ways to pay for it myself. DJing is as good a place as any to start.

But with every track, every measure, every note, comes a new set of fears: That I'll never be able to afford Fulton. That I won't get a scholarship. That Crow and Nicky will go to the conservatory of our dreams and I'll be stuck in Coletown forever, folding towels and swiping membership cards and slowly rotting to death. All because Britt decided she didn't want to play soccer anymore. All because our parents put her first.

CHAPTER 32

I can barely stand to go to work the next day. Everything about the gym—the ugly fluorescent lights, the sweaty stucco walls, the persistent stink of rubber, bleach, and feet—feels like a prison. I'm afraid that if I even look at my parents I'll explode, my shell of rage falling open to reveal the raw, pulsing hurt beneath. I can't lose my cool—not here, not now—so I bury my nose in my laptop and download more tracks for Electri-City, distracting myself with a fantasy where a wealthy benefactor catches my set and offers to pay my tuition at Fulton and buy me a set of CDJs and a Rane mixer too.

At three o'clock, when afternoon ensembles let out, I FaceTime Nicky at camp. He's in the lounge, and I catch the blurry outlines of Regina and Brian behind him, playing a card game and laughing.

"Has your family ever lied to you?" I ask, glancing around the gym to make sure my parents are out of earshot. "Like, about something big?"

"Um." He turns his eyes skyward, thinking. "They pretended to be cool when I came out, even though I overheard my mom sobbing to my dad later about how I'd never give them grandchildren," he says finally. "But at least they tried, you know?"

I bite my lip. That's not exactly what I'm talking about. If anything, it's the opposite.

"Who're you talking to?" Crow comes up behind Nicky, peers into the screen, and sees me. "Oh," she says, turning to go.

"Crow, wait!" I call after her.

She freezes. I count four agonizing beats of looking at the back of her plaid vest before she turns.

"Atta girl," Nicky says, pulling her down next to him. "It's about time you two talked."

Crow blinks behind her glasses. I take a deep breath.

"Listen, about Visitors' Weekend." I pick at the edge of a fingernail. "I'm sorry, okay? I shouldn't have been so harsh about it. I was just having FOMO."

"Having what?" Crow cocks her head.

"Fear of Missing Out," I explain. My stomach twists; it was Yelena who taught me that word.

"Oh!" Crow's brow unfurrows. "I really like that."

"Am I forgiven?" I ask.

Crow adjusts her fedora. "I guess," she sighs. "Just don't do it again."

"Thanks." I melt a little at her crooked smile. "I missed you."

"I missed you too, jerk," she says affectionately. "Hey, did Nicky tell you about his new romance?"

My eyes shoot to Nicky. His face is scarlet. "Tell me every-thing. Now."

They launch into a detailed account of flirtations in the dining hall, mushy duets in the practice rooms, and a first kiss down by the lake. By the time they're through I've lost my desire to tell them about Britt. I don't want to ruin their fairy-tale summer with my drama, and there's nothing they can do to fix it anyway.

"I wish you were here," Nicky laments, still rhapsodizing about his boyfriend. "I told Sidney all about you. He would *love* you."

"I wish I was there too," I sigh. FOMO balloons inside me, pulsing in my chest. As happy as I am for Nicky, it hurts not to be there for his first love.

Then again, it's not like he's been here for mine.

Suddenly, I want to see Derek more than anything. It's been three days, and our endless text-message chain doesn't feel like enough right now. I want the solidity of his body, the grainy warmth of his laugh. I want to remind myself that at least one thing in my life right now is genuinely good.

When I text to see if he can hang out after work he says he's visiting his mom in Westchester and can pick me up after. A month ago I would have been embarrassed to meet him in the sad shopping plaza where The Gym Rat is nestled between a Chinese takeout place and a Payless ShoeSource, but we're beyond that now. What we have is too deep, too real, to be hampered by the lame reality of my hometown.

I impatiently count down the hours until five o'clock, then freshen up in the locker room and practically vault into his van.

"Hey, beautiful," he says, leaning in for a kiss. "Is the mall here any good?"

"You want to go to the *mall*?"

He nods like an eager puppy. "I haven't been to a mall since high school. Please tell me they have a food court. And a Hot Topic! Oh, and I need socks."

"You're nuts." I shake my head, the anger of a day cooped up in the gym already dissipating. "But, yeah, it has both of those things. And probably socks."

"Great!" He pulls onto Route 17. "The mall it is. We can pretend it's the '90s. And wait'll you hear my good news!"

"Good news?" I feel like I haven't had good news in ages. For a moment, all thoughts of Britt and Windham and my family's lies drift away.

"About Electri-City." He pulls up to a stoplight and gives me a quick peck on the cheek. "I got you a pretty sweet rate. How does five hundred sound?"

My jaw falls into my lap. "Five hundred *dollars*. Oh my god. Derek. Really?"

His laugh ripples through the van. "Of course, as your manager I'll be taking fifteen percent. . . ."

"Five hundred dollars?" I repeat. That's more money than I've ever made at one time. If I can get more gigs like that, paying for Fulton on my own might not be such a pipe dream after all. "You're amazing."

"Damn right. And don't you forget it." He reaches over and squeezes my knee. "I got your set time too."

"Yeah?" I lean forward. "When is it?"

His eyes flicker over to me, then back to the road. "Friday. Six p.m. Don't hate me—it's the best I could do."

"Oh man." My stomach drops. "You told me it was the weekend after my audition. You didn't tell me it's the same *day*."

He frowns at the road. "What time is your audition? Early, right?"

"Three." I wince. "That's cutting it *really* close."

"But it's in Manhattan, right? You'll be fine. You worry too much," he says, ruffling my hair.

I scratch at a bug bite on my knee. "It's a lot to worry about," I admit. With almost anyone else I'd pretend it's no big deal—I wouldn't let them see me lose my cool. But I'm past that with Derek. He's seen me at my most vulnerable, and I'm not afraid to let down my guard with him anymore. "It was already going to be the most important day of my life."

"So now you'll kill it at two things instead of just one." He keeps his hand on the back of my neck. "I have total faith in you, Mira. You just need to have faith in yourself."

"Thanks." I close my eyes and let his touch transport me to a fantasy where I've already aced my Fulton audition and am at Electri-City, about to drop my new track for a thousand screaming fans. . . .

"Hey." My eyes fly open. "Can I play you something?"

He raises an eyebrow. "Another mix?"

"Even better. A new track."

"Get out. You're producing?"

"Sort of. I was over at Shay's the other night and this happened." I plug in my phone and find the rough cut of our song, keeping an eye on Derek as bass rolls through the speakers. His face stays blank as the track builds and swells and drops into a breakdown, finally tapering into drumbeats, then silence.

"What do you think?" I ask anxiously. He's staring straight ahead at the road, giving nothing away.

"I don't know." He drums his hands on the wheel. "I wouldn't play that at Electri-City if I were you."

Disappointment leaks through me, making me deflate. "It's missing something, right?"

"Not just that." Derek's lips go thin. "It's too experimental. This is your first set at a major festival—you should be playing shit people already know and love."

"Well, I mean, of course it sounds experimental. It was an experiment. And Shay says she has a friend who'll master it, and she's going to play it at this Pine Barrens party this weekend and maybe it'll be different over a real system, and I still think I can figure out what it's missing. . . ." I'm babbling, I realize. I trail off and glance at Derek. His eyes have turned to stone.

"What's wrong?" I ask.

He sighs, pulling into the right-hand lane and following signs for the Tri-County Mall. "No," he says, shaking his head. "I promised myself I wouldn't do this."

"Do what?" I ask, my shoulders tensing.

"Dammit." He slaps the steering wheel once, making me jump in my seat.

"Derek." I rest a hand on his shoulder. "Tell me what's wrong."

"Fine." He grimaces as he pulls into the parking garage and finds a spot on the second floor. He parks carefully and lets the engine tick into silence before turning to me, his eyes troubled. "You really think it's a great idea to be spending so much time with Shay?"

"What?" I sit back, stunned. "Is this because she's your ex or something?"

"No!" He shakes his head. "It's not about that at all. We're cool. But how well do *you* know her?"

"Pretty well." I twist my hands in my lap. "I mean, we've hung out a bunch and she taught me how to DJ and I met her friends and stuff."

"Sure." He sighs. "Look, don't take this the wrong way, but it doesn't sound like you know her that well at all. Trust me, you'd stay far away from her if you knew what she was really like."

"Shay?" I scratch the bug bite harder, leaving thin lines across the welt. The girl Derek's describing doesn't sound anything like the Shay I know. "Are you sure?"

His eyes slide toward me. "Remember how upset you were after your Silent Disco set?" he says. "When you'd just slaughtered the dance floor and gotten booked for your first major festival and should have been on top of the world, and instead you were worried because Shay was giving you the silent treatment?"

I nod, twisting my hands until my fingertips turn pink.

"Then she didn't speak to you for, what, a week?" he continues. "Without even telling you what was wrong? Even after you practically watched Yelena die? How immature is that?"

I look down at my hands, coiled in my lap. "She said she was sorry," I murmur.

"Sure. And everything's cool for a little while. And then you'll do something else to piss her off and it'll be the same shit all over again. You really want to get caught up in that?"

"I don't know." I untwist my hands and shake feeling back into my fingers. Shay's reaction felt normal to me; I might have done the same if I'd watched my friend get something I'd always wanted and hook up with my ex at the same time. But Derek's known her longer than I have. Maybe I'm not as good a judge of character as I thought. "I guess not," I say slowly.

"So you'll stop hanging out with her?" he asks, taking my hands in his.

I pull them back, startled. "I didn't say that."

"Oh." His face contorts. "So you'll just keep putting up with her shit, and listening to her when she says terrible things about me, and . . ."

"Wait a minute." I sit back in the bucket seat, struggling to reconcile this new side of Derek with the gentle, easygoing guy I fell in love with. "Is that what this is about? You're worried she's going to talk shit about you?"

"Man, I don't know." Derek sighs and drops his hands into his lap. "I wouldn't put it past her."

"She won't, okay?" I cross my arms over my chest. "Maybe she was different when you guys were dating, but she would never do that now. And even if she did, I wouldn't listen."

"You mean that?" He looks up cautiously, eyes brimming with hope.

"Of course I mean it." I uncross my arms. "Don't you trust me to make up my own mind?"

"I guess." There's a long pause. Finally he reaches for me, pulling me onto his lap and resting his head on my shoulder. When he speaks again his mouth is against my neck. "I'm sorry." His voice is muffled. "I don't mean to be like this. It's all my mom's fault, and seeing her today . . ." he sighs into my skin. "I told you I have trust issues."

"I know."

So *that's* what's behind this side of him—why he's acting like I'm going to betray him just by hanging out with my friend. His mom made him like this. I should have guessed.

I rest my head on top of his and his scent wraps around me as the tightness in him loosens, letting me back in. "But you don't have to be like that with me," I whisper in his ear. "You can trust me. Always."

CHAPTER 33

"Ooh, Panda Express *and* Chick-fil-A!" Derek exclaims as we stroll through the food court, pausing in front of each. "How should we clog our arteries tonight?"

"There's always pizza," I suggest. "The Domino's here makes it extra bland."

He laughs and throws an arm over my shoulder. "I guess we're not in Bushwick anymore," he says, steering us toward Subway. We order sandwiches and manage to find a table that's not covered in spilled soda or fast-food wrappers. Even on a Tuesday the food court is crowded with families having loud, messy dinners and packs of the type of people who like to call me Sad Trombone at school. Derek's talking about Electri-City again, about how I'm on after some electronic jam band, and I'm nodding around a mouthful of turkey when I feel a tap on my shoulder.

I whirl around, strands of shredded lettuce flying from my sub. Gabriella Lawson towers above me, flanked by Missy Meyer and Grace Wu. Jamal Robeson and Brian D'Angelo are behind them, horsing around in glossy athletic shorts and comically large basketball sneakers. I wonder how I'm going to explain the inevitable slew of Sad Trombone comments to Derek.

Gabriella leans over and plants a big, fake kiss next to my cheek. "Mira, *hi*!" she says like we're best friends. "I haven't seen you all summer!"

Of course she hasn't. Aside from the fact that we go to the same high school, Gabriella and I barely inhabit the same planet.

"I've been busy," I say cagily. I expect her to make some snide comment about how I've been busy face-planting all over the football field. Instead she pulls up a chair and settles herself on the edge, leaning both elbows on the table. "Oh yeah?" Her eyes cut from me to Derek, lingering on him for a beat too long. "Doing what?"

"Just . . . working and stuff." I inch my chair away from hers, legs shrieking on the waxy floor.

"You work at that gym, right? The Gym Rat or whatever? God, I should go there. I'm so out of shape!" She flips her glossy brown hair over her shoulder, her eyes drifting back to Derek.

"You are *not*," Grace pipes up behind her. And she's right: even my parents would approve of Gabriella's body fat ratio.

"Whatever, I really need to start working out before lacrosse season." Gabriella sits back, crossing one tanned leg over the other. "So who's your friend? Aren't you going to introduce me?" She shakes her head and gives Derek a look, like the two of them are adults and I'm a slow child.

It takes every muscle in my face not to glare at her. "This is Derek," I say, keeping my voice measured. "He's . . ."

But what is he? My manager? The guy I'm hooking up with? We never defined our relationship, so I can't say he's—

"Her boyfriend," Derek finishes for me. He crumples his sub wrapper and stands, offering me his hand. "Come on, babe," he says, wrapping an arm over my shoulder and giving me a noisy kiss on the cheek. "I still want to buy you that thing we were talking about."

He nods ever so slightly in Gabriella's direction before turning both of us away and ambling in the other direction.

"What thing we were talking about?" I ask when we're safely out of earshot.

He grins and pulls me closer. "There isn't a thing. I just wanted to see the look on her face."

I rest my head on his shoulder, my body shaking with laughter. "How are you so amazing?"

"I just am. And don't you forget it." He stops at the entrance to Bloomingdale's. "Let's pop in here for a sec. For those socks."

He leads us through racks of dresses, each more sparkly and ridiculous than the last. We're almost out of the ladies' department when he stops so suddenly I slam into his hip.

"Damn," he says, picking up something stiff and iridescent. "You should wear this for Electri-City."

"That?" I laugh. Derek's holding a gold bandage dress, wide triangles cut in the fabric.

"I'm serious." He lays it against my body, the brush of his fingers on my collarbone sending sparks across my skin. "Try it on."

"Uh-uh." I shake my head. "That is so not my style."

"Why?" He rests the dress against me, smoothing it over my hips. "Don't you want people to see how beautiful you are?"

Heat spreads from my cheeks all the way down through my toes. What *would* it be like to rock a dress like that? To have

that kind of confidence, to be able to strut into a room showing that much skin?

"Just try it on." He looks around for a dressing room. "No
one has to see but us."

I open my mouth to protest but he's already leading us to the
back of the store, talking to a woman in a black polo shirt and too
much hair spray who ushers me and the dress into a fitting room.

"Promise you'll show me," he says.

"I promise nothing," I tell him, shutting the door.

I stare at the dress. I could just wait in here, come back out
in five, and tell Derek it didn't fit. The dress glimmers back at
me, a portal to another world.

I inch my shirt over my head, step out of my shorts. The
dress has triangles cut in the upper back and sides. I won't be
able to wear it with a bra so I unhook that too, already prepar-
ing my speech about how horrible it looked, how I couldn't
even get it over my head.

The dress slides easily over my shoulders. I find the arm-
holes and tug it down, facing away from the mirror so I don't
have to see. Once it's plastered to my skin, I hold my breath
and turn around.

It looks . . . not bad, actually. The bandage fabric hugs my
boobs and butt, making my curves look curvier and my legs
look longer. For a moment I can almost see myself wearing it
at Electri-City, strutting on glittery heels to the DJ booth and
taking my place behind the decks as fans scream my name. . . .

"Can I see?" Derek asks from outside.

I think of him seeing my breasts for the first time, the look
of awe on his face. I think of him telling me I'm beautiful. I
open the door.

His jaw drops.

"Mira." His voice is an octave lower. "You look . . ."

"Trashy?" I volunteer.

He shakes his head. "Gorgeous."

The compliment makes me feel light-headed—or maybe it's just the dress cutting off circulation to my brain.

"Take a good look." I spin around, letting him see me from all sides. "Because this is the last time you're going to see it."

"Then we may as well make the most of it." He steps forward and kisses me long and hungry, inching me back until we're both in the dressing room and my back is against the mirror, the door closing behind us and Derek's fingers getting stuck in the open triangles as he reaches for my breasts.

"Hey!" The associate calls from outside. "Only one person at a time in the fitting rooms!"

"Sorry." I grin, pushing Derek away. "We'll have to finish this some other time."

The associate pounds at the door as he kisses me again, his tongue opening my mouth like we have all the time in the world. "Don't make me call security!" she threatens.

"Go." I wriggle away from him and shove him at the door, my face burning.

A minute later I'm back in my own clothes. "It got stuck," I mutter to the associate, shoving the dress in her hands as I hurry toward the exit. "He was just helping me get it off."

"*Sure* he was." Her glare is as ferocious as Derek's smile. I lace my arm through his and we practically run out of Bloomingdale's, giggling all the way to the van. I'm already in the passenger's seat when he remembers he forgot socks.

"Can you wait here?" he says. "I'll just be a sec."

I nod and blow him a kiss. My heart is still racing from our mad dash through the store, the memory of the dress and his hands warm on my skin. I tip my head against the window frame, listening to the rhythmic *kerthump* of a skateboard rolling across the pavement. My tongue *tsks* against the roof of my mouth, adding snare.

I'm halfway through working out a new beat in my head when Derek clicks the van door open, a large bag swinging from his arm.

"Miss me?" he asks.

"Terribly." I eye the bag. "You *really* needed socks, huh?"

"Socks . . . and this." He removes a white cardboard box and sets it on my lap.

A thrill travels from the back of my skull down through my neck . . . excitement, but also a warning. My fingers feel clumsy digging through layers of tissue paper until something stiff and sparkly emerges. The thrill in my neck is icy-hot, insistent. "You didn't." I pull out the dress and hold it up, pinpoints of glitter catching the parking lot's lights.

"I did." He slides into the driver's seat. "You deserve it."

"But I can't wear it." My heartbeat makes its way into my voice, making it shake. "I told you, I'd never have the guts."

His hand inches higher. "Maybe not now."

"Probably not ever."

"Mira." His smile is gone now, his voice serious. "I wish you could see yourself the way I see you."

"Which is how?" I barely trust myself to speak.

He smiles. "Only as one of the hottest, most beautiful girls in the world."

CHAPTER 34

Driving to the Pine Barrens party feels like careening into the middle of nowhere. The roads keep getting smaller until I'm jouncing down a dirt track barely wider than the LeSabre. Pine needles brush the roof softly and my car feels like it's full of ghosts in the dark, lonely night: Yelena yelping and bouncing in the back seat. Grandpa Lou holding a cigarette out the window as he fiddles with the tape deck. Britt cracking a joke and putting her feet on the dashboard, and Crow and Nicky arguing over who was better: Billie Holiday or Ella Fitzgerald.

But as lonely as it is driving through the darkness of rural south Jersey, it's better than staying home in our house made of lies. I feel like if I exchange more than two words with Mom, Dad, or Britt I'll turn into a puddle of ugly-crying, accusation-flinging emotion—the same Sad Trombone spectacle I've spent the last three years trying to avoid. Instead I've been escaping to Brooklyn once my Gym Rat shifts are over, bringing my laptop so I can practice DJing in Derek's room and then sinking onto his bed and letting my body dissolve into his and my anger dissipate under his touch.

Just as I'm beginning to wonder if I made a wrong turn somewhere, I hear the faint pulse of drumbeats ahead. A violet light draws me in, the sound growing deep and rich until I can make out strains of reedy electric melody. I pull into a parking lot that's really just a ring of dirt, cars and vans and a few psychedelic-painted school buses parked in haphazard lines. Beyond it the party glistens between slender tree limbs. I lock the car and start through the forest, under fabric triangles that dance with video projections, pink and green fractals branching endlessly into the night.

Through a clearing I find a larger stage covered with painted plywood butterflies. A thick crowd dances enthusiastically to a driving, tech-heavy track that reminds me of factories and assembly lines, grease and metal and concrete. Shay bounces up to me from inside a puddle of shifting turquoise light.

"I'm so excited!" The gold chains around her neck jingle as she gives me a hug. "My friend Bo mastered our track—I can't wait to hear it over this system." She looks over my shoulder, then all around me. "Where's Britt?"

I try not to let her see how much Britt's name rankles. "I don't know. Probably in the city or something."

"Bummer." Shay pouts. "Is she doing okay?"

I shrug. I don't want to think about Britt right now. I'm here to get away from her, and my parents, and their lies.

Shay looks like she wants to say something more, but thinks better of it. Instead she asks if I want to hang out in the booth during her set. I hesitate for a moment—if Derek sees me there, will he be upset? Then I shake the thought out of my head and accept her offer. I told him I wasn't going to stop hanging out with Shay, and I meant it. He's just going to have to get over his trust issues.

Shay leads us to the DJ booth, which is really just a small plywood platform next to a cluster of trees. As she messes with her equipment I train my eyes over the field of bobbing heads, looking for Derek. But it's dark out here, darker than it was in the warehouse or at Summerfest. In the drifting lights I can barely make out the difference between bodies and shadows and trees.

Shay's first track settles over me like a warm bath. It's one I know well and my hips start moving to the beat. But when I look out at the crowd I notice she's losing her dance floor—the clumps of people are breaking up, wandering away toward the vendors.

Her tongue sticks out from between her teeth as she transitions. Her new song has a lilting, ethereal melody of distorted pan flute, with jungle sounds swinging through the beats like monkeys on a vine. I love this track, but I can tell right away the dance floor doesn't. There are big dark spaces between the dancers now, large patches of nothing but pine needles.

Shay notices too, and her face falls. She curses quietly as she flips through her tracks, tiny beads of sweat popping up on her forehead.

"Maybe they want something harder?" I suggest. Her music sounds too light and delicate after the last DJ's industrial mayhem; it's throwing the dancers off.

"Fuck." Shay wipes her forehead. "I planned this whole, like, fairy-music set. I mean, look at this place!" She gestures at the towering trees, the twinkling lights, the butterflies above the stage.

"Yeah." I bite my lip. "But . . ."

"I know. It's not working." She turns to me. "Did you bring thumb drives?"

I nod. I've been keeping them on my key chain.

"Want to tag in?" She shakes her head in disgust. "Maybe you can get them going. I read this crowd all wrong."

There's a note of bitterness in her voice, and I flash back to Derek's words in his van. *Is* Shay a jealous person? And if so, is she going to be jealous of *me*?

"Come on." She's already yanking out one of her thumb drives, gesturing for me to plug in. "I just need a couple minutes to regroup."

I fish my keys from my pocket. I'm pretty sure I know exactly what to play right now, a perfect way to bridge Shay's ethereal world-music with the harder sound I think these people are looking for.

I plug in my thumb drive and cue up the track, bringing in a beat that's all tribal, organic bongos that meld with Shay's jungle sounds. Then the effects come in: the ping of hammers on steel, the steamy chug of the bass. I feel the dancers pick up their heads and sniff the air like hound dogs sensing meat; people who have been chatting on the sidelines start to drift back. Shay shoots me a tense smile.

For my next track I go even harder. More people stream onto the dance floor and they hit the ground running, feet churning pine needles and dirt. A sense of power rises in me like a mushroom cloud. I think about what Derek said: I have great instincts, and dance floors love me. Maybe he's right. Maybe I really was made for this. Because right now, I find myself loving the dance floor right back.

Shay taps my shoulder. Her eyes are gleaming, all traces of bitterness gone. "I can tag back in," she offers, so I hand her the headphones and watch as she mixes in the next track, my body one step ahead and already anticipating the beat.

This time she nails it. She drops a tech-heavy banger that has the dancers packing in like sardines and turns the clearing into a whirlwind of shuffling feet and drifting dust. I know the perfect song to come after it, and even though Shay's back in the driver's seat I can't help shuffling through my tracklist and finding it.

"Hey." Shay's at my elbow, holding out her headphones. "Want to tag back in?"

My grin blossoms like flowers after a rain. It feels like the whole world is spinning in perfect sync: me and Shay and the dance floor, all hurtling together on the same spaceship into the great unknown. I take the headphones. Shay starts flipping through her tracklist. And just like that, we're tag-teaming.

We spend the rest of the hour going back and forth, building from deep and techy to whimsical and wild, the crowd hanging on every note. When the next DJ appears in the booth we look at each other and nod. We still haven't dropped our track yet, the one we wrote together, and with only ten minutes left we both know it's time. By now we've worked the crowd into a lather; I can smell their sweat and excitement in the sharp night air.

I try not to hover as Shay cues it up, but my eyes are glued to her fingers flying over the rig, one hand on the jog wheel and the other working the levels. I can hear our beats in my head even before she turns the volume up, bringing it in steady and sure. I glance out at the crowd but they're oblivious, still dancing like tonight will never end. So slowly I can feel each beat stretch out like a rubber band, she slides the crossfader to the right, drowning out the old track and bringing the new one in. The night fills with the music we created from scratch, each note swelling until even the treetops seem to sway along.

The crowd notices. The crowd responds.

They throw themselves into the music like children diving into a ball pit, faces split open with joy. Their hands grasp the air, reaching for the next note.

They reach. They keep reaching. And then they stop.

Because it's not there, whatever it is they're reaching for. It's so close—we can all sense it, the intangibility of whatever this song needs. But even on the big sound system, even with a packed dance floor, even with the volume turned all the way up, this track is still missing something.

And I still can't figure out what it is.

I can feel Shay's disappointment radiating off of her, echoing my own. We are so close with this. But we're just not there.

The dancers sense it too. Their shuffling slows; their arms begin to look tired. They haven't left the clearing yet, but we'll lose them if we don't drop something else soon. The next DJ paces in tiny circles below us, looking worried.

I turn to Shay. "'Just a Little Lovin'"? I suggest. It's the track we first bonded over back at the warehouse, the one that made the whole crowd leap in the air.

Shay nods. She cues it up and brings it in fast, and just like it did in the warehouse, it gets the dancers back on their feet. The next DJ looks relieved.

"Come on," Shay says as we palm our thumb drives and high-five the new guy on our way out. "Let's go dance."

I can tell she's still trying to shake the disappointment of our track falling flat as we jump from the lip of the stage into the crowd, into the fray.

As the last notes of "Just a Little Lovin'" pour honey-sweet into my ears people start coming up to tell us they loved the set and ask what our duo is called. We look at each other and shrug. Are we a duo now, I wonder? If Derek is right about Shay she would never want to share the spotlight, but right now she's as happy as I've ever seen her, hopping in circles and giving me a big sideways hug.

As the next DJ mixes in I push my way through the crowd, looking for Derek. I finally find him at the edge of the dance floor, leaning against a tree with his nose buried in his cell phone.

"Hey, babe!" I tap him on the shoulder, prepared with my biggest, sweetest smile.

He doesn't return it. "Oh," he says, slumping further against the trunk. "Hey."

I feel the smile fall from my lips. He doesn't peel himself off the tree, doesn't take me in his arms or give me a kiss.

"Is everything okay?" I ask.

"As okay as it can be, I guess." He shoves his phone into his pocket, crossing his arms.

"What's wrong?" I ask.

"Nothing." He shakes his head. "It's fine."

"It's obviously not fine." I straighten my shoulders, trying to hold on to the rosy afterglow of our set even as it slips away. "Just tell me what's wrong."

"No." He shakes his head. "You'll be mad."

"I won't be mad," I assure him.

His eyes cut to the DJ booth, then back to me.

"Hold on," I say, as it slowly dawns on me. "Is this about Shay?"

He looks down at his shoes, his voice quiet. "I knew you'd be mad."

"I'm not *mad*," I try to explain, even as something hot and bitter rises in my chest, something that actually does feel a bit like anger. "I just want to understand."

"I can't believe I have to spell this out for you." He gives a deep, wounded sigh. "First you tell me you're going to stop hanging out with Shay, and next thing I know you two are tag-teaming?"

I stumble back, my mind reeling. "I never said that."

He steps forward, until we're almost nose to nose. "Yes, you did. You promised me, at the mall the other day. Did that mean nothing to you?"

I shake my head. I feel like I'm going insane. "You must have misheard me. Or misunderstood or something."

"Are you calling me a liar?" His eyes bore into mine, and I can feel his breath hot on my cheek.

"*No.*" A hot, sticky tar of frustration fills me, slowing my thoughts. "I don't understand why you're being like this. I didn't do anything wrong."

He looks at me for a long time as lights flash blue and green over our faces. We're eye to eye, nose to nose, our breathing heavy and synced. Every time I've been this close to Derek it's felt wonderful; it's felt absolutely right.

Now it feels all wrong.

Finally Derek deflates, like the fire's been extinguished from his chest. "Why am I even wasting my time on you?" he mutters.

Then he turns and stalks into the forest, leaving me alone at the edge of the dance floor with a hard little pocket of tears lodged in my chest.

CHAPTER 35

I slump against the tree trunk, breathing hard. I don't want to cry, not here at a party when I've just come off the kind of DJ set that should keep me smiling all night. But Derek's words clang against my heart.

Does he really think he was wasting his time on me? I thought I understood what we had, but now it seems like he wants things from me that I don't know how to give him, like every word that comes out of my mouth is wrong.

I pull myself off the tree and start into the crowd. I can't stay here at this party, pretending to be happy when my heart is shredded. My tears blur the lights into watercolor streaks and I can't find the parking lot and I feel like I'm going in circles, getting further away from what I want with every step.

In the darkness between clearings and I stumble over roots and fallen branches, using my phone as a flashlight and cursing myself for ever thinking this party was a good idea. A cloud of blue light blooms in the distance. I've almost reached it when I hear my name, scratchy and broken, from the ground.

I jump back, a scream bursting through my lips. Tangled in the roots at my feet I see Yelena's big patent leather boots, her lacy midriff-baring top and silver belly chain, her flouncy miniskirt. Her backpack lies between her legs, the doll's face smeared with dirt.

My heart flings itself at my rib cage and I feel dizzy, nauseous, weak. This isn't like imagining Yelena's ghost in the back seat of my car. This is real.

Then I see the corkscrew hair and tawny, muscled thighs. It's not Yelena's ghost lying prone against that tree. It's my sister.

"Britt!" I throw my arms around her shoulders, forgetting for a moment that I'm furious with her for almost ruining my life. "I didn't know you were going to be here. Did you catch my set?"

Britt makes a strangled, croaking sound. Her skin is cold, slimy with sweat. "Are you okay?" I ask. Her shoulders are tense and I can feel her heartbeat through her shirt, erratic and way too fast.

Britt doesn't respond. Her head lolls against the tree bark, her skin waxy and her eyes unfocused.

"Britt!" I scream, waving my hand in her face. Her eyes swim into focus and I breathe a sigh of relief.

"I don't feel good." She's grinding her teeth hard, her jaw working into grotesque positions. Her pupils are huge, eclipsing all but the thinnest rim of golden-brown iris. She looks terrified.

"You took something." I try to keep the anger, the fear, the frustration out of my voice.

Britt doesn't try to deny it. "Yelena would have."

"Of course Yelena would have," I mutter. "Stay here. I'm going to find you some water."

"No!" Her hand claws the air and lands on my arm, cold fingers scrabbling at my skin. "Don't leave me here."

"Then you have to come. Can you walk?"

She bites her lip. I look around and the blue light ahead of us swims into focus. It's a geodesic dome, I realize now, with a few figures silhouetted inside.

"Come on." I point to the dome. "Just over there."

I stand and help Britt up, supporting her under my arm as the bulk of her weight collapses against me. "I feel like I'm full of bees," she mumbles as we half walk, half stumble toward the light.

Two women and a man with a long, scraggly blond beard sit in camp chairs in the dome, illuminated by ghostly blue rope lights. They're older, maybe in their late twenties, and they all have dreadlocks even though they're white.

"Jesus." One of the women stands and hurries over to help. We get Britt settled in an empty camp chair and the woman grabs a plastic gallon jug of water, holding it up to Britt's mouth so she can drink. Britt swallows and coughs, sending water spluttering down the front of her shirt.

"What'd she take?" the man asks.

"Molly," I tell him. "Right, Britt?"

Britt groans, and a sickly feeling settles over me. "Britt?" A note of panic creeps into my voice. "Oh my god. What did you take?" I think about Yelena and the meth and butylone, about Miles Davis and heroin and cocaine. It feels like drugs are infiltrating my life from every corner, destroying everything and everyone I've ever cared about.

Britt's head rolls to one side, but she manages to look up at us. "Just molly," she gasps. "I swear, that's all it was."

The guy snorts. "Like hell it was."

"What do you mean?" I glance up quickly.

The woman next to him shakes her head. "You think pure MDMA makes you feel like *that*?" She points to Britt, whose eyes are rolling back, leaving nothing but milky slits.

"So maybe she didn't take pure MDMA?" Suddenly *my* legs feel like jelly, and *my* body feels full of bees. I lean against the dome.

"Jesus, you kids." The guy picks something out of his beard, examines it, and flicks it away. "Of course she didn't. It's never pure. There's all kinds of adulterants in molly these days . . . cough syrup, cannabinoids, meth, butylone . . ."

Butylone. Meth. Like the drugs Yelena took, the ones they found in her system after she died.

"Get a test kit already," the guy sighs, shaking his head. "They're like forty bucks on Amazon."

I ignore him and turn to my sister. "Britt." My voice is cut glass, slicing through the night. "Where did you get that pill?"

She says the name so quietly it might as well be a pine needle drifting to the ground.

I make her say it again.

This time I can't help hearing it, and wishing I could un-hear it, and knowing I never can.

The woman who's been helping her clucks her tongue. "Oh yeah. We don't buy from that guy anymore. His shit is the worst."

My entire body goes rigid. My head starts to spin and I grab one of the dome's supports to steady myself . . . and then I hear gagging. I turn just in time to see Britt lunge over the side of the camp chair and launch a sticky green stream of vomit on the ground.

CHAPTER 36

I race to Britt, yanking her hair from her face as jets of puke splatter around her. The woman who's been helping us jumps back, silently handing me the water jug. I rub my sister's back as the streams turn to trickles and finally dry heaves, then help her take a long, shaky sip.

"Told you she got some whack-ass shit," the man says. He sounds smug, and even though I know he's only trying to help I kind of want to wrap his white-guy dreads around his neck.

I crouch next to Britt. "How are you feeling?" I ask.

She looks up at me from under sweat-slick spirals of hair. Her face is damp and pallid, but the terror is gone from her eyes. "Like shit," she says.

"Think you can make it to the parking lot?"

She gives me a jerky nod. I get directions from the hippies and try to return their water jug, but the woman tells me to keep it. Britt leans heavily on my arm as we trudge through the forest. I've never been happier to see the LeSabre in my life.

"Think you'll be okay here for a sec?" I ask once I've settled her into the passenger's seat. "I just need to grab something real quick."

Britt moans, leaning her head against the seat. "Leave the doors open," she begs. "I need air."

I settle the water jug at her feet, kiss her waxy cheek, and tell her I'll be right back. The party feels like it's pressing in on me as I fight past the main stage, bushwhacking through a thicket of churning dancers. I finally spot Derek hanging out by a smoothie bar at the edge of the forest, talking to a pair of girls in leather halter tops. The three of them are laughing, the colored feathers in the girls' hair catching the light as they throw their heads back. I plow into their conversation, grabbing Derek by the wrist.

"I need to talk to you." My voice is low, urgent. As soon as he sees me his smile drops, and his eyes go wide and soft. The girls exchange a look and melt away.

"Mira!" He grasps my shoulders. "I've been looking all over for you."

I shake his hands away. "What the hell is in your molly?"

His eyes harden. "What are you talking about?"

The fury inside me grows molten, overflows. "My sister's out there puking her guts out from the shit you sold her! What the fuck, Derek?"

"Oh, Mira. I'm so sorry." He reaches for my hand. "It must be dehydration. Did you get her water? Where is she now? We should make sure she's okay."

"It wasn't dehydration." I spit the words in his face. "I know you sell bad pills."

His face darkens, and I feel the air around us tense. "You don't know what you're talking about."

"I know what I saw."

"You're totally new to this." His voice drips with disdain. "You've never even *done* molly."

My hands are shaking. I ball them into fists, holding them tight at my sides so he can't see. "Have you ever even tested it?"

He shrugs. "I've never had any complaints."

"Yeah, well . . . Britt's complaining. And Yelena probably would be, if she were still alive." Tears rush to my eyes and I turn, stumbling on a root and righting myself, desperate now to escape him and get back to the parking lot.

"Mira, wait." His voice is close behind me, pleading. It's the same tone he used when he told me about his mom, that wide-open vulnerability that puts the two of us in a bubble and shuts out the rest of the world. "Talk to me." His fingers catch the sleeves of my dress. "I want us to be okay."

I rip away and push forward, tears streaming down my cheeks. The light from the parking lot peeks through the trees and I run to it. I can see the LeSabre, the toe of Britt's boot kicking at the dirt.

Derek catches up to me, his breath hard on the downbeat. He doesn't try to touch me this time, just stands there with his chest rising and sinking, his eyes wide and blue and lost. I try not to see how beautiful he is, to tamp down the tiny sting of longing that still pierces my skin.

"Just tell me what you want," he begs. "Whatever it is. I'll do it."

Britt turns slowly toward us, her eyes more black than gold.

"Whatever I want?" I ask.

He nods. He looks broken. Not that I care.

I gather in air, the breath shuddering through my lungs. "Stop selling shitty drugs." I climb into the driver's seat, go to pull the door closed.

"Mira, wait." His wedges his hand in the door. I turn back, steeling myself against his eyes.

"I love you," he says. And then he releases the door and I slam it shut, my body shaking harder than the LeSabre as it shudders to life and kicks up a plume of dust peeling out of the parking lot.

CHAPTER 37

I'm still shaking as I start down the dirt road. Derek's face looms in my memory, his final words screaming in my ears.

He told me he loved me.

He poisoned my sister.

He called me a waste of time.

He might have killed Yelena.

Enough is enough. He can't keep doing this to people. I need to stop him.

But what if he really didn't know what was in his pills? What if the whole thing with Shay was just a misunderstanding, if he really does love me, if what he said was true?

Maybe he meant what he said. Maybe he'll stop now. Maybe he'll do it for me.

The LeSabre's wheels clatter against the washboard road. I wait for Britt to say something, anything, but she just rests her head against the window, her breath making a small circle of steam against the glass. I don't know what I expect from her—a tearful confession? An apology?—but I can't deal with her silence. Now that the danger is past, all my fury from the past week comes bubbling up, roiling just below the surface like hot lava in a long-dormant volcano.

"Molly?" I finally erupt. "Really, Britt?"

She digs her nails into her leg. "You're seriously going to judge me for that?" Her fingers release, leaving pale half-moons on her skin. "Seriously, now?"

I clutch the steering wheel tighter. "It just seems like a really weird choice to keep taking drugs after they killed your best friend."

We hit the end of the dirt and the car jolts over the concrete lip, wheels smoothing out on pavement. Britt sighs and lifts the backpack from the floor, cradling the doll to her chest. "You wouldn't understand."

"No, I don't understand." The lava inside me froths and blisters, filling my voice with fire. "Please, help me understand."

Britt tucks her chin over the doll's head, rocking the two of them back and forth. She mumbles something, but all I catch is Yelena's name.

"What?" I snap.

"Yelena would have understood."

I smack the steering wheel. "So you're going out every night getting high because that's what Yelena would have done?"

I expect Britt to flinch, or cry, or apologize. But she just looks away from me, resting her head on the window. "It's like she's there sometimes." Her voice is so thin I have to strain to hear. "Dancing with me. Holding my hand."

She sags against the window, looking small and frail as a wisp of smoke. I open my mouth to scream at her to stop chasing ghosts, that all the molly in the world won't bring Yelena back. But then it hits me—nothing I can say or do is going to change Britt's mind. She's still in denial. She never made her way to the next stage.

It's why she keeps wearing Yelena's clothes, why she carries Emma wherever she goes, why she listens to DJ Skizm's set on repeat. It's why she keeps partying, even when everything else in her world is screaming at her to stop.

And I can't keep pretending this is a normal stage of grieving, I can't keep hoping she'll snap out of it and life will just go back to normal. I can't keep ignoring what this is doing to our family, to my future . . . to my sister.

It's time for the lies to stop, I decide as I pull onto the highway and point the LeSabre back toward Coletown. Our parents need to see that Britt isn't their golden girl anymore. I need them to understand what's happening. I need their help.

Our wheels roll smoothly over pavement and Britt goes slowly limp in the passenger's seat, her back rising and falling in gentle waves. I'll do it tomorrow, I think, cracking the window and letting ribbons of crisp night air slice across my face. Our parents close the gym at eight on Sundays and I'll make us all sit down as a family as soon as they get home. I'll make Britt tell the whole story, starting with the soccer team at Pepperdine. I won't let her leave anything out, and I won't let her lie.

My sister's asleep by the time we pull into our driveway, tiny snores drifting from her lips and puttering against the windowpane.

"Wake up," I say, gently nudging her. "We're home."

"Hmmmm?" She startles, her eyes drifting open. "Aw. You let me sleep."

"Come on." I help her out of the car, keeping a hand on her elbow as we go up the stairs. "Let's get you into bed."

I maneuver her into her room and she sighs in the darkness, lying back like a rag doll as I unlace her boots and pull them off her feet.

"You're a good sister," she murmurs, snuggling into her pillow.

But am I?

CHAPTER 38

Are we cool?

I ignore the text and pick up my trumpet. Derek's been blowing up my phone since last night, sending strings of texts and leaving long voice mails.

He says he's sorry about what happened to Britt.

He says he'll stop dealing.

He says he loves me.

He says a lot of things. I wish I knew what to believe.

I ignore my phone and go back to the trumpet, trying to improvise along with my metronome. I want the music to quell the jitters about what I have to do when Mom and Dad get home from work today, but all it's doing is magnifying my anxiety: not just about what will happen, but about Derek and molly, about Fulton and my music and my future.

Crow and Nicky come from camp tomorrow and our audition is in three weeks and two days. I should feel ready by now, but instead everything feels uncertain, like I've stacked my dreams on a fault line and the slightest tremor could send them tumbling to pieces.

My phone lights up. Derek again.

You promised me you wouldn't do this. You said I could trust you always.

My hands shake as I fling the phone back onto my bed. That had nothing to do with molly. That was before my sister puked her guts out from his pills.

"That was about *Shay!*" I scream into the mouthpiece of my trumpet. It blasts through the bell as a series of angry blurps.

Then it hits me. Derek didn't want me talking to Shay about him—he didn't even want us hanging out. At first I took his fears at face value, another symptom of his trust issues. Now I wonder if it was something else.

I pick up my phone and text Shay. *I need to talk to you,* I message her. *Can I come over?*

She sends me back a GIF of a gnome riding a unicorn and screaming YES!

I laugh to myself as I grab my car keys. This is the person Derek called bitter and jealous?

Before I leave I peek inside Britt's room. She's curled around Yelena's backpack, her eyes closed and a chunk of the doll's hair in her mouth. What's going to happen to us after tonight, I wonder? Will she start resenting me like I've always secretly, just-a-little-bit resented her? Will she hate me for yanking the life she chose out from under her? In a way, I want her to know how that feels. But a tiny kernel of doubt also nudges me, burrowing beneath my skin. What if our parents don't believe me? What if they still take her side?

The chorus of doubts and worries sings in my head as I drive to the Bronx, where Shay greets me wearing a zebra-striped bikini and carrying a beach bag. I follow her up to the roof and she lays out two towels and puts on an Ibiza-style house mix that sounds like blender drinks and palm trees and miles of white sand.

"It's not quite the beach, but it'll do, right?" She stretches out on a towel and works sunscreen into her legs, squinting at the Manhattan skyline. "At least the view's almost as good."

I sprawl out on the towel next to her as she fills me in on the rest of the DJ sets from last night, who killed it and who cleared the dance floor. It's so nice to be with someone who doesn't seem to want anything from me, someone who isn't damaged or injured or just inherently fucked-up.

"Personally, I feel like we had the best set. Not that I'm biased or anything." She rummages in the bag and hands me a Sprite, popping a second for herself. "We should tag-team again. That was fun."

"I'd like that." We fall into a comfortable silence, listening to music and catching rays until my skin starts to feel warm and tingly from the sun. I wish I could stretch this moment forever, not just to enjoy the music and sunshine but to postpone the conversation I have to have with my family tonight: the one that could destroy my relationship with my sister forever, and also maybe save her life.

"So," I say, turning to Shay. "I need to ask you something." I take a deep breath and force myself to continue. "About Derek."

"Uh-oh." She props herself up on her elbows. "Is he being shady with you?"

"Shady." I turn the word over in my mind. "Yeah, I think so. Was he shady with you?"

"Oh yeah." Shay laughs. "All the time."

My stomach tightens. "Like, how?"

"I don't know." She stretches, reaching for the sunscreen again. "Are you sure you want to hear it?"

"Yes," I tell her. "I'm ready now."

"Okay. I don't know if it was me or what, but . . . anyway." She pours lotion into her palm, rubbing it into her shoulders. "At first it was just little things. Like, he wouldn't text me for a week, but then he'd get mad if I didn't text him for a day. Like he was doing these little mind-control tests to see if I'd go for it."

I think about the beginning of our relationship, how he went a full ten days without texting. I'd assumed he was busy, or I wasn't the first thing on his mind. But maybe it was something else.

"Then he started getting weird about my friends," Shay continues. "He said they were losers and were holding me back. Like, these people I've known since ninth grade—you met them all. Later I figured out it was because they hated him and he could tell."

The bubbles in my Sprite sting my throat. This is all too familiar. It's almost exactly what he said to me about Shay.

"I should have just listened, you know?" She sighs and caps the sunscreen. "They told me he was creepy, but—I mean, you know how he is. He's got those eyes and those tats and he'll tell you a whole sob story about his life. Did you ever meet his mom, by the way?"

"No." I lean forward, shielding my eyes against the sun. "Is she as awful as he says?"

"Oh my god, *no*." Her brows levitate over her sunglasses. "She's like the nicest lady and all she could talk about was how proud she was that he goes to NYU and how much she liked my hair. Then she figured out Instagram just so she could like all my pics."

I feel like I've been slapped. I set my Sprite down hard. Some of it splashes on my hand.

"You okay?" Shay asks.

I shake my head, wiping Sprite on my towel.

"He pulled that shit with you too," she says gently. "Didn't he?"

I try to speak around the lump in my throat. "Why didn't you tell me?" I ask finally. "If you knew what he was really like?"

"Girl, I'm sorry." She hugs her knees. "I thought maybe it was just me. Maybe we were just bad together. And you seemed so happy, and then everything happened with Yelena and I just thought it would sound petty if I started bad-mouthing my ex, and . . . yeah, you're right." She sighs. "I should have said something."

"It's okay." I laugh softly. "I probably wouldn't have believed you anyway."

"He gets under your skin, right?"

"Yeah." I look past my toes, out at the city. "I lost my virginity to him, you know."

"Holy shit." Shay sits up straighter. "When?"

"At Summerfest." I wiggle my toes against the skyline. "The night we played the Silent Disco."

"Dude," she says. "I saw him that night. He was rolling balls."

My toes stop wiggling. "What?" I ask.

"He was high as fuck. On molly. I saw him backstage at the Lip Smacker stage. He sold a bunch of pills and took like three and then he stole a bottle of champagne and ghosted."

She laughs. "That champagne was supposed to be for the DJ. What a dick, right?"

My head fills with static. "He was on drugs that night?"

"Yeah, you couldn't tell?"

I think back to Summerfest, the most magical night of my life. Derek's eyes just a rim of blue around huge pupils. How I made fun of him for chewing gum while drinking champagne.

"I'm an idiot," I groan, hiding my face in my hands. It was a lie, all of it: how he said I was different, his whole line about how he could tell me anything. About how everyone in the world was a pain in the ass but me. That was the drugs talking, not him—he probably would have said the same thing to the guy selling Belgian fries.

And I was too dumb and naïve and in love to realize it.

Fury rises in me, breaking through the layers of sadness and confusion and humiliation, leaving a rich copper taste on my tongue. Suddenly I have too much energy, too much anger, to sit for another second. I leap to my feet and pace to the edge of the roof, the wind finding my hair and lifting it around my face.

"Fuck you, Derek," I say, almost to myself.

"Yeah!" Shay leaps to her feet and scrambles to join me. "*Fuck* Derek."

Her words are like backup singers to my melody, making it more real. "*FUCK YOU, DEREK!*" I scream off the edge of the roof, and my voice goes tumbling over the rooftops and flying away on the air. I scream until my throat hurts and I feel like I've been emptied out, like I'm clean and hollow inside. When I'm done I collapse back on my towel, breathing hard.

"Do you think he's done this to other girls?" I ask, reaching for my Sprite.

"I don't know," Shay sighs. "I was so new to the scene when he found me. Me and my friends were like these giggling little kids going to their first warehouse parties, and he was this cool older guy who knew everyone and always had pills. I was so psyched he was into me, it didn't even occur to me to ask questions."

I think about pills, about Yelena, about Britt. "When you were dealing," I ask her. "Did you know what was in your pills?"

"What do you mean?" she picks at the tar paper, peeling it off the roof. "I mean, molly's just MDMA."

"Not necessarily." I tell her about Yelena's autopsy report, Britt's near collapse last night, what I heard from the hippies in the dome.

"Jesus." Shay sits back, looking stunned. "I hope I didn't do that to anyone. I had no idea."

"Do you think Derek knew?" I ask. "He told me he didn't."

"Honestly?" Shay picks harder at the tar paper. "I think Derek just does whatever it takes to make money and get laid."

Her words hit me like a bucket of cold water. I shiver in the late afternoon sun.

"He said he'd stop," I say quietly. "After I told him about Britt."

Shay takes off her sunglasses and looks at me. "Do you believe him?" she asks.

"I don't know." The weight of her words, of his promise, of everyone out there he could be hurting, sink like a wet blanket on my shoulders. "I honestly don't know."

CHAPTER 39

Mom and Dad, I need to talk to you.

You guys need to sit down. We need to talk about Britt.

There's a big problem in our family, and I can't believe you're too clueless to see it.

I practice saying the words out loud on my drive home, but there's no right way to start this conversation. I pull into our driveway with less than two hours until my parents get home, no closer to a solution than when I left the Bronx. As I cut the engine, I realize our house is shaking.

At first I think maybe it's me. I'm so nervous about what has to go down tonight that I'm trembling, and it feels like the world is shaking with me. But then I hear the bass. I open the car door and it puddles around me, that same fuzzy distortion I've grown to know all too well.

DJ Skizm. Again.

"Britt!" I fumble with my house keys. "Turn that down! The neighbors are going to kill us."

The music drowns out my voice, trembling the glass in the photos along our walls: Britt at her first soccer tournament, Britt winning MVP, Mom taking first place at a CrossFit tournament, Britt at a sports banquet, me at the Visitors' Weekend recital at Windham two years ago. Synth tumbles down the stairs and echoes off the walls, filling the house with a sound like the sizzle of lightning.

"I didn't know your speakers went up this loud," I say, starting up the stairs. "It's all distorted."

The only answer is a wailing reverb.

"Britt?" I reach the second floor, and something cold and sticky starts to weave through my gut. It's dark up here, the only light coming from our bathroom. The light catches a scrim of sparkles embedded in the carpet, like sunshine on the snow. I kneel slowly. Our carpet has never sparkled before.

I run a hand over it and glitter sticks to my skin, grainy and cool. The chill rises from my gut and spreads through my chest. The sparkles are gold and silver, reminding me of Britt and Yelena's eyelids as they danced their way through warehouses and festivals, holding hands and spinning and rolling and laughing. It looked almost natural on them then, like they were born to shine. But it doesn't look like that now.

"Britt?" I peek into the bathroom. There's makeup scattered everywhere: lipstick open on the edge of the sink, a blob of it smeared across the porcelain; eyeliner pens on the floor and toilet seat and one sticking out of the sink drain. A broken compact spills inky eye shadow in the cracks between tiles.

"Britt!" I call again, a quiver in my voice. She was sleeping so soundly when I left, I didn't think there was any chance she'd get up and go out again by the time I got home. I wanted her to be here when I talked to our parents; I didn't want to have to do it behind her back. But if she's already out at another party, I might not have any choice. I feel like I have to do this as soon as possible, before I lose my nerve.

"Did you go out again?" I shout down the hall.

The only answer is the music snarling back at me.

I don't bother knocking on her door. I throw it open, my heart leaping into my throat.

Britt's room is trashed. Her posters have been shredded, bits of the US Olympic Soccer Team clinging to the walls and staring up from crumpled piles on the floor. Trophies litter the carpet. There's a hole in her wall where it looked like one of them was flung against it, and another lies at the base of what used to be her full-length mirror and is now just a few shards of glass sticking to a frame. The rest of the mirror lies in pieces on the floor, turning the room into a twisted disco ball.

And then there's my sister.

"Britt!" I scream her name and run to her, sinking to my knees. She lies spread-eagle on the floor, hair fanned out in a messy halo and closed eyes coated in clumpy glitter. Her skin is clammy and ash-colored and she's wearing Yelena's clothes again, her favorite black lace minidress and platform boots. Emma lies next to her, almost as if the two of them had spun around until they got dizzy and fell down, just like me and Britt did when we were kids.

"Oh my god." I reach for the doll. Its belly is unzipped and the contents have been gutted. They lie amidst rumpled tissues and jagged bits of broken glass: Britt's cell phone and Yelena's favorite eye pencil, a sparkly wallet stuffed with crumpled singles, a flyer for a party in New Haven that's supposed to start in a couple hours.

And an empty plastic baggie with grayish dust smeared inside.

"Britt, what did you do?" I scream. I reach for the baggie, shoving it in my pocket. I don't want to think about what was in there, how many of the same horrible pills that made her sick last night. I never should have gone to Shay's, never should have left Britt alone. I should have known this conversation was too important to wait.

Now it's too late.

I'm too late.

Britt's skin is tacky with dried sweat as I feel for her pulse, cursing myself for not paying more attention to the first-aid unit in freshman health class. It takes me a half dozen tries but finally I find it buried deep in her neck. It's weak and limping, like it wants to give up. I clap my hands in front of her face and yell her name one, five, twelve times, but there's no response. I can barely feel her breath against my neck.

9-1-1. I need to call 9-1-1. My fingers shake so hard that it takes me two tries, and each ring seems long enough to be a song of its own. Finally the operator picks up, and I tell her what happened, that I suspect it was an overdose. I beg them to hurry. I give her my address through choking sobs. At one point she asks me to move away from the music and I jolt up, startled. I'd forgotten Britt's stereo was on, forgotten the sickening drumbeats shaking my stomach. I turn it off and stay on the line, watching Britt and trying to answer the operator's questions until I hear sirens in the distance, so faint at first that I'm sure I'm just conjuring them out of blind hope.

We hang up and I sink to the floor. The siren sounds louder, wheels screaming around the corner and into our driveway.

I take Britt's dry, chilly hand and try to warm it in mine. "Please," I say to her, even though I know she can't hear. "Please just be okay."

Chapter 40

I'm in a hospital waiting room full of hard plastic chairs, a television blaring talk shows over my head.

My sneaker squeaks painfully and I realize I'm kicking the floor. A mother with a moaning, pasty-faced toddler gives me a dirty look.

"Sorry," I mumble.

A burst of cheesy string music blasts from the TV: a commercial where a little girl goes from rocking a toy doll to galloping off a school bus to throwing her graduation cap in the air to cradling a baby of her own. I grip the chair's arms. What if Britt never graduates from college, never holds her child in her arms? What if the last image I'll ever have of her is gray-faced and unconscious on a gurney, rolling through a set of double doors?

The doors to the waiting room fly open and my parents rush in, still in their gym clothes. I start to stand, but then I see their faces.

They look like they've aged twenty years. The tiny wrinkles around Mom's mouth have turned to crevasses, and Dad's eyes are hollow pits. I notice flecks of gray in Dad's stubble that were never there before, flashing silver in the light. For a moment, he looks so much like Grandpa Lou it's like seeing a ghost.

They run to me, sweep me off the chair and into their arms, and I find myself clinging to them like a little girl who fell off her tricycle and scraped both her knees. I can smell the fear under their dried sweat, can feel Mom's heart trembling in her chest. I hug them tight, not wanting to let go, and the tears come back until I'm a heaving mass of flesh and snuffles and snot.

"What happened?" They sit on either side of me, leaning forward with their hands on their knees. Dad smoothes invisible wrinkles from his athletic shorts while Mom's toe taps a non-rhythm on the floor. I grip the chair, anchoring myself in the grit of plastic against my palms. None of us can stay still.

"She overdosed." I can't meet their eyes so I look down at Mom's sneakers, which are pink and turquoise and so stupidly cheerful they make me choke up all over again. "Or like . . . the pills she took, they were laced with something. Maybe meth, or it could have been other stuff. . . ."

"Whoa, hold up." Dad raises a hand. "What pills?"

Mom's sneakers stop dancing on the floor. "Britt never took pills."

"Molly." I grasp the chair harder. "Or at least, she thought it was molly. . . ."

"You're talking like a crazy person." Mom stands abruptly. "We need to find a doctor. Excuse me . . ." She stalks to the admitting desk, taps her fingers against the glass. "I need to see my daughter."

The nurse looks up. "Ma'am, she's with the doctors right now. As soon as she's ready for visitors, someone will let you know."

"But I need to see her *now*!" Mom bangs harder on the glass. "We don't even know what happened. I'm her *mother*!"

"Please sit down, ma'am." The nurse tucks her three chins together, giving Mom a disapproving stare. "We'll let you in as soon as we can."

"Beth." Dad stands and drapes an arm over Mom's shoulders. "Please."

"But I need to *know*!" Mom stamps her foot like a child. "Why won't anyone tell me what's going on?"

"I'm trying to tell you!" I leap to my feet, my anger rushing to the surface. "You're not listening!"

"I'm listening." Dad turns to me. "What kind of pills?"

"Molly." I sink back into the chair, my voice going small. Mom remains standing, her hand around Dad's wrist. I can see the rapid rise and release of her breath under her shiny turquoise sports tank. "It's like, this drug . . ."

"Like Ecstasy?" Dad asks.

"Yeah."

Mom barks out a laugh. "Britt wasn't doing *Ecstasy*."

"There's a lot about Britt you don't know."

Mom stands taller. "Don't tell me I don't know my own daughter."

"Beth." Dad rests a hand on her arm. She shakes it off.

"What *really* happened?" she demands.

"I told you. She took molly—Ecstasy—whatever you want to call it—and she took too much and it was bad to begin with. And she knew it, and I should have known she was going to do it, and I should have stopped her, and . . ."

"Whoa, slow down." Dad holds up a hand. "So she'd taken it before?"

"Yeah." I can't look at them. Tears drip down my nose and onto the floor, leaving a pattern of tiny puddles.

"This is ridiculous." Mom marches to the front desk and raises her hand to knock on the glass again. The nurse looks up, shakes her head. Mom lets out a long bellow of breath and comes back to us, glaring at me through slit green eyes. "She doesn't . . . she would never . . . I mean, she's an athlete, for god's sake."

"I'm sorry," I say, because I don't know what else to say. The ghost of Britt's voice flits through my head, begging me not to tell Mom and Dad. I never should have listened. I never should have left her alone.

Mom sits down hard. "I don't believe this," she insists. "I just don't . . ." She makes a noise that's somewhere between a sob and a gasp and her hands fly to her face, covering it. Dad kneels in front of her and she wraps her arms around him and weeps into his chest. I want to reach for her, to tell her that it's all going to be okay. But I can't make any more promises.

I don't know how long we stay like that, Dad kneeling in front of Mom as she cries into his shoulder, me a stiff and helpless lump. It could be minutes or hours of my thoughts playing on the same pointless loop of *I wish* and *I hope* and *I should have* and *if only* until finally the doors swing open and a doctor emerges, her hair pulled back in a severe French braid.

"Ms. Alden?"

Dad stands. Mom scrambles gracelessly from her chair.

"I'm Doctor Chopra." She extends her hand. "You're the parents?"

They nod, wordless and obedient. A numb, tingling rush fills my veins. I don't feel myself pushing off the chair and taking a step forward, don't notice I'm standing until I'm face-to-face with the doctor, taking in the tiny strands of gray laced through her dark hair.

Dr. Chopra smiles weakly. "Good news: your daughter is awake and responsive."

Relief floods my limbs. I grab Dad's shoulder to steady myself.

"What happened?" Mom squawks.

"She seems to have ingested something toxic," Dr. Chopra says.

"On purpose?" Mom's puffy red eyes scrunch into a skeptical scowl.

The doctor's mouth twists. I look from Mom to Dad but they're both staring at her, waiting for answers.

"This." I find the baggie in my pocket, my fingers trembling, and hand it to her. "She thought it was MDMA. But it could have been anything."

"Mira!" Mom gives an exasperated sigh. "This again?"

Dr. Chopra thanks me and takes the baggie, carefully slipping it into her white coat. "We'll send this to the lab for testing," she says, then turns back to my parents. "We pumped her stomach and stimulated her heart rate and respiratory system. She's responsive now and seems to be stabilized."

"Can we see her?" Dad asks, impatient.

She nods. "Come with me."

Mom doesn't stop fuming and Dad doesn't let go of her hand as we follow Dr. Chopra through the swinging doors and into a long, bright hallway that smells like alcohol wipes and disinfectant. Her shoes sigh to a stop in front of a doorframe covered in a flimsy blue curtain.

"Britt." She knocks on the doorframe. "Your family's here."

From behind the curtain I hear a long, low groan. Mom lets go of Dad's hand and rushes into the room, slapping the curtain away so it whooshes against my cheek. Dad follows and I stand there for a moment, rubbing my face where the curtain smacked it. Then I take a deep breath and step inside.

Britt looks even worse than when I found her. Her lips are dry and cracked, caked with orange vomit, and her skin is practically translucent. A tube runs under her nose and an IV drips into her arm, connected with a bag of something white and milky dangling from a stand above. Next to her bed, a hulking machine hums like it's tired of being here.

But she's here. I'm seeing her. She's alive.

Unlike Yelena, she's alive.

"Baby." Mom can't stop touching her. She wipes her forehead, tucks hair behind her ear, strokes her shoulder. "Oh my god, my sweet baby. Are you okay?"

She rests her head on Britt's chest, hugging her awkwardly around the tubes and wires.

"You're fine, sweetie," Dad says, taking Britt's hand. "We're here. Everything's going to be just fine."

I find a spot at the foot of her bed and grasp the cold metal railing. Britt's eyes lock on mine and I see guilt and terror between the gold flakes. She shakes her head so gently it could just be a trick of the light, like she's trying to ask me something. Or tell me something.

"What happened, baby?" Mom asks, kissing her forehead.

"I don't know." Britt moans. "I just want to sleep."

"Of course you can sleep." Mom strokes her hair. "Just tell us what happened."

Britt's eyes flutter. "I must have eaten something bad."

"See?" Mom turns to me, her voice sharp and triumphant. "It's food poisoning!"

"Britt . . ." I say.

"What did you eat?" Mom asks. "We'll sue their pants off."

Britt looks down at her knees, two blue-and-white mountains under the hospital gown.

"Tell them the truth," I insist.

Britt closes her eyes, moves her head weakly from side to side. Her voice is so small we all have to lean in to hear. "Just leave me alone."

"Mira, what is wrong with you?" Mom steps forward, her chest heaving. "Your sister almost died of food poisoning."

I ignore her, moving closer to Britt. "What were you thinking?" I ask, my voice cracking. "You knew there was something wrong with those pills!"

Britt burrows her head deeper into the pillow, whimpering like a hurt animal. "Stop," she begs.

But I can't stop. "How could you?" I gasp, words and tears tumbling out of me in one big, messy rush. "After what happened to Yelena? After what happened last night?"

"Mira . . ." Mom starts to step forward, but Dad puts an arm across her chest, blocking her. Waiting to hear what Britt has to say.

Britt's lips tremble. Her eyes go liquid. "I just wanted to see her again," she whispers.

"See *who* again?" Mom demands.

I remember what Britt said in the car last night: *It's like she's with me sometimes. Like she's holding my hand.*

"Yelena," I answer for her.

Britt doesn't say anything. She kneads the hospital blanket where it bunches at her knees.

"You know you can't bring her back, right?" I say softly. "No matter how many pills you take."

Britt's head drops. Tears gather at the corner of her eyes.

"Britt." Dad's voice is quiet and gentle, like he's talking to a scared kitten. "Are you in the hospital because you took drugs?"

Britt blinks hard. She looks at the ceiling and the humming machine and the blue curtain on the door. "Maybe," she says. The tears threaten to fall.

"Well that just takes the cake!" Mom slams her hand down on the edge of a table, making a plastic tray jump. "You had everything going for you! A full scholarship and awesome grades and . . . and you threw it away to do *drugs*?"

Britt's shoulders start to shake. "It was just too much," she whispers.

Dad leans close to her. "What was too much?"

"Just . . . you guys." A tear snakes down her cheek. She doesn't try to wipe it away.

"*Us*?" Mom steps back, her hand to her chest.

"Just like—pushing me. You were always pushing me." Another tear falls, and then a third.

"We only pushed you because you could handle it," Mom says.

Dad nods. "We just wanted you to do what made you happy."

Tears stream down Britt's face, too fast for me to count. "Sure: as long as I was happy the way you wanted." Her voice goes thick. "Like playing soccer and winning all the time. You were never that way about *her*."

Her eyes are on me.

"Mira?" Dad asks.

"Yes, Mira!" Her voice trembles. "She could just do her own thing and like be this jazz weirdo and you'd leave her alone. That's all I ever wanted."

"That's not—" Mom starts.

"*Mira* didn't have to be perfect!" Britt cuts her off, sobbing. "Just me. All the pressure was on *me*."

"Oh, honey." Mom reaches down and takes her hand. "We never meant for you to feel that way."

"But I *did*," Britt weeps. "I always did."

Dad heaves a shuddering sigh and launches into a speech about how all they ever wanted from Britt was for her to be herself and do her best, but I'm only half listening. Instead I'm playing my sister's words over in my head, listening and pausing and hitting Repeat.

She could just do her own thing and you'd leave her alone, Britt said. *That's all I ever wanted.*

I look at my sister huddled in a hospital bed, her face caked with tears and snot and vomit. I've spent my entire life envying Britt. It never occurred to me that this whole time, she could be jealous of me too.

CHAPTER 41

The three of us stay in Britt's hospital room for hours, finally having the conversation we should have had months ago: the one about Britt's scholarship and her drug use, about parties and Yelena. About lies and evasions, our savings account and Pepperdine and Windham and Fulton, and how our parents always treated Britt versus how they always treated me.

The one where I finally tell them how much it hurt that they went to all of Britt's games and almost none of my recitals.

The one where they actually apologize.

"You never seemed like you needed us," Mom confesses, wiping mascara-tinted tears from her cheeks. "You always seemed so confident. Like it didn't matter if we were there or not."

"It mattered," I tell them, my eyes watering. "It still matters."

With every word I feel the ball of rage I've been carrying all summer unravel just a little more. I know my family can't go back in time and change anything, but it helps to know that they never meant to hurt me, that they were just doing what they thought was right.

It's almost eleven by the time we're done talking. The doctors want to keep Britt overnight for observation, and Mom and Dad prepare to spend the night in the waiting room.

"You should go, Mir-Bear," Mom says as I stifle a yawn. "Get some sleep."

I'm too tired to argue. I stand and kiss Britt on her cheek, resting my head for a moment against hers and savoring the feel of her breath, shallow but warm and alive, against my face.

"I'm sorry," she whispers, so quiet only I can hear.

"It's okay," I whisper back, the very last of my anger ebbing away. "I'm just glad you're okay."

Dad gets up to give me a hug.

"We love you, Mir-Bear," he says.

Mom goes next. "To the moon and back," she adds.

We hold each other for longer than usual, their smell and the feeling of their arms reminding me of how it felt to be a little kid, when I really believed they could protect me from anything.

"I love you guys too," I say.

I turn and make my way through the muted hospital halls, driving home through the still, warm night. As I let myself into the house and start up the stairs I notice glitter winking up at me from the carpet. A shard of broken mirror catches the light, reflecting the chaos in Britt's room.

Right. Britt's room. She must have trashed it before she collapsed. And now it's a mess, just when it's starting to feel like everything else in our family is finally coming together. As tired as I am, I don't want them returning home to this.

I enter Britt's room and pick her soccer trophies off the floor, arranging them in neat rows on top of her bureau. I find the caps for Yelena's eye pencils and tuck them into her makeup bag, fold her clothes into her suitcases and zip them shut and take them to the garage. I find rubber gloves and contractor bags and start in on the broken mirror, careful not to let the jagged edges touch my hands. A fractured mosaic of my face stares up at me: curls limp with fatigue, dark circles under my eyes. I look older, I think as I toss pieces into the trash bag, dissembling my face bit by bit. I look like I've lived through a year in the last night.

I look like my mom, and my dad. I look like Britt.

I take out the trash and lug our old Hoover up the stairs, falling under the spell of its dull roar as it sucks flecks of glitter from the carpet. I read once that a vacuum cleaner has the same frequency as the inside of a womb—some parents even use it to soothe babies to sleep. Right now, I believe it. I'm practically asleep on my feet.

The Hoover bumps the edge of Britt's desk and her computer comes to life. DJ Skizm blares through her desktop speaker, overpowering the vacuum with chomping beats and shrieking chords. It jolts me out of my trance, making my ears ring and my stomach do angry somersaults. It feels like it's inside me, clawing at my guts and trying to swallow me whole.

I dive at Britt's desk, trying to find the mute button on her keyboard, but my palm slides over her mouse pad and I trip on the vacuum cleaner's cord. My knee hits the floor, slamming into a sliver of glass. It lodges in my flesh. Blood gushes from my leg.

The music gets louder, the beat throbbing along with the pain. A wave of pure hatred crashes over me then: not just for DJ Skizm but for the music itself, for this track and this set and every other song made on a computer and peppered with drum machines.

If it weren't for the music I never would have let myself get sucked into this scene. I would have tried to stop Britt from partying instead of going to parties with her; I would have run to our parents the second I found out she was taking drugs.

But the music seduced me: the music, and Derek, and the lights and glitter and magic of diving feet-first into a brand-new world. It blinded me so I didn't see all the ugliness beneath the surface, deafened me so I didn't hear the wake-up call when Yelena died. Instead of turning away and dragging Britt with me, I went in deeper. I let the music be my guide.

My hand scrambles on Britt's desk, knocking her keyboard to the floor as the music blares on and on and on. I can't believe how naïve I was, thinking there was more to this world than canned rhythms and sketchy drugs. Thinking I had a place here, a future. Thinking it could maybe even change my life.

Hot tears leap to my eyes. I rise to my feet and clamp my hand over the speaker until I feel it vibrate against my palm, through my veins and into my chest.

I heave the speaker against the wall.

It cracks the drywall and slides to the floor and I leap on it, stomping until the sound goes fuzzy and distorted.

I am done with this music: not just here and now, but forever. I am done listening to it, done mixing it, done making it. Electronic music has done nothing but distract me and lie to me. This world has given me nothing but heartache.

The speaker's plastic shell finally cracks under my feet. The music grinds to a halt and a thin plume of smoke drifts up from the speaker, almost like a sigh. The white noise of the vacuum cleaner fills the room again. I yank its plug from the socket.

I look down at the bits of speaker littering Britt's carpet, the blood trickling from my knee and pooling in my shoe. It hurts, but it doesn't hurt as much as the music did.

I slide down the wall and onto the floor, breathing heavily. Silence covers me like a coat.

CHAPTER 42

My world shrinks to the size of my trumpet.

There is nothing but the flow of breath through brass, the click of notes finding their place on the staff, the *tock* and *whoosh* of my metronome. I push everything else to the side, where I can't hear it and it can't touch me. My audition is three weeks away.

Crow and Nicky come home the day after Britt's overdose. They try to tell me about camp but I don't want to talk; I only want to play. We jam until Crow's music room is thick with sweat, stop to eat sandwiches and crank the A/C, then go again. I didn't realize how far I'd fallen behind: their sound is mature and polished, gleaming like fine, old wood. It's what happens when you spend eight weeks practicing, when you have instructors correcting every note. I've been on my own all summer, and compared to them I sound raw and wild.

My audition is two and a half weeks away. I have a lot of work to do.

Britt has a lot of work to do too. She's grounded for the rest of the summer, only allowed to leave the house to see her new grief counselor or meet with her substance abuse group. Our parents have started taking turns coming home early from the gym, so she won't be lonely. So she'll feel like they're there for her, no matter what.

There's no more talk of her rejoining the soccer team, and she's even questioning whether she'll go back to Pepperdine. Her counselor suggests taking a semester off, maybe taking a few classes at community college while she figures out what comes next. And for once our parents aren't talking to her about pushing herself or winning; they've been reading the books her counselor sent home and are speaking a new language now, one that's all about living life as it happens and taking things one day at a time.

My audition is two weeks away. I'm up until dawn putting the final touches on my composition portfolio, staring at Sibelius for so long that even when I sleep, black notes swim in front of my eyes. I have no time to think, no time to socialize, no time for anything but this. I'm already too far behind.

I erase the DJ software from my laptop. I hide my thumb drives and delete all my new tracks. Sometimes I still find snippets of dance music echoing in my head, haunting my jazz compositions with the guttural throb of bass or teasing me with the promise of creating something new. I push it all away.

My audition is a week and a half away. I tell Shay she can take my set at Electri-City. She refuses at first but caves eventually—it is, after all, her dream. I don't tell Derek. He can find out when she takes the stage. I tell myself I don't owe him anything, not after all his lies. I delete his texts and voice mails.

My audition is one week away. I'll be playing "Lou's New York," the piece I debuted in the band room on the last day of school. I thought about playing one of my compositions from this summer but they all bring up too many memories: the jingling of Derek's keys, the swing of Yelena's hips, the sweetness of holding a dance floor in the palm of my hand. I can't afford to get emotional during my audition. Any distractions could ruin the most important ten minutes of my life.

My audition is one day away. My recital dress is clean and pressed, my sheet music neatly labeled, my trumpet polished until it gleams. I know my piece backwards and forwards; the compositions in my portfolio are printed out and perfect.

The electric buzz of summer is so far behind me I can almost believe it never happened. The warehouses and festivals, the lights and speakers and dancing crowds, are hazy as a distant dream. I've wiped every emotion from my mind; I push forward on autopilot, thinking only of the music and only of reaching my goal. My Fulton audition is tomorrow, and it's the only thing left that matters.

CHAPTER 43

"Here it is!" Crow cries. "The bastion of all our dreams!"

I pull up in front of a white stone building with the Fulton Jazz Conservatory's purple banner rippling over the entrance and wait for the rush of adrenaline to kick in. Crow and Nicky leap to the sidewalk, anticipation radiating from them in waves. I try to catch some but it's elusive, twitching away from my grasp.

I grab my trumpet from the trunk and hope excitement comes soon. This is my big day, the moment I've been prepping all summer for. Surely I'll start feeling *something* any minute now.

We enter the building in hushed, reverent silence, our footsteps echoing on the marble floor. A woman sitting at a large wooden desk hands us each a placard with our name, proposed major, and audition time.

"You're on soon." She points to a series of practice rooms. "Better warm up quick."

We follow her finger past a dozen other nervous-looking high school students clutching their instruments on stiff wooden chairs. Alone in my own tiny practice room I play scales and wait for the jitters to begin.

This is it, I tell myself, fingers flying over the valves. *You're finally here.*

I want to shock myself into feeling something, but my palms aren't sweating and my throat isn't dry and I don't feel like I'm going to throw up. Over the past three weeks I've worked hard to tamp down every emotion, to turn myself into a machine with nothing but this moment on my mind. I guess I've succeeded too well. Now that I want to feel something, I'm not even sure I can.

I'm cool, I realize. After all these years of trying, I'm finally cool.

I segue into my audition piece. Back in the band room at the beginning of summer it felt so alive, like the music was a wild animal desperate to burst from my trumpet. Now it feels sparse and flat, as empty as this room.

I place my trumpet gently on a stool and run my hands over the braids Mom put in my hair this morning. I've probably just played it too many times, the way if you say a word over and over in your head it loses its meaning. Everyone says this piece is great. I just need to believe in it. I just need to nail this audition and get that callback, and then my life can start up again. I'll start feeling things, start falling back in love with jazz. It'll be like this summer never happened.

I run through my piece a few more times and take a seat in the hallway. I can hear the faint trill of scales coming from the other practice rooms, the swish and creak of bodies moving on old wooden chairs and the gentle swish of traffic outside. I close my eyes and a beat starts to emerge from somewhere deep in my chest, pulsing and electric, filled with energy and heat. It jogs alongside my heart, bass layering in and merging with the sounds all around me until I find myself nodding along. My tongue *tsk*s with imaginary snare.

A shadow falls over my face and my eyes fly open. Crow and Nicky are standing over me. The track grinds to a halt.

"Sorry," Nicky whispers. "Were you going over your audition piece?"

I nod. It *should* have been my audition piece. "You guys ready?" I ask.

"Ready as I'll ever be." Crow bounces on her toes, the feather quivering in her fedora.

"Same." Nicky looks pale. "I think I'm going to throw up."

"You'll be great." I pat his arm just as the doors to the concert hall open and eject a girl with a clarinet and an expression of blissful relief. A skinny man follows her, shoulder-length hair tucked behind his ears. "Crow Cutler?" he calls. "Double bass?"

"Good luck!" Nicky and I whisper as Crow hurls herself at the concert hall. The doors shut behind her with a somber click.

"This is seriously going to be the longest ten minutes of my life." Nicky paces back and forth, each step jerkier than the last. I wish a nervous spark would fly off of him and kindle something in me.

Nicky abruptly stops pacing and drops into the chair next to mine. His leg keeps bouncing, his knee going a hundred eighty beats per minute and setting off a drum-and-bass rhythm in my mind. The squeak of his chair forms a melody of ancient creaks and cartoonish shrieking. I look down at my hands and see that I'm drumming along.

Nicky notices too. He looks at my hand and I stop, clutching the fabric of my dress instead. He gives me a sympathetic nod. He thinks I'm nervous, like him.

If only.

The double doors open and Nicky grasps my arm. Crow flies out, her wing tips clattering on the floor. She wears a flustered smile.

"Nicky Soriano?" the man calls. "Double major in drums and sax?"

"Break a leg," I whisper as he stands, his tiny body almost vibrating, and makes his way to the doors.

"How'd you do?" I ask Crow, bending my head close to hers.

"Good, I think." She slumps back, knees splayed around her bass. "They're hard to read."

"I hope Nicky's okay in there," I say. "He looked like he was going to shit his pants."

A guy clutching a French horn shoots us a dirty look. From a practice room down the hall I can hear a trombone practicing "It Don't Mean a Thing." The beat of Nicky's jittery leg rushes back, its rhythm fitting snugly under the melody. I imagine cutting the trombone's phrases into little bits and sampling them over the beat.

It don't mean a . . . don't mean a . . . don't mean a thing.

"Mira Alden, composition and trumpet."

My name echoes through the hallway and Nicky's coming toward me, hand outstretched for a high five. He looks elated, his cheeks glowing pink. I stand, my head spinning, and suddenly all the nerves I haven't felt all day, all week, all month crash over me and I'm practically paralyzed with fear.

My hands pool sweat around my trumpet, soaking my composition portfolio.

"Go!" Crow hisses, scooting me forward.

"You got this," Nicky says, his voice barely audible over the ringing in my ears.

"Come on in," says the long-haired man, and then I'm the one disappearing through the double doors.

CHAPTER 44

The concert hall is massive. Rows of chairs fan out around a high stage; a vaulted, chandelier-studded ceiling soars above. The man leads me down an endless aisle and introduces me to the faculty sitting behind a table in the front row. I hand over my portfolio and try to smile as my palms pour sweat.

"You can give your rhythm part to the drummer, and begin when you're ready," the long-haired man says.

I nod and walk to the stage, my feet feeling a size bigger with each step. My hands shake as I hand the drummer my music; when I let go I can see the damp outline of my palm. I look out over the room and it feels like the vast space is closing in on me, like the soaring ceiling is collapsing and taking all the oxygen with it.

Play it cool. I have to play it cool.

"Ready when you are," the drummer says.

I struggle to take a breath. There's no clock in this room, but I feel a ticking deep inside me as I place my own part on the music stand. It's the strong, bone-deep tock of the band-room clock, the thud of Derek's heart against mine, the tribal pounding of drum machines calling me from five stages at once.

I force air through my lungs. There's no room for those beats in this room.

The drummer raises his sticks. The concert hall stretches in front of me, empty and sterile and static. I bring my trumpet to my lips and in the moment before we begin I close my eyes and imagine the room filled with dancers and pulsing with beats, the energy surging off the dance floor and into my fingers.

I open my eyes and begin. One note. Five notes. A phrase. Something's wrong.

The tempo's too slow, like the piece is dragging through mud. It's not the drummer's fault. This is the tempo I asked for, the one I've always played. But now it feels as old and slow and used-up as a broken-down bus. The piece needs more life, more energy, more beats, deeper beats, stronger beats. The need propels my fingers faster over the valves and I speed up, passing the drummer and gaining on the curve. I feel him hesitate, and in his hesitation I pause and lose focus. I miss a phrase, struggle to catch it, and blast the wrong note.

In the front row, the faculty winces. I miss another note, choke on my breath, and sputter through the next few bars until I'm lost and tangled in my own piece. There's nowhere to go and nothing to do but stop.

I stop.

The drummer plays a few more measures, realizes he's lost me, and drags to a halt. Silence fills the room. The long-haired man clears his throat.

"Miss Alden," he says. "Would you like to start again?"

I don't want to start again. I want to sink into the stage, to disappear, to pretend this audition and Fulton and my trumpet and jazz and even Grandpa Lou never existed.

"Okay," I say, so quietly I can barely hear my own voice.

I beat out the tempo against my leg, a fraction faster than it was before. This time we get through the piece, but there's no joy in it, none of that alive animal feeling I got from playing with Crow and Nicky in the band room just twelve short weeks ago. The beat feels wooden and forced. It feels like every note I breathe has to be trucked in from so far away it's lost its flavor by the time it arrives.

It's still a piece of music, but there's nothing musical about it. When it's over it's a relief: not just for me, but for everyone in the room.

CHAPTER 45

Crow and Nicky can tell from my face. They're silent as we leave the cold white building, falling into step beside me as a cello solo chases us out the door like the punch line to a bad joke.

"Do you want to talk about it?" Nicky asks when we've settled into the LeSabre, city noises beeping and huffing outside.

"No." I tilt forward, resting my forehead against the steering wheel until it leaves a dent in the skin. Maybe I'll just stay like this forever, parked and going nowhere.

"It probably wasn't as bad as you think," Crow says tentatively. "You've always been a perfectionist."

I lift my head. "If I told you I lost the drummer, played a really bad wrong note, and had to start over, would you believe me?"

"Shiiiiiit." Nicky releases the word in a long, slow breath.

Crow's hand flies to her mouth. "Oh my lord." She looks like she's going to cry.

"Yeah, so." My voice comes out flat. "There goes that."

The Fulton Jazz Conservatory banner flutters in the corner of my eye. There's no point staying here. I don't belong here anymore.

I find my keys and start the car.

"Maybe you can petition," Nicky says as I pull onto 116th Street. "I mean, if you tell them what happened with Britt. . . ."

"No." We ease into traffic, the sun at our backs illuminating specks of dust on the windshield. "I don't want their pity."

"You could try again next year?" Crow suggests. "Like, take a year off after high school and just . . ."

"Just what?" My voice comes out sharp. "Work at the gym? Live with my parents?" I shake my head. This was my ticket out of Coletown, the only one I had. There is no Plan B.

Crow slumps back. "I was going to say practice," she says.

"You could live with us!" Nicky's leg is jittering again, the same rhythm as before. Slick trombone notes float through my head: *it don't mean a . . . .don't mean a . . . don't mean a thing.* "We could still get that place off campus. You could get a job or something."

"Yeah!" Crow perks up. "You could take time to practice and jam with us every night and then audition next year. . . . You'd only be a year behind!"

"Yeah, maybe." I try to picture the loft we've always talked about, with the little stage and the big windows and instrument cases piled against the wall. But it's morphed over the summer, into some combination of Derek's place in Bushwick and Shay's basement studio. "I don't know."

"This doesn't have to be a setback." Nicky's leg shakes harder, driving the beat like a wedge into my head. I can hear the melody now, almost like it's in the car with us. It goes with the beat like ice cream with cones, like tires with asphalt. "It's not the end of the world."

"You could work at a music store," Crow suggests.

"Sneak onto campus and audit lectures," Nicky adds.

"We'll steal you food from the dining hall. . . ."

I tune them out and wait for tears to come. I should be sobbing right now, mourning the future I just lost. But I've spent so much of this summer crying, maybe I don't have any tears left. All I feel is empty, hollowed-out. Ready to be filled in again.

I swing the car onto Harlem River Drive. The East River sparkles in the sunlight, and I can just see Brooklyn in my rear-view mirror. Above our heads a road sign announces the next few exits: *Willis Avenue Bridge. 135th Street. Randall's Island.*

I check my watch. Shay will be going on at Electri-City soon, taking the slot that was supposed to be mine. I hope she kills it out there. I hope it launches her career and makes all her dreams come true, so she can spend the rest of her life playing clubs and festivals and getting all the fame and fortune and love she deserves.

I hope somebody's dream comes true today. Even if it isn't mine.

Nicky reaches over and pats my leg. "It's going to be okay," he says.

I don't answer him. I open the window and let the air cool my face, feel the hum of motors and thump of tires on rough road fill the empty hole inside of me with sound. The city will always make music, I think as I accelerate around a curve. There will always be the rattle of the subway, the thrum of electricity through underground lines, the melodic lilt of conversation in every language.

A sign for the Randall's Island exit swims into view. I put my blinker on and cut across one lane of traffic, then two.

Nicky's head jerks around. "What are you doing?" he asks.

"We're getting off here." I take the exit. "There's something I need to do."

CHAPTER 46

"Have you gone off the deep end?" Crow's eyes are wide with shock in the rearview mirror. We've made it to the island and a tangle of beats engulfs us, the woolly thump of bass from far-off stages mingling with a half dozen DJ mixes trickling from the open windows of cars around us.

A guy in an orange vest directs us to a spot at the edge of a vast parking lot. Girls in tiny shorts and clear backpacks hurry past; guys high-five as they lope toward the gates, their goofy, excited grins mirrored in each others' sunglasses.

"Who are these people?" Nicky scrunches up his nose. "What are we doing here?"

I climb out of the car. "My friend is on in like twenty minutes. I just want to catch her set. Then we can go."

"And you're just going to leave our instruments in the car where anyone can steal them?" Crow crosses her arms over her chest.

I sigh. "Nobody's going to steal our stuff."

"We don't know that," Crow argues. "We don't even know these people."

I check my watch again. Eighteen minutes until Shay goes on. I don't have time for this.

"So just bring them, if you're so worried." I grab my trumpet from the trunk. "See? No big deal."

Crow scowls. "It IS a big deal. My bass is huge!"

I can feel myself unraveling. After everything that's happened today, I can't handle Crow's drama, too.

"Then just stay here," I snap. "I'll be back soon."

"Crow." Nicky gives her a look. "C'mon. Mira's having a tough day."

"Okay, *fine*," Crow huffs, dragging her bass from the car. "I can't believe I'm doing this."

"I can't believe it either," Nicky confesses, clutching his saxophone case. "But here we are. At some rave thing."

I ignore my friends, as well as the looks we get crossing the parking lot: three jazz nerds in our finest recital clothes, lugging instruments while everyone else skips toward the entrance in crocheted vests and fairy wings. A month ago I would have died of embarrassment, but now I don't care. I'm not here to make friends or impress anyone. I just want to see Shay.

At the gate I plunk down my emergency debit card and buy three day-passes. It's practically all the money in my account, but it's not like I have anything to save it for anyway.

"Electri-City," Nicky reads the banner above our heads, twisting his bracelet and huddling close as we wait for a team of beefy security guards to pat us down. Huge signs at the entrance remind us that Electri-City is a zero tolerance event; anyone caught buying or selling drugs will be punished to the fullest extent of the law.

The guards paw through our instrument cases and spit us out into the festival, where the crowd fans out into a street lined with vendors. Nicky sniffs the air, taking in the scent of Red Bull and sunscreen. "So this is what you've been doing all summer without us?" he asks.

"Kind of, yeah." We reach a junction and I find a sign pointing to the NRG stage. Eleven minutes until Shay goes on.

"Whoa." Crow pauses as a gaggle of girls carrying neon Hula-Hoops flits by, their fiber-optic plumage sending sprays of light across our faces. "This place is *nuts*."

"Kinda cool, right?" I turn left, toward the stage.

"I didn't say that," she grumbles.

There's a band playing live progressive house jams on the NRG stage: DJ, electric bass, drum set, and keytar. LED lightning flashes and plumes of fire shoot up whenever the beat drops, orange flames tickling the sky.

The beat enters me, steadying me, and I think back to that trombone in the practice room: *It don't mean a thing, if it ain't got that swing.* It's almost too much here, with the band jamming on stage and the beats all around me and the music in my head.

I push through the crowd.

"We're really going in there?" Nicky says in my ear, his short legs pumping as he hurries to keep up.

"Yeah." I want to be right up front when Shay goes on. I want to hear her set in the place where the sound is brightest and loudest and most immediate, and I want her to see me and know I'm there.

I lead us past tight circles of friends dancing together or taking photos, trying not to jab anyone with my trumpet case, Crow grunting and lugging her bass behind me. People move aside; whether it's because we take up so much room or just look so out-of-place is anyone's guess. We're just a few feet from the front now: I can see the spot I want, directly in front of the DJ booth.

Then someone moves in front of me, slight but muscular in a loose black tank top and sleeves of tattoos. My heart stops and my blood stops and I stop. I'd know those tattoos anywhere.

CHAPTER 47

Derek doesn't see me. His back is to me and he's talking to a girl with long blond hair that sweeps the skin below her tube top, their heads bent close in conversation. I watch him dig a bag from his pocket, count a few pills into his palm, and press them into hers.

The pills are flat and grayish. Like the powder inside Britt's baggie. Like the pills that almost took my sister's life.

I surge forward, slamming into the girl. The pills fly from her hand.

"Hey! Watch it!" She turns and glares at me before crouching down, reaching for the pills scattered in the mud. I put my foot over them.

"Mira!" Derek's eyes go from hard to soft in the space of two syllables. "What are you doing here? You should be backstage."

"You don't want those," I lean down to shout in the girl's ear, so she can hear me over the music. "They're laced."

"So?" She sneers up at me and I notice with a shock that she's even younger than I am. She can't be more than fifteen. "Let me know if you find any shit that isn't."

"With *meth*," I tell her.

"Ew, really?" She looks from me to Derek. "Is that true, dude?"

"I—" Derek starts.

"He has no idea," I tell her. "My friend died on his shit."

"Okay, god." She straightens up and gives him a dirty look. "That's fucked up, dude," she says before scampering off into the crowd.

I whirl on Derek. "You told me you were going to stop!" My head swims as I realize how many pills he must be carrying right now, how many people at this festival could end in the hospital like Britt...or like Yelena. How many other parties has he been to since the Pine Barrens, I wonder? How many innocent people have ended up sick, or hurt, or worse?

"Yeah, and then you ghosted on me anyway." Derek's eyes go cold, the blue turning to ice. "What the hell, Mira. After everything I did for you?"

"Everything you did for *me*?" I can't help laughing. "Like poisoning my sister? Killing my friend?"

His eyes narrow as he gestures toward the stage. "Like getting you this set? Making you a star?" He shakes his head, his lips twisting in disgust. "Why aren't you backstage, anyway? You should be setting up."

"I gave the set to Shay. How are you still selling that crap?"

"You weren't going to tell me?" Hurt percolates in his eyes.

"After you almost killed my sister? No, sorry, I had more important things on my mind."

He shakes his head sadly. "I see what this is really about," he says, so quietly that I have to strain through layers of beats to hear him. "You let Shay get to you. After you promised me you wouldn't."

For a moment all I can do is stare at him, dumbstruck. A tornado of fury starts in my stomach and whirls through my chest, up into my throat.

"You're making this about *Shay*?" I say finally, when I find my voice. "I'm talking about the fact that you're literally killing people with your shitty drugs, and you're turning this into some petty ex-girlfriend drama?"

"Mira . . ." He reaches for my hand. "Don't be like this. Don't ruin what we had."

I yank my hand away. "I know why you didn't want me talking to Shay." My hands are shaking, but to my surprise my voice is calm. "You were worried she'd tell me the truth."

Derek's eyes flash. There's anger there but something else too. Just for a moment, he looks afraid. "Because she lies," he mutters, his face reddening.

"Did she lie about Britt needing her stomach pumped?" I look at the bulge in Derek's pocket, the bag I know is full of pills. I think about the young blonde girl out there somewhere in the crowd, about all the people who will buy whatever he sells them and swallow his pills without knowing what they are. "Did she lie about what happened to Yelena?"

"That was an accident," Derek mutters. But I'm not listening anymore. I know, now, that no matter what he says, Derek isn't going to stop. He isn't going to stop selling drugs, and he isn't going to stop preying on girls who are too young and naïve and awestruck to realize he's weaving a web of lies.

Girls like Shay. Girls like me.

I don't know why he's like this. Maybe it really is his mom, or maybe it's just the way he is, someone who's so addicted to having money and power and connections that he doesn't care who he hurts along the way. All I know is that he's not going to stop. Not unless I find a way to stop him.

I think about the signs outside the festival gates, the security guards who rifled through our instrument cases. Something hard and jagged crystallizes in my chest. I know what I have to do.

"Is everything okay?" Nicky's hand on my arm makes me jump. I'd almost forgotten he and Crow were here.

"Yeah. I'm done here. Come on." I spot a security guard leaning against the stage. I start toward him but Derek grabs my wrist, yanking me back.

"Ouch!" I try to pull my hand away, but his grip is hard and cruel.

"Come on," Nicky says, a warning in his voice. "She told you she's done."

"But I'm not done with *you*," Derek snarls, his eyes boring into mine.

"Get your hands off of her!" Nicky screams, smacking Derek's arm.

Derek bats him away like he's nothing more than a fly. "You'd be nothing without me," he tells me, his eyes glinting ice. "You were just this little loser until I came along and made you what you are." His face reddens and his chest puffs up and I'm suddenly aware of the fact that he's no taller than I am; he's no longer larger than life. "I eat girls like you for breakfast," Derek spits as I struggle in his grip. "You think I can't do better than you? You were just some dumb toy for me to play with until something better came along."

His words are like a quick smack on the cheek. By the time they stop stinging, the hurt is gone.

"She's not a loser." Crow appears on my other side, towering over Derek. "*You're* a loser. Who even talks like that?"

Derek stares at us, his chest rising and falling with quick,
angry breaths.

"Your friends are freaks," he says, letting go of my wrist.
"And so are you."

He backs away, bumping into a group of girls taking selfies.
As he turns to them with a thousand-watt smile I push my way
through the crowd, to the front of the stage.

I find the security guard, say a few words in his ear, and
point to Derek.

He picks up his walkie-talkie and begins barking commands
just as the band finishes playing and Shay takes the stage.

CHAPTER 48

"That was Derek, wasn't it?" Nicky asks when I'm done talking to the security guard.

I nod. Shay steps up to the decks, pink and blue lights sweeping across her face. "You won't be seeing him again," I tell them.

"What a dick!" Crow gasps. "What were you thinking?"

From the corner of my eye I watch Derek emerge from the crowd. A squad of security guys moves in around him, broad backs in black polo shirts swallowing him whole.

"Hey, I get it." Nicky gives my shoulder a comforting pat. "He's a *hot* dick."

Shay taps the mic. The crowd strains behind me, waiting for the beat to drop. A security guard slaps a pair of plastic handcuffs on Derek and leads him away.

Shay spreads her arms like a bird about to take flight. Her smile is so huge, so genuine and happy it feels like it could light the dance floor on fire. She has no idea what just happened to Derek, no idea that I'm here, but I know exactly what she's feeling now. I can sense the nerves beneath her calm, can see her sizing up the crowd as she tries to ride the delicate line between giving them exactly what they want and playing the songs in her heart.

She brings in her first track, soft and low. The beat enters me like water, lifts me over the crowd. It slides from the speakers like liquid silk, wrapping the whole crowd in its web.

Tears gather in my eyes as my hips start to move: tears for the set I'm not playing and the music Shay is, for the future I left behind at Fulton, for Britt back at home trying to put the pieces of her life together, and for Yelena who will never have that chance. I cry for Derek, who will never be the person I fell in love with. And for myself, because I fell in love with a lie.

I feel a hand on my shoulder and look over to see Nicky swaying next to me, Crow dancing with her bass on his other side.

"Hey." He stands on tiptoes to reach my ear. "This actually isn't so bad."

Next to him, Crow nods in agreement.

"Thanks," I say, smiling through my tears. "I think?"

I watch Shay choose another track and I ache to be up there with her. I yearn for the feel of knobs and dials under my hands, the tangle of beats in my headphones. Snippets of music flash through my head, layering beneath Shay's beats: Nicky's leg jittering a drum-and-bass rhythm. The keytar player and bassist from the last set. The saucy strut of that practice-room trombone. *It don't mean a thing, if it ain't got that swing.*

Above me Shay glows with stage lights and sweat and something more, something so pure and joyful it turns us all into a sea of stars. Spotlights sweep the crowd. I open my mouth and let my voice fly free, calling her name, raising my hands to the heavens. A spotlight lingers on my face, warming my skin and making spots explode in my eyes.

The beats. The trombone. Yelena's arms in the air.

The bass.

My trumpet.

The band.

The spotlight.

Shay. Nicky. Crow.

It hits me like a high A-sharp, suddenly and smack-dab in the middle of my head.

I know what that track was missing.

I jump up and down, waving my arms and calling Shay's name. But everyone's yelling, everyone is jumping up and down. Of course she doesn't notice me.

The spotlight is still on me. I just have to catch her eye.

I undo my trumpet case, hands shaking as I snap my instrument together and wave it in the glare. My heart thrums and the spotlight starts to move away, and just as I think I've blown it Shay squints and takes a step back. Her eyes land on the glare from my trumpet. The light moves away. And then she sees me.

She does a double take.

And before I can change my mind I'm scrambling over the lip of the stage and Shay is pulling me up, her face opening in a laugh as her arms open wide, circling me in a hug.

"Mira Mira, in the house!" she screams into the mic, diving back behind her rig as I motion for Crow and Nicky to join me.

"What is happening?" Crow demands as I yank at her sleeve, trying to pull her up behind me.

"Get up here." I'm breathless, my heart pounding as the stage vibrates beneath my feet.

"I don't think . . ." Nicky starts to say.

"Just do this." I cut them off. "I just blew my audition and had my boyfriend arrested. So please, just do this for me."

They look at each other and shrug, then scramble onto the stage.

"Get your instruments out," I beg, excitement squeezing my words into gasps.

"You're acting crazy," Nicky says, reluctantly opening his case.

"I know!" I reply. But I can't help it—I can't stop moving, pressing the valves on my trumpet, hovering over Crow as she pulls her bass between her knees, hopping behind the decks to join Shay.

"What's happening?" she asks, her eyes cutting from me to Nicky to Crow and her double bass.

"Our track." I don't have time to explain. "It was missing something."

"This?" Shay looks from our instruments to the crowd. A field of curious eyes gazes back, no doubt wondering what a trio of musicians in recital clothes is doing up on stage with the DJ. "Mira, I don't know. . . ."

I know what she's thinking: that this is her big break, and I'm probably about to ruin it.

Maybe she's right. I don't know anymore. All I know is that this is what I want more than anything else in the world, and we only have one chance to get it right.

"Can you cue it up?" I beg. "If it doesn't work we'll leave the stage and pretend nothing happened."

Shay's tongue pokes out from between her teeth.

"I guess. . . ."

"Great." I turn to Crow and Nicky before she can change her mind, maneuvering them into place behind the microphones where the keytar player and bassist stood. "You two just follow my lead."

They both look at me like I've grown a second head. Shay cues up the track. I clutch my trumpet. My heart races.

Out beyond the festival the sun has dipped below the horizon, leaving peach-colored streaks in the sky. The crowd is a blanket of blinking lights, faces softened and blurred by darkness. Shay brings our track in, light and easy as summer rain. My heartbeat sprints past it, pounding through my body and into my fingers, making them thrum with music and desire.

The beat builds through four bars, then eight.

At twelve I bring my trumpet to my lips.

Here goes nothing, I think.

I take a breath and blow, my fingers coming down on a low, rich D that vibrates across the dance floor and disappears like a memory on the end-of-summer air.

Note by note, I spin a phrase. It catches on the beat, not quite falling into step, and for a long, terrible moment I'm back at the Fulton Jazz Conservatory's grand hall, blowing that and now this. Over the bell of my trumpet I see people gathering their things to leave.

This can't be happening. Not again. I've already lost everything: my spot in the conservatory, my chance to be a DJ, my boyfriend and Yelena and almost my sister and, if this doesn't work, probably my friends.

I need this to work.

I pause and close my eyes, filter out the rest of the world until all that's left is the rhythm and me. Once it's embedded deep as my own blood I raise my trumpet and belt out the melody again.

This time it sticks. The melody and rhythm fall into a groove and I feel the crowd pause, considering. Giving us a chance.

My eyes find Crow and Nicky and I nod them in. Crow brings her palm down flat on her bass as Nicky's sax soars over the lip of the stage.

The crowd shifts. People who were starting to walk away drift back again. I can feel the pull of interest from the out-skirts, dancers flitting back to our music like moths. They find their footing in the beat; feet start to tap, hips start to sway. Shay adjusts the levels. A smile breaks like sunrise across her face.

I lead us into a chorus, notes falling fat and glistening from my trumpet. They illuminate the dance floor, turning every limb to gold. The crowd swells forward and rises, lifted by the music, transformed.

Sweet, hot jazz pours from our instruments and mixes with the beats booming from the speakers, and I close my eyes but this time I'm not in Harlem and it's not 1944. I am right here, right now, in this year and this day and this moment. I don't need to close my eyes anymore because the dancers are right here in front of me, losing their minds and screaming my name and flinging themselves into the air.

The music sounds just like it did in my head. The missing pieces fit together in a combination of jazz and dance music that I realize was always there, just inside of me waiting to bubble to the surface. It's like nothing I've ever heard before—nothing any of the thousands of people out there have ever heard before—but it's perfect and complete, total and whole and mine.

I look at Crow, red-faced and smiling above the strings. Nicky raises his sax in a salute. I glance at Shay and she flashes me a secret smile and I know this won't be the last time we make music together, not even close. I can tell this is just the beginning.

I look out at the crowd, a mass of churning limbs and blissed-out faces, then past them to the edges of the festival, the edges of Randall's Island, the city, the world. My future spreads out before me, full of possibilities. I could live with Crow and Nicky in New York. I could try for NYU or Juilliard, or Berklee in Boston—any number of conservatories that haven't had their auditions yet.

I could keep DJing. Shay and I could be a duo, tag-teaming our way across the continent. I could keep producing. I could strap on a backpack and travel the world, picking up jobs wherever I land and learning music from every culture, checking out the jazz scene in cities like Paris and New Orleans that Grandpa Lou dreamed of visiting, and hitting up dance music festivals in Croatia and Berlin that he never could have imagined.

All I know is that wherever I go and whatever I do, this is my music now. I've found my sound—and the people I want to make it with—and now that I have it I'll never let it go.

Shay eases the volume up on the track and we segue into our final notes, all of us rising together in a glorious finale that explodes like fireworks over the crowd. I set down my trumpet and raise my arms, soaking up applause. When I walk to the front of the stage the cheer grows to a chant, a sea of thousands calling my name.

I bow my head and the chant swells, rising up over the island and filling the sky, reaching from Bushwick to Harlem to all the places I have yet to go.

I spread my arms, rise to my toes, and leap into the crowd. They catch me, holding me over their heads, and I fly.

ACKNOWLEDGMENTS

Writing is like DJing: you mostly do it alone in your room, but you need other people to bring it to life.

Thanks first and foremost to my wonderful agent, Eric Smith, for responding to my query in less than ten minutes (on your birthday, no less!), believing with all your heart and soul in this book, and for being a friend and spirit guide in publishing and parenting.

To my wise, insightful, and delightful editor, Becky Herrick: you were always right, even when I didn't want you to be. I cannot thank you enough for your unflagging passion and thoughtful feedback as an editor and band geek. Thanks also to the rest of the team at Sky Pony Press: Emma Dubin, Kate Gartner, Bethany Bryan, and Joshua Barnaby. You are all magical flying unicorns.

When the Beat Drops was fortunate to have a great group of early readers: Tina Wexler, Bernie Barta, Lauren Scobell, Emily Settle, Sunny Lee, Claire Taylor, Shani Petroff, and particularly Danielle Rollins and Leah Konen, whose fingerprints are all over the story in the best possible way.

I'm equally lucky be part of the inimitable Electric Eighteens debut group and the unstoppable #TeamRocks, who help me face the always-questionable decision to become an author with laughter, medicake, and way too many emojis.

I am eternally grateful to Candice Montgomery, Shannon Luders-Manuel, and Nena Boling-Smith, my team of brilliant diversity editors, for adding depth and dimension to this book. Thanks also to Samantha Isom for inspiring Mira's biracial identity, and for graciously answering my questions about hair.

Hustle is as important in publishing as it is in dance music—and Liane Worthington, Savannah Harrelson, and Crystal Patriarche at BookSparks are the classiest hustlers of all. Thanks for making my little book feel like a big deal.

My parents, Zeke and Linda Hecker, brought me up reading (or at least, raised me in a house without television so I didn't have much choice). Thanks for your unflagging belief in me as a writer—and thank you, Dad, for your early read and formidable musical knowledge.

This book was inspired in no small part by my vibrant family of DJs, producers, party people, and dance floor freaks. Thanks to the beautiful people of A Cavallo, Alien Underground, The Armory Podcast, Asylum, Bangarang, The Blackbird, The Bunk Police, Camp D, Charlie the Unicorn, Container Camp, DanceSafe, The Danger, De Menthe, Distrikt, Disorient, Empire Breaks, Figment, Freeform, Gemini & Scorpio, The Get Down, Gnome Camp, the Grampagers, Gratitude, Hooping NYC, House of Yes, Icarus, Illeven:Eleven, Kostume Kult, Mobile Mondays!, Mysteryland, New Amsterdam Village, The NYC Bass Collective, NYC

Decom, NYC*Ravers, Opulent Temple, The Paper Box, PEX, Playa Del Fuego, Pink Mammoth, Prismatik, Punks Music, Rat Camp, Rubulad, my Secret Santas, The Sexy Tramps, Smoochdome, The Space Cowboys, Sparky's, SRB Brooklyn, Tasty Noodles, Transformus, Winkel and Balktick, Wonderland, Zone Records, and all the other beat-fiends and burners. Extra shout-outs to Agent 137, DJ Assault, Aston Harvey, The Beatslappaz, Been Jammin', Big Daddy, Deekline, DivaDanielle (whose rainbow unicorn vibes may or may not have rubbed off on DJ Shay), DJ Icey, DJ ICON, Douggie Style, Justin Aubuchon, Kellye "Mohawk" Greene, Lady Waks, Lee Mayjahs?, Mafia Kiss, Martin Flex, Martin Hørger, Philip Evans, DJ Shakey, DJ Shooey, DJ $mall ¢hange, The Stanton Warriors, Tanya Everywhere (who still isn't a DJ), The Teknacolor Ninja, Wally Whatever, Wavewhore, Wylie Stecklow, Zach Moore, DJ Zinc, and everyone else with whom I've broken bread in the name of breaking beats.

Finally, thanks for eight years of pure magic to my Vitamin B crew: Tektite, Illexxandra, Anna Morgan, VJ DoctorMojo, Guncle, Sammycakes, and, of course, Tim the Enchanter— my favorite DJ and favorite husband.

And thank you, Jack, for being the sweetest distraction of them all.

ABOUT THE AUTHOR

Anna Hecker grew up at the dead end of a dirt road in Vermont. She holds an MFA from The New School and spent a decade writing ad copy and chasing beats before returning to fiction, her first love. She lives in Brooklyn with her husband, son, and fluffy bundle of glamour, Cat Benatar. Follow her @ HeckerBooks on Twitter, Instagram, and Facebook.